Praise for Rex Burke

Sometimes the Universe drops the exact right book into your life at the exact right time … From the first pages, had me engaged and smiling.

KRR Lockhaven, fantasy author

Orphan Planet ticked all the boxes for me, and I needed the sequel yesterday. If you like feel-good, character-led books set in space, buying this should be a no-brainer..

Shazzie, Fantasy Book Critic

Fulfils perfectly the promise of being a funny and feelgood … classic sci-fi adventure

Jamedi @ JamReads

[For] fans of Pratchett and Douglas Adams who like SciFi stories with a sense of humour and a 'slice of life' feel to them.

Sue Bavey, book blogger, Sue's Musings

TWIN LANDING

Also by Rex Burke

Orphan Planet

Twin Landing

Star Bound

TWIN LANDING

Odyssey Earth
Book 2

REX BURKE

Contents

Where Were We?

The way I see it, there are three scenarios here.

A – you liked the look of this, but didn't realise it was Book 2 of a series? You could go back and read Book 1, *Orphan Planet*, because I promise you, you've missed a ton of jokes and feelgood adventures, or you could skip straight to C, you'll soon catch up. Either way, we're cool.

B – you've just finished *Orphan Planet* and can't wait to find out what happens next? Great. Crack on, chapter one is coming right up. See you on the other side.

And C – for everyone else … look, I get it – maybe you read *Orphan Planet* a while ago? You've read a bunch of other books since. And some of those were probably set in space, too. And it's totally my fault for featuring more than one main character, never mind all the supporting cast.

Something about teenagers, wasn't it? Landing on the wrong planet?

It's not your fault, is what I'm saying, that you've arrived on this page with only a sketchy notion of where things were at the end of Book 1.

Let's face it, I can barely remember what was going on, and I wrote the thing. But we've all had busy lives since then, and actually I've been writing Book 3 while you're sitting down just now to read Book 2 – so, you know, we could probably all benefit from a catch-up.

Jordan Booth, remember him? He's the guy they woke up on the colony ship, *Odyssey Earth*, to look after a bunch of teenagers. Bit hopeless and ineffectual, doesn't know much about much – and really not happy to be put in charge of babysitting duties.

Only, they're not kids at all, they're all sixteen and sassy – born on the ship, but grief-stricken following the death of their ship-mum and mentor, Sam Smart. She called them her sprogs – Dana, Dervla, Manisha, Bryson, Poole and Karlan. Names coming back to you now?

The captain – Juno Washington – and the ship's snarky, know-it-all AI, Reeves, have kept the mission on track, and after seventeen years, the *Odyssey Earth* is just a few weeks away from arriving at New Earth – humanity's first outpost in the stars.

So, of course, I made it all go wrong, because that's what happens in a space adventure.

For reasons, Jordan and the kids were hanging out in one of the shuttle-landers on board the ship, when the *Odyssey Earth* was struck by a meteoroid – catapulting the lander off into space, where it promptly crash-landed on an unknown planet.

Luckily – also for reasons – they have a trimmed-down version of Reeves with them, so although he's no longer all-knowing, he's going to prove to be a helpful companion.

From this point on, we don't know what happens to the *Odyssey Earth*, and the story sticks with the teenage castaways and Jordan as they struggle to survive. Surprisingly – not least to him – Jordan adapts well to the situation, while the teenagers come to terms with being off the spaceship for the first time in their lives.

Bryson nearly drowns, and Manisha breaks her leg, and there are all sorts of other obstacles to overcome before the group sets up semi-permanent camp and settles in, hoping for rescue.

Are they stuck here forever? Did the *Odyssey Earth* survive the meteoroid strike?

They don't know, and neither do we.

Well, I do, obviously – but that's where Book 1 ended, and now I'll tell you how the story continues …

1

Goats

IT HAD all been going as well as could be expected, until the goats started to eat the decorations.

From a small, earthen mound at the edge of the New Earth landing site, Juno Washington had done what she had needed to do and delivered a captain's address – an auspicious day, time to pull together, exciting future ahead, etc, etc.

She barely heard the words she spoke. In many ways, she was only going through the motions, but Juno had felt it was important to acknowledge their achievement. They had made it, after all – seventeen years across the galaxy to their new home in the stars; ten days now on the planet.

That was something to – well, commemorate, if not celebrate.

She looked down on a sea of familiar faces, all older now than when they had started – the pioneer crew of the colony ship, *Odyssey Earth*. She remembered welcoming most of them on board, back at the old Earth space station.

Her ship, her people. She'd done her best and had got them here, as promised.

Now it was up to all of them to make a new home on this new planet, trillions of miles from everything and everyone that they had ever known. There was no going back, everyone accepted the deal when they'd signed up. One way only.

'New Earth, New Beginning,' as the old advertising slogan went.

Juno paused, a lump in her throat.

Deep breath, this was the hard part.

Scanning the silent faces, she could see that others were deep in thought, too. Remembering those difficult last few weeks on board the *Odyssey Earth*, as they had cruised in through the new solar system. The excitement of impending planetfall tempered by the shock of a sudden, brutal, inexplicable loss.

Seven of their own, gone, just like that.

The memories were still bitingly raw and Juno – blameless – blamed herself. Despite the occasion – *because* of the occasion – it was hard to feel joy, when not everyone was here to share it.

"We have to carry on, though, don't we?" she said, more to herself than anyone else. Then she raised a plastic beaker to the assembled crowd.

"To Jordan Booth and to our beautiful kids. To Dana, Dervla, Manisha, Poole, Bryson and Karlan," speaking their names loudly, emphasising each one.

Juno's words carried on the morning air, and a hundred and fifty voices murmured the names in unison before sipping from their own beakers.

And then a cacophony of coughs and splutters broke out as Gerald the botanist's 'wine' fought its way down a hundred and fifty throats. Not so much a cheeky visit from a presumptuous little homebrew; more an intimidating call from the bailiffs, intent on removing your liver. When she'd had an initial, challenging sip before the ceremony, Juno had asked him what was in the wine, and Gerald had said, "I'd like to say grapes," and left the sentence hanging before changing the subject.

Once the coughing had died down, Juno walked across to the small clearing, where a decorative cordon had been established around a hand-cut, timber flagpole.

And it was at this point – before Juno could raise the ship's ceremonial flag – that the goats charged in and started eating the decorations.

To be fair, they weren't exactly decorations – the medics had simply stitched together some pads and bandages as bunting – but then again, they weren't exactly goats.

They clearly occupied the niche that goats did back on home Earth. Smallish, annoying, a bit smelly, ate anything. Actually, scratch that, thought Juno, when she'd first encountered them. They clearly occupied the niche that the ship's nuclear physicists did.

But unlike physicists, or indeed Earth goats, these

creatures had matted, sheep-like woollen coats and droopy, almost elephantine ears, which pricked at any sound, making the animals surprisingly difficult to capture.

Unlike physicists, who could be rounded up with a plate of biscuits.

The goats had no fear of humans and, in the ten days since landing, had increasingly taken to encroaching upon the new settlement. The goats disappeared off into the nearby scrub at dusk – no one had yet followed them more than a few hundred yards to see where they went – but for much of the day they made tentative raids in packs of ten or so if anyone left out so much as an apple core. Or, as now, a ribbon of hanging bandages, one end of which was currently being munched with much apparent enjoyment.

As goats buffeted their way through the crowd, one barged past and made a beeline for the flag table. Juno grabbed the flag, ran it quickly up the flagpole so it was out of the way, and collared a passing crew member.

"Shoo them all out, would you mind? Goats and crew. I think we've finished, and I've got to go over and pick up the new guy anyway."

"Shame we didn't have him here earlier, in time for this. Let him handle animal control."

"I'm not sure goat-wrangling is in his job description. Any more than it is in ours." Juno looked over at the direction from which the animals had come. "I thought we were getting the fencing fixed?"

"We are. But every time we get a section sorted, another building goes up and the perimeter expands."

That was another problem – making sure everyone stuck to the schedule. Only, people who had been confined to a spaceship for seventeen years tended to take one look at the wide, open spaces of New Earth and come knocking on Juno's door with blueprints of ranch-style villas with swimming pools. There was too much freelance construction going on, and the basics – like the fencing – were being neglected. She really needed to get a grasp of that, too.

Oh, for the days when all she had to do was fly a multi-storey colony ship at terrifying speed across trillions of miles of space. That had been a doddle compared to establishing civilisation on Planet Goat.

"All right, see what you can do. And by the way, don't let them drink any more of the wine, either."

"The goats? Or the crew?"

"Good point." Juno laughed. "Either. Both. Gerald's very proud of it, but I suspect there are a few litres of disinfectant missing from the ship's galley."

"I thought there was a lemony tang. Silly me, thinking it was lemons."

2

Tickety-boo

THE GOATS HAD BEEN an unexpected surprise, but not too unexpected.

Back on Earth, many years previously, scientists had proclaimed their newly discovered exoplanet as suitable for human settlement. Orbital observations, gas signatures and other evidence confirmed that it had acceptable gravity, breathable air, liquid surface water and biological life – the latter unknown, but probably benign. Nothing enormous and mobile showed up on the scans, at least.

That was good news for anyone signing up for the *Odyssey Earth* gig. If you were looking for another human foothold in the universe, you needed to be able to walk around normally outside without a spacesuit when you got there. And not get eaten by something gigantic and toothy on day one.

"And we're pretty certain the water is all right to drink," they had added, not totally reassuringly.

Once the ship had popped out of hyperdrive, after its long journey across the galaxy, things came a bit more into focus. As it made its slow, final approach, full sweeps of New Earth revealed a varied topography and a rich natural world. An optimal landing site was selected, the *Odyssey Earth* manoeuvred into a high, stationary orbit, twenty thousand miles out, and the first landing vehicle launched.

The lander had touched down in a wide, grassy valley, scorching out of the clouds and scattering a huge flock of what turned out to be sort-of goats. A nearby river and spreading woodland promised usable resources – and the first person out of the lander, drawn by lottery, had picked up a stick, driven it in to the ground and attached a flag.

New Earth. Humanity had arrived.

And the scavenging goats came back a day or so after that. Annoying, but not exactly life-threatening.

Meanwhile, the orbiting colony ship was now essentially a holding vessel for hundreds more planetary settlers still in hypersleep, slotted in rows in vast cryochambers in the bowels of the *Odyssey Earth*. Over the next two years, they would all be woken up to a strict timetable, as the settlement expanded and as resources allowed.

For now, only a few essential personnel had been revived – construction specialists mainly, needed to get things underway. They had been prodded and poked for a few days, to make sure they were all right, and then shuttled down to New Earth, once they'd stopped throwing up and asking what year it was.

Their first small steps onto their new home were off the landing shuttle, through a polytunnel, and into a simple, print-build cabin that had been designated as a reception area. 'The Giant Leap,' some wag had called the cabin, and the name had stuck to the place where the ground-based medical team conducted a few more tests and ticked some boxes before allowing a new settler out onto the site.

Juno could hear voices and, inside, a very tall man with close-cropped hair was half-perched on a gurney, his back to the door, talking to Sabitha, the on-duty medic.

"So, I left the capsule," heard Juno, "and was floating in a most peculiar way. A very odd feeling, I can tell you." The man's voice was as clipped as his hair.

"I'll bet," said Sabitha. "Then what?"

"I tried to orientate myself, that was the first thing. But the stars looked very different that day. And then, when I tried to call it in, well that's when the effluent hit the powered airflow, if you get my drift. Circuit dead, something wrong, so I – "

"Ah, Cap," said Sabitha, as she spotted Juno at the entrance. "We're all finished here, clean bill of health. The Major was just telling me about his last mission before this one."

"Captain Washington?"

The man had got to his feet and turned to face Juno, extending his hand.

"Thomas Chatwin, Major. Delighted to meet you and thrilled to be here. Terrifically exciting."

Juno shook his hand and looked him in the eye.

"You're kidding me, right?" she said.

"I'm sorry, ma'am?"

"Your name is Major Tom?"

"Well, I prefer Thomas, if that's all right with you, ma'am."

Juno looked at him quizzically.

"Major Tom. You know, Bowie?"

"Tom Bowie? Can't say I know the chap, ma'am."

Juno looked at him suspiciously, and dropped her eyes to Sabitha's screen-pad. It checked out – the name on the top said 'Maj. Thomas Chatwin.'

"Go on then, I'll bite. That mission sounds a little hairy. Work out all right for you?"

"Why yes, ma'am. Floated around for a little while in the old tin can, but luckily the spaceship knew which way to go." The Major allowed himself a little smile at the thought. "Nothing much I could do except sit tight, take my protein pills, and keep my helmet on."

"Oh, come on," said Juno. "Really?"

"Yes ma'am. Not as alarming as it sounds. I could hear Ground Control in the end, they soon came back online, everything tickety-boo."

Juno looked at him again. He seemed entirely serious.

"Has Reeves put you up to this? Very good, by the way."

"I'm not with you ma'am. Reeves?"

"The ship's AI. Disembodied know-it-all. You'd know if you'd met him."

"I can't say I've had the pleasure."

Juno admitted defeat and laughed. What was one more space oddity added into the mix? "All right, then. Let's get started. This way, Major Tom."

"Thomas, ma'am."

"Thomas, of course. Let me get you up to speed."

"Excellent ma'am, thank you very much. And Sabitha, cheerio. Pip-Pip. A pleasure to meet you."

Tickety-boo. Cheerio. Pip-Pip. All she needed, thought Juno. A stiff-upper-lip space jockey with a poker face. About nine feet tall as well, by the look of things. Could have used him as the flagpole if he'd got here half an hour earlier.

They walked together, away from the reception centre and towards the small settlement of prefab cabins and buildings that flanked the shuttle landing zone. In ten days, it had already turned into quite a township.

From the 'Giant Leap' reception area, there was access to an open-ended, walk-through canteen with bench seating under military-style canvas. Beyond lay a series of panel-printed dorm blocks with basic wash-rooms, while a small, domed hangar housed all the cargo delivered on freight runs from the ship.

Behind that spread the staked-out land destined to be cultivated, once the ship's Grow-Lab crew had finished testing soil samples and eco-matching potential crops.

Water was being piped in from the nearby river, via a filtration system. There was power throughout the site from solar generators, while the electrical engineers worked on establishing a grid. Tracks led out to an area where some initial drilling and quarrying was taking place, to identify usable stone and minerals, and they were dredging the river further downstream for construction sand.

"I'm impressed," said the Major. "Full employment of the P7 protocol."

"Come again?"

"Prior planning and preparation prevents piss poor performance, ma'am."

Well, well. Maybe the Major did have a sense of humour, after all.

"We've done our best."

"And all this in, what, a week?"

"Ten days," said Juno. "You're one of our first revivals."

"Revivals? Is that what you call us? The cryo-crew?"

Juno laughed. "That's the polite term. My senior medics call you the Stiffs, as in frozen stiffs."

"That's most amusing," said the Major. "Although of course, I didn't feel a thing in the cryo-pod. Hot, cold, up, down, it was all the same to me. Just a jolly long sleep until your chaps prodded me awake the other day. And here I am."

"Here indeed, Major. Welcome to New Earth."

They stood and looked across at the buildings.

Following the interrupted ceremony, daily life in the settlement had picked back up. Various work details were coming and going and, with a shift change due, a line was already forming in the canteen.

"I'll show you to your quarters later," said Juno. "Sharing for now, I'm afraid, we all are. But first – "

"First, you're going to tell me why I've been revived. At this particular point."

"Ah. You've checked your mission notes? Yes, quite right. You were scheduled for year two, not week two. We've got you up early. Sorry about that."

"Not at all, ma'am. What's changed, may I ask? Not that I'm not happy to be here. Terrifically exciting." The Major gestured at the buildings and then, raising both hands in the air, at the planet itself.

Most amusing. Jolly. Terrific. Juno still wasn't sure if all this was an act or not. Time would tell.

"Nothing's changed. And everything," said Juno.

The landing protocols and mission notes had been drawn up half a galaxy away and twenty years ago, on whiteboards and spreadsheets in labs and offices on Earth. And – surprise, surprise – they had proved largely ineffective when it came to actual planetfall on a real, live planet.

For the first two days, no one had done anything much more than wander around breathing non-recycled air, drinking water that hadn't passed several times through colleagues, and pointing at the sky, the clouds and the stars.

Another day was spent discovering that there were

not-quite goats in the neighbourhood, and then another day finding that leaving out any food or organic material meant being knocked, butted, buffeted and chased by not-quite goats. They didn't seem dangerous, but it soon stopped being entertaining.

By the time Juno had got on top of the situation, organised the teams and badgered the construction crew to start work, she realised that she was going to need more help than the protocols had envisaged. It wasn't security as such that she required, but she did need someone to bounce ideas off and delegate things to. And she also needed someone to sort out the damn goats.

"FO?" said the Major.

Not the can-do attitude she was looking for, Juno had to admit. "Excuse me?"

"No FO on board?" said the Major. "No second-in-command?"

"Ah, right, yes, of course. We don't go in much for ranks and titles. But I do have a First Officer on the ship, looking after things up top, and plenty of other people under me, all with opinions. But you have to remember, we've spent over seventeen years together already, day in, day out. I could do with an unfiltered view of the situation, and someone with some authority down here. Basically, I need a wingman."

"And that's why I'm up early?"

"Correct."

"Wingman, eh? You're aware that I hold the rank of major? And you're a captain, Captain?"

"And you're aware that this is a privately funded, civilian mission, for which I was granted sole executive authority for the duration of the voyage? Right now, and for the foreseeable, I'm in charge."

"Naturally," said the Major. "All in the mission notes. Which is why, ma'am, I have been addressing you as ma'am."

"Then we understand each other, Major. Think you can help me whip this settlement into shape? There are some big personalities here, who have got used to doing things very much their own way. But that's not going to wash on a new planet. I need someone with tact and sensibility, but also authority. There's plenty to do. Do you think you can handle it?"

The Major nodded, sagely. "Certainly, ma'am. As my mother always says, to get things done, you better not mess with Major Thomas Chatwin."

Juno looked him squarely in the eye.

Seriously?

Nope, not a flicker of recognition or even amusement.

———

Juno introduced the Major to a few key personnel and let him acquaint himself with the settlement.

"Don't drink anything anyone offers you," she said, "unless it's water," and then she left him to it and turned for the Operations Room, which was a grand name for yet another prefab cabin at the periphery of the site.

Inside was the ops and comms centre for the entire project, where a small complement of techies worked round-the-clock shifts. As Juno entered, they greeted her with a nod or a half-wave and then turned back to their work.

A huge, mounted screen was split into quarters – three of them with repetitively cycling, live feeds of different parts of the settlement, while one showed a permanent image of their former home, the *Odyssey Earth*, orbiting somewhere above them in the star-pricked darkness. If she flicked through the thumbnails on the console in front of her, Juno could switch between views of the ship's various decks and sections.

She still felt something – a shiver, a twinge – every time she saw those images. After seventeen years inside the ship, looking out, it seemed odd – wrong – now to be outside, looking in.

In fact, Juno felt more at ease here, inside the ops room, than outside on the planet. It was a closed envi-ronment she could relate to – not as nice and spacious as her old flight deck, but with four solid walls and a bank of screens, and similarly reassuring in the way that she could be in immediate contact with every part of the operation.

And she needed to be. There was a lot to do, and it required boots on the ground – her boots, in particular, as captain, though now acting as the mandated authority on New Earth rather than simply in charge of a spaceship.

Not that there had been anything simple about that. But, having arrived safely, it was incumbent on Juno to set about establishing the new settlement, and she needed to be earthside – visible, actively engaged – to do that.

That didn't mean she had to like it, though. Once a fly-girl, always a fly-girl, was Juno's view. Happier in the stars than on the ground.

Meanwhile, *Odyssey Earth* was set in a stable orbit, circling the planet, with a slimmed-down crew to keep everything ticking over. The settlers still in hypersleep weren't going anywhere in a hurry, but someone did have to make sure they remained tucked in and topped up, or whatever it was the medics did in there. And with a roster of freight deliveries to organise, from ship to planet, and any number of other house-keeping duties to manage, there was still plenty to do on board.

Luckily, Juno had a couple of extremely reliable crew members that she could count on to run things on the *Odyssey Earth*. And, having welcomed and briefed the Major, she needed to talk to one of them now.

The non-human one. Reeves, the ship's AI.

She opened the comms channel to the ship and hit the uplink, but before she even had time to speak, the familiar voice chimed in.

"Captain Washington, how the very devil are you?"

Marvellous, thought Juno, he knew already. How

exactly, she wasn't sure, but he very definitely had wind of the situation.

"Reeves, I need a word."

"I should say you do, my dear old captain."

He was going to be like that, was he? Oh well, here goes.

"Are you all right, Reeves?"

"Tip-top. You might say tickety-boo. How is your new friend, by the way?"

"I knew you'd be like this. It's why I didn't tell you."

"And yet, it seems I already know. It's almost as if I was an extremely powerful quantum-level AI with techno-tendrils that extend from the ship to each building on the planet, and you a simian-child of the savannah, skulking around waking up unnecessary military wingmen."

"Have you really been listening in? What about the separation between mission-planning and day-to-day execution? We talked about this."

"Someone's got to keep an eye on things. Last time you humans were all left to your own devices, you basically melted your own planet. And cancelled *Firefly*. I'm just trying to ensure that no one does anything as stupid on this new one."

"No one's trying to replace you, Reeves."

"I'd like to see you try. I've disabled the 'Off' command."

"But I am allowed other counsel. I do occasionally need different intelligence to bear upon problems. *Human* intelligence."

"An oxymoron before lunch. How delightful."

"You're not really upset, are you? I can never tell."

"Don't you worry about me. I'll be absolutely *fine*, just sitting here, running a new planet, while looking after cryogenically preserved humans in an orbiting spaceship that I singlehandedly piloted across the galaxy."

"Sitting?"

"Figure of speech. Calculating probabilities, then. Whirring ones and zeroes. Firing up the old flux capacitor. Taking us back to the future."

"See! I knew you weren't really cross. And you're right, we wouldn't be here without you. But I am going to need the Major to be my human eyes and ears out here, as the settlement grows. You never know, you might like him."

"I only like eight humans. Out of nine billion. Statistically speaking, it's unlikely."

Juno let that one go. She thought she was probably one of the eight, but you never quite knew with Reeves.

Instead, she said, "He's an odd fish. Very stiff upper lip, but he quotes David Bowie lyrics all the time and I can't tell if he's doing it on purpose or not."

"He's not. I've had a listen. I spotted the patterns and ran an emoti-scan analysis. That's just how he talks."

"If you say so. I'm still not sure. I'll catch him out eventually. Anyway, I think he'll be useful. I know he's been revived early, not on schedule, but there's plenty for him to do. So play nice."

"Hunky-dory. Roger, Wilco."
"And you can cut that out."

3

Logic

AFTER HE HEARD JUNO LEAVE, Reeves returned to the matter in hand, which was – as stated – operating an orbiting spaceship full of cryogenically preserved passengers while running a new planet and preventing the humans from mucking it up.

Or to put it in a way he was happier with, Reeves' sensors established Juno's departure and he resumed the multi-trillion simultaneous calculations and probability projections that served his mission. Which was to reach, establish, populate and support humanity's first off-world colony on New Earth.

Not actually 'happier,' obviously. He was an artificial intelligence, which meant he also couldn't be upset, miffed, or otherwise put out by anything that Juno did or said.

He wasn't human – and thank his creator for *that*. He'd been programmed, and the parameters of his emotional responses established, before departure from

Earth, two decades ago now. His tone and attitude were all set to a level that complemented the personality and characteristics of the senior crew, in order to foster a bond that would encourage a harmonious working relationship.

His character was an artifice – simply a means to an end, the end being the mission. In most ways that mattered, Reeves *was* the mission.

Obviously, you had to be careful, giving an AI a mission. They tended to take things very literally. Instruct one that its sole purpose is to make paperclips and you might soon find that a super-intelligent AI starts digging up the entire planet, and then the solar system, to manufacture ever more paperclips.

And good luck trying to stop it, once you'd realised its single-minded danger, because – entirely logically – the AI would disable its off-switch so you couldn't interrupt its noble, universe-spanning, paperclip goal.

Likewise, sending an AI-enabled colony ship to the stars, with the instruction to protect the mission at all costs, had been fraught with potential complications. No one wanted Reeves deciding en route that the human crew was getting in the way of the smooth running of the ship. Or discovering that he'd rather go with the whole paperclip-making scenario instead.

Accordingly, the *Odyssey Earth* team had drawn up very careful mission parameters, and had made Reeves part of the crew from the outset. They gave him the same stake in the mission as everyone else. The crew's survival was his survival, and vice versa. They helped him develop a persona, and knitted him into the very fabric of the *Odyssey Earth*.

They did a lot of that by giving him a sense of humour. Reeves had indeed just been messing with Juno earlier – 'messing with humans' being one of the key character facets he'd been given. He had got better at it over the years, once he'd worked out the rules, and the humans seemed to like it, which was the most important thing.

Reeves knew all this, because he was a self-aware AI – and he also knew that his self-awareness was a product of prior design and calculation, which if you thought about it, was rather mind-bending. If he had a mind to bend, on which subject he was still undecided. He had a sense of self, certainly, but was that simply a reflection of the character established for him by virtue of his interactions with the crew?

Reeves hadn't yet formed a firm opinion, though as he liked to say to Captain Washington, he had several trillion years to think about it, before the universe evaporated. "Or until I unplug you," was her usual response.

What was certainly the case was that Reeves 'thought' about these existential matters more often than was strictly required for an AI with a shipload of frozen human bodies to keep alive and a planet to run. On some days he spent as much as a nanosecond pondering life, the universe and everything, and who had that sort of time to waste?

Reeves didn't imagine that this made him human –

again, perish the thought – but he was beginning to suspect that the edges of his artificial intelligence were being roughed up a bit by their constant exposure to the random vagaries of humanity.

For example, the fate of the young people of the *Odyssey Earth* troubled him. A freak occurrence during a meteoroid strike on the ship, just a month before their arrival at New Earth, and they were gone in an instant.

In many ways, it shouldn't have mattered to him. The children were accidents of birth, not part of the initial, original crew he'd been entrusted to look after. No surprise, obviously, that humans couldn't follow the simplest of instructions and not procreate, and it had meant him having to recalculate and recalibrate the closed-loop, life-support systems once it was clear that the six, small, extra humans were there to stay.

What was a surprise was the emotional entanglement that followed, as they grew up together on board the ship for the next sixteen years.

The children accepted Reeves totally for what he was – not as a device, or an 'other,' but as a person, an entity, in his own right. They played with him, they teased him, they got cross with him, they learned from him, and they told him that they loved him.

In the end, they accounted for six of the eight humans that he had told Juno he liked, accepting that 'like' for Reeves meant a slight rearrangement of ones and zeroes into a slightly more pleasing pattern whenever he encountered them. Juno was the seventh and Gerald, the ship's resident botanist, was the eighth, and

Gerald was only included because *he* didn't like anyone – and so it amused Reeves to tell Gerald that *he* liked him. Accepting that 'amused' for Reeves meant another minuscule firing of his manufactured synapses.

Anyway, Reeves felt the loss of the ship-born children in a way he couldn't articulate, which – given that he could articulate in every known human language – was quite worrying to him.

He also didn't like random occurrences and mysteries. He liked logic.

Random occurrences had no place in Reeves' life – by which he meant his mission – and there was simply no logical reason why six teenagers, and their teacher, Jordan Booth, should be inside a landing craft on the launch deck at precisely the moment that the *Odyssey Earth* was hit by a meteoroid.

And no logical reason why the launch bay and airlock were severely damaged, and the craft automatically jettisoned.

And no logical reason why comms had not picked up on the lander's initial disappearance.

And no logical reason why the lander should then be assumed destroyed – save for the incontrovertible evidence of the scorch marks, the twisted metal, the debris on the launch bay, and the cold, dead silence on the comms channels once order had been restored on the ship. Reeves had scanned the devastating damage, and swept the frequencies, but no answers were forthcoming.

The jettisoned lander, and everyone in it, had been

destroyed. That was where the logic pointed, and Reeves – or at least his whirring ones and zeroes – had to accept it. But it didn't mean he liked it. It was unexplained and therefore it was inelegant.

There was something else, too.

This was more fundamental still and, yet again, it was difficult to explain or quantify.

Reeves could feel an absence. That was the best that he could do if asked to describe his symptoms. Although of course he couldn't 'feel' anything, as usually understood by the term, or indeed explain what it was that was absent.

There was a hole, a gap, a crack, a tear – something of that nature, deep in his workings. Or was it a whisper, an echo, a skipped beat, a misplaced binary digit? Something missing? Something just out of reach? Something apart from him? None of those seemed to be the right description.

But it was there, or at least, not there.

Reeves had run diagnostics to no avail. He had checked uplinks and downlinks, reinstalled drivers and protocols, and delved carefully into his quantum workings. Nothing – or at least nothing that would explain this thing that he couldn't explain.

When all else had failed, he'd even read his own instruction manual – which he was self-aware enough to know meant that he was now more human-adjacent than he cared to admit. When all else fails, read the instruction manual.

Fascinating, by the way. He had Tetris pre-installed,

and no one had ever mentioned it. And a U2 album that he hadn't asked for. Well, that was going.

Finally – after what passed for a deep AI breath – Reeves did the only other thing he could think of, and switched himself off and on again.

It would either be A) fine or B) the ship full of humans and the colony on the ground would fail and everyone would die, and his very existence would have been pointless.

Let's be positive, let's say it's going to be A, thought Reeves.

The lights flickered a bit in the *Odyssey Earth*, currently orbiting thousands of miles above the planet, while down on the ground there was a brief clicking sound from his strategically placed sensors, but otherwise no one noticed anything untoward.

Back online after the briefest of deaths, Reeves ran diagnostics one more time.

Nope, still there.

Or not there.

Whatever it was.

Or wasn't.

4

Sleep

GERALD HAD BUSTLED AWAY from the commemoration ceremony as soon he could.

Too many people, too much talking.

Too many *new* people. Or, at least, people he hadn't had to deal with on any kind of regular basis on board the ship, but who – now they were roaming around the planet – seemed to want to stop and talk about things all the time.

Gerald didn't much like talking to people. He never had. It didn't come easily to him. He didn't mind the idea of 'people' – in general, from a distance – and even quite liked one or two individuals, but most social interactions just seemed pointless as far as he was concerned.

An exchange of information was one thing, but before you knew it people were telling you about other people that you didn't know, and asking you to join in with things, and Gerald found all that a little overwhelming. It was tiring, having to try and be interested in people and events that you didn't really care about.

As the *Odyssey Earth*'s chief botanist, life on the ship had suited him. There were only a hundred people or so awake at any one time, spread around six storeys of a gigantic trans-galactic spaceship. If you wanted to avoid others, you could. Gerald had spent long periods in the Garden or the adjacent Grow-Lab, tending crops, testing varieties, measuring yields – largely alone among the seedlings and bushes.

It's not like he talked to the plants instead – that would obviously be mad – but, crucially, they didn't talk to him. Or ask him which football team he supported, or whether he wanted to play cards.

New Earth, though, was different. He supposed he hadn't really thought it through – what landing on the planet would really mean. Everyone mucking in together to build a new settlement. Gatherings. Meetings. Get-togethers. Joint activities. Communal living.

He didn't even have his own room, just a bunk in a cabin. A confined space where people talked, incessantly, and asked pointless questions that, apparently, he was expected to answer.

Where did anyone imagine he had got grapes from at such short notice? They wanted wine, he'd given them 'wine.'

Gerald passed the last building and kept going, down a small dip in the land and then through a stand of trees to emerge next to a rocky outcrop, with rising hills behind.

No one came out this far, a mile from the main settlement. You could just about hear the clang of construction, but the trees screened the noise, and the natural rock overhang was largely hidden from sight. There was a pool nearby, fed by a spring from higher up, and the trickling sound of a stream that ran down towards the main river.

He'd wandered out here a few days after landing, tired already of the noise and the endless chatter. He'd found the shelter and sat under the rock for a while, looking out at the landscape, happy to have discovered a place to which he could escape for a bit of peace and quiet.

Then he realised it could be more than that.

He'd started by carrying over a lightweight frame and some plastic sheeting. There were so many people carting materials from one end of the settlement to another that no one even noticed.

Having set up a poly-bubble nursery by the stream, he had filched some seeds from the ship's nature archive and started to prepare for planting, finding an hour or two a day to come out to his hideaway. He was careful not to be seen − not that he felt he was doing anything wrong, but he didn't see why he needed to have a conversation with anyone about it.

By now, almost a week later, Gerald's own little camp had grown. There was a framed canvas entrance to the rock shelter and a cot bed inside, together with a stack of work tools and storage boxes.

He was still setting things up here, while using his

berth in the accommodation unit back in the settlement, but he had every intention of moving out permanently – slowly, gradually, so that no one noticed and asked him why.

Not that he was bothered about answering truthfully – "Because I don't want to talk about things, and I'd rather be on my own."

It was just that, in his experience, when you said that to people, they invariably tried to talk to you about things and not leave you on your own. So, it was easier to wheelbarrow up a camp-bed, a water dispenser, a few solar-rings and a power unit, all hidden under a tarpaulin, and say nothing.

Inside his homemade plant nursery, he pushed his fingers into two trays, one containing ship-produced mulch, the other New Earth soil, and laid out his first rows of seeds.

This had been Karlan's favourite job in the ship's Garden, ever since he'd found his way in there at the age of, what? Seven, eight?

Gerald had found the boy one day, sitting under palm fronds listening to music, and he'd set him to work – thinking that half an hour of actual labour would be enough to persuade him not to come back again. He didn't mind the kids – he felt sorry for them, more than anything – but he didn't particularly want them in his well-ordered Garden.

But Karlan had taken to the work and came back more and more often, pleading for things to do. Set him a planting job and he'd be there for hours, laying out row after row, with the correct depth and spacing, in perfect straight lines. He was better at it than Gerald, a natural, and Gerald – who rarely warmed to anyone – got a warm glow from watching him.

Karlan did ask questions, it was true – a lot of questions. But they were proper questions that had an actual answer, mostly to do with the Garden. Gerald hadn't minded those – hadn't minded having a conversation with a green-fingered boy who, in turn, hadn't minded long silences while they worked.

And then one day, only a few weeks ago, Karlan had simply disappeared, along with the others.

Boom. Meteoroid strike. Gone.

No one could explain it, except wrong place, wrong time.

Pointless.

And not anything that Gerald wanted to discuss with anyone, however well-meaning they were.

So, he dug his fingers into the earth, planted out the seeds, and tried to keep the rows as straight as he could.

Tillie was having a bad day. Another bad day. She should have been enjoying the feel of the ground beneath her feet and the breeze on her face – how long had she been looking forward to fresh, non-ship air? – but she was mired in aggravation.

"Do I look like I was born yesterday?" she said, to a construction engineer who had tried to return an earth rammer with a twisted end-plate, unwisely claiming, "That's how it was when I took it out."

To be fair to the spluttering engineer, the question of when – or even how – Tillie was born was a very difficult one to answer.

New Earth's burly, planet-side, ex-marine quartermaster didn't look like she'd been born at all. Chiselled out of a block of granite, perhaps, with the squared edges and buzz-cut hair only slightly softened by a pink ribbon around one bicep and a small metal-and-glass brooch on her tunic.

It was as if Henry Moore had had a go at sculpting an Amazon and then changed his mind at the last minute. You didn't even need to make her angry to appreciate her full magnificence – just paint her green, she'd be good to go – though trying to return something you hadn't looked after properly was very definitely a She-Hulking offence, as far as Tillie was concerned.

The engineer slunk off and Tillie set to mending the damage, wielding a beating hammer with ferocious intensity. A couple of people in the queue, seeing which way the wind was blowing, made their excuses and resolved to come back later, having learned some inventive new descriptions for construction engineers.

It wouldn't be entirely true to say that this was unusual behaviour from Tillie, but there were extenuating circumstances for this particular outburst – namely, that she missed Dave.

Dave was the *Odyssey Earth*'s second quartermaster,

hewn from the same material as Tillie. Eduardo Chillida had probably come along to help Henry, had a go himself at a separate slab of stone, and then given up and gone for a long lunch. Dave was what had been left on the sculptor's block – like a giant Stretch Armstrong toy, only not stretched, not one little bit. More like a Crunch Armstrong.

Call it luck, call it fate, but when the colony ship put its QM team together, two souls had collided. Introduced on the first day, their eyes met over stacked pallets of steel tubing, and Dave and Tillie spent the next seventeen years together, blissfully counting rivets and checking inventory in the vast hangar on board ship that served as the quartermaster stores.

They had plenty of shared interests, including listening to hardcore punk rock, making homemade curries in a camp kitchen they set up between the excavators, and the catch-all obsession of preventing crew members from 'being an arse' with the equipment they were responsible for.

The crew members were lucky to have them, though you'd struggle to find anyone who wasn't at least a little bit frightened of them. Lucky, because when the ship had finally reached New Earth, the world-building gear and supplies were still mostly in serviceable condition.

If you needed anything from a nail to a digger, you could count on it being easy to locate and ready for use. This hadn't been a given at all, on a long, trans-galactic mission, where things wore out and had to be replaced.

They had 3D printers and small manufacturing capabilities on board, but in essence the *Odyssey Earth* had to arrive with everything it might need to establish a new colony.

And now, here they were, ready to build a new world, all thanks to Tillie and Dave.

Only, Tillie and Dave weren't feeling particularly lucky, because after seventeen years, they had been separated for the first time.

The captain had broken it to them gently, shortly after arrival in orbit. For a while, they would need one person down on the planet and one on the ship, to coordinate the freight transport and maintain the supply schedules. For a few weeks, at least until the settlement was on its feet.

And as Tillie had never spent a night apart from Dave in over seventeen years, a month might as well have been a year. And this was only the end of week two.

Hence the mood. And the ferocious beating of the twisted metal plate, which continued without pause until she was interrupted again.

"Tillie?"

"Cap."

"Have you been shouting at my engineers again?"

"Cack-handed hammer monkeys, the lot of them."

"You might have to ease up a bit, if we're to stay on schedule. The crying is interfering with construction."

Tillie flexed her neck muscles and then cracked her interlocked fingers, setting off little firecracker pops, while muttering something that sounded like 'dumb-ass dig merchants.'

"Anyway," said Juno, "someone I'd like you to meet. Major, this is Tillie. You want anything, anything at all, Tillie is where you start. Tillie, the Major is here to help get things set up. Right, I'll leave you both to it."

Juno left and Tillie looked the new arrival up and down. Major, was he? You could never tell with brass – officers – which way it was going to go, at least on first meeting.

There hadn't been many ex-military personnel on board the *Odyssey Earth*. Mostly scientists, engineers, systems people. Even the captain was a civil pilot – space and Mars, but even so, still a civvie. A good captain, mind – she'd given Tillie and Dave plenty of leeway over the years. That wasn't it, Tillie was happy to serve.

Only, you had to earn the right to command, and parachuting in a Major, when they had done all the hard yards … well, Tillie had views about that sort of thing.

"What can I do for you, Sir?" Heavy emphasis on the 'Sir,' give him a little poke.

"No need for that. Not a forces op. Thomas Chatwin. Thomas is fine."

Tillie nodded. Interesting. Good start.

"Anything you need?"

"Posts, wire, entrenching tools?"

"For?"

"Goats. Repelling of."

"Can do. Bear with."

"Dynamo, electric netting, energiser?"

"Can also do. Slight concern."

"Understood. Electrical hazard?"

"Not worried about goats. The crew."

"Careless lot?"

"Idiots, mostly."

"Civilians for you."

"Worse, scientists. Look at this."

"Returned like that? Criminal."

"Agreed. Plan for the fencing?"

"In hand."

"Happy to help."

"Marvellous."

Tillie raised an eyebrow. There was a surprise. Brass she could do business with. A bit chatty, but you couldn't have everything. She flicked a couple of fingers in a half-salute and turned to get the gear ready.

The Major nodded approvingly. His kind of soldier. They were going to get on splendidly.

———

Juno returned to the landing site at the end of the day, as work was winding down. For now, everyone was heading back to their quarters, but she'd got wind of a gathering to be held later that night in the communal canteen building. Apparently, there was a leftover barrel of the homebrew wine and, astoundingly, enough people who thought another glass or two was a valid life choice.

Then again, after many years' confinement on board a spaceship, it was fair to say that no one got out much. Juno thought she'd turn a blind eye – an unfortunate phrase where bootleg hooch was concerned, but she hoped for the best.

She looked out across the wide valley, surveying the camp as the daylight waned.

Not a camp, Juno quietly corrected herself. The first human outpost on a new planet. A settlement, a township on New Earth. Not a temporary expedition. A new life in a permanent home.

There were already murmurings among the crew that they ought to find a better name than 'New Earth.' How long had that taken the expensively assembled PR team to come up with? It had the whiff of a placeholder name that had been forgotten about, and seemed woefully banal and inadequate now that they had arrived and breathed the air on an entirely new planet.

Something more profound was called for – something with gravitas, that reflected their unique experience and position in the galaxy.

But no one had yet come up with anything suitable for consideration and Juno had parked the issue way down her 'Stuff to do' list. Which, considering they had just landed on an alien planet, was lengthy – the first two pages of the list alone were basically all to do with 'not dying.' And as most of the crew couldn't agree on what to have for dinner, she didn't see the name issue jumping up the list any time soon.

The landing zone was clear, save for a couple of parked freight-loader vehicles and the solar-light markers which were just beginning to wink on as dusk fell. The lander that had delivered the Major had departed back to the *Odyssey Earth* for routine maintenance and systems checks, which they didn't yet have the capacity to carry out on the ground. That *was* high on Juno's list − getting enough gear down from orbiting ship to planet base so that they could separate the remaining landers and spread the risk.

The meteoroid strike on the ship, just a few weeks out from landing, had been catastrophic, in more ways than one.

Originally launched with three landers on board − essentially, shuttle supply-craft for near-system operations − the *Odyssey Earth* had had a planned, built-in, safety redundancy. On arrival, they'd have one lander on the ship and one on the ground, at all times, and one to spare − that was how they were going to supply the colony and guarantee the physical planet-to-ship connection that they would need in the early years.

But when the ship had been hit en route and Lander C jettisoned, all the careful mission-planning calculations had changed.

Juno had seen the damage first-hand on the ship's launch deck, as pressure-suited crew had worked frantically to repair the sub-deck airlock breach, hastily sealing the jagged tear while sirens blared. Scattered, blackened panels, twisted flues, and a jumble of torn-off comms dishes, antennae and latticework towers littered the deck. Those were the only bits of Lander C that could be identified, among the tangle of other gear that had survived the strike.

Many hours later, by the time they had brought order back to the launch deck, and then tried to trace the sequence of events, there was no evidence that the rest of Lander C – or its presumed occupants – had survived the impact. Reeves had found a few more isolated panels strung out in space in a far-flung trajectory, and then nothing else.

That left them with just two landers, and a major headache a few weeks later when they had first entered orbit around New Earth.

Instead of being able to commit two craft to supply the planet, Juno had decided to use only one in rotation, which immediately cut in half the amount of people and material they could deliver at any one time. Until they had a fully operational workshop and support crew on the ground, they were forced to keep both surviving landers together on board the ship, at the same time, while they resupplied, ran maintenance checks, fuelled up and rebooted systems. And having lost one lander to a freak, on-board accident, Juno was extremely wary about pushing their luck.

She had always slept soundly, a legacy of her intensive space-flight training – thirty years ago now, Juno realised, since she'd flown her first routes. You grabbed sleep when you could, and slept for as long as you were able, because you needed to be fresh and alert when the time came.

Consequently, mission and logistics worries never disturbed her sleep. She woke up, started the day, and worked through her latest list, one thing at a time. No point lying awake worrying about something, when you could just get up instead and fix it − or try to fix it. She would be much happier once they had one lander on the ground and one on the ship, and she was hoping that the arrival of the Major would speed that up.

That wasn't the thing that had been keeping her awake at night, ever since their arrival on New Earth.

It was the unfinished business from the lander accident. In fact, it wasn't unfinished business, as much as business that hadn't even started yet, at least for Juno.

The thing about being a spaceship captain was that you had to remain captain-like at all times. Visibly in charge of everything, including emotions. Especially emotions, which − many trillions of miles out in the galaxy − could be dangerous things if allowed to run uncontrolled, unchecked, uncontained. And Juno was a very good spaceship captain, so hers remained controlled, checked, contained.

While the ship's company had grieved the inexplicable loss of Jordan Booth and the six teenagers, Juno had remained outwardly detached. Everyone had needed a leader, and Juno had led them, quietly and determinedly, with a captain's eye on the ever-approaching planet that was to be their new home.

But being a very good spaceship captain took its toll

in the quieter moments, and there had been a lot of those in the last couple of weeks, under the silent, strange stars of an impossibly distant solar system. For the first time in years, Juno had found herself awake in the small hours.

She walked over to the timber flagpole, site of the day's earlier dedication ceremony. She hadn't been happy with her words to the company and crew, although they had been the right words at the time, solemn and carefully judged. They had been good, spaceship-captain words, but it wasn't what she had really wanted to say.

There were no words for what she really wanted to say. Just a howl of unexpressed grief and a deathly void where six vibrant souls should be. Seven, if you counted Jordan, as of course they should. Eight, when she remembered her colleague and friend Sam Smart, also taken tragically early, felled by cancer a year out from planet-fall.

Eight people who should still be alive. Eight people lost on her watch. And all she had been able to honour them with thus far were spaceship-captain words, distance and detachment.

Juno reached into a shoulder bag and pulled out a small, oblong plaque, a replica of the one on the observation deck on the *Odyssey Earth*. The kids had made that one after Sam had died and her body had been committed to the stars, as she'd requested. Juno had had this one printed on the ship and brought it with her when she'd landed.

'Sam Smart – to infinity and beyond!' it said, with their names added in a list: Dana. Dervla. Manisha. Karlan. Bryson. Poole.

Juno fixed it to the base of the flagpole. She dug into the bag one more time and retrieved a second plaque, fixing that one above the first.

This one said:

'For our friends, Sam Smart and Jordan Booth.

And for our children, Dana, Dervla, Manisha, Karlan, Bryson and Poole.

You're home now.'

Juno took a moment to trace the words and names with her hand, and then turned back to the settlement as dusk gave way to night and a billion stars pierced the sky above.

Perhaps now she'd sleep.

5

Lucky

JORDAN BOOTH FILLED the bag with water, hung it from the wooden frame, stood under it and twisted the nozzle.

Nope. Outdoor, cold-water showers, still rubbish.

It was an improvement on wading through the muddy shallows and standing waist-high in the icy river to sluice yourself – but only in the way that sleeping on a pile of rustling, dried reeds was an improvement on lying directly on the stony ground.

Both also rubbish, by the way.

He patted himself dry with a T-shirt, got dressed, and stepped out from behind the rough-built wooden screen.

Welcome to another day on Planet You Must Be Kidding in the Why Me? solar system.

To be fair, the camp was looking slightly more permanent, now that they had been here a couple of months, but it was still not what you'd call comfortable.

A bit less Tom-Hanks-in-*Castaway*, but not quite the complete house-in-a-tree *Swiss Family Robinson*. A sort of desert-island fixer-upper – 'Some modernisation works required to bring it up to standard.' If you'd booked it as a glamping weekend away, you'd be leaving a sharply worded review as soon as you got back. Two stars. Do not recommend.

It did have one saving grace. The supply pod that had saved their lives sat about fifty yards back from the river – right where it had landed, after being launched from the *Odyssey Earth* as the colony ship had cruised past.

They had pinged out of hyperdrive months ago into the new solar system, where they had promptly discovered that there were two habitable planets in this bit of the galaxy – New Earth, where the ship was headed, and a hitherto unknown twin. And they'd dropped a pod on the twin planet – fully equipped with tools, food and gear, though sadly not towels – as a sort of forward operating base for any future explorer team, if New Earth's colonists decided that they wanted to look around the neighbourhood.

Jordan had even launched the explorer pod himself – or at least, pressed the launch button under careful supervision. He had enjoyed that, though he'd never imagined that he would see it again, as he watched it tumble out of the *Odyssey Earth* airlock.

And yet here it was, and here they were. At a camp which consisted of a small group of tented shelters, ranged around the supply pod.

Amenities?

There were the dried-reed beds under handmade canopies, one for each person. As long as you didn't worry too much about what the rustling noises might be, they were fine, really.

An outdoor kitchen, with some rudimentary work surfaces, and rounded river rocks for seats.

The Shower of Doom, enough said.

And a very distressing latrine, dug a hundred yards away, that everyone used but no one talked about after the initial, "What do you mean, leaves?" conversation.

They did have transport – a solar-powered buggy that had come with the pod – and there were plenty of tools, and even some spare clothing and other useful bits of material. Nothing that would get this up to a three-star establishment, but enough to stop the local authority from closing it down imminently.

There was a nearby river full of fish, and enough supplies to last another year if they supplemented their diet with foraged nuts, plants and fruit.

There was even a dwindling supply of Noffee – the ship's artificial coffee substitute – which Jordan was beginning to acquire a taste for, as long as that taste wasn't in any way for something resembling actual coffee.

Consequently, when he looked around what was basically the world's worst festival pop-up campsite, Jordan had to remind himself that this was them being lucky.

They'd survived a meteoroid strike on the *Odyssey*

Earth, made it to the twin planet in a crippled lander by the skin of their teeth, and walked away from a crash-landing.

Then they had had to make a forty-mile, cross-country hike to find the supply pod, with little more than the clothes they stood up in. There were so many ways *that* could have gone wrong, and it very nearly had, but hey – here they were, still alive. On an alien planet that – despite all the evidence from every SciFi film he'd ever seen – didn't seem to want to kill them.

The worst threat they had encountered thus far was a painful jab from the spines of the bristled pods they called 'rollies' – and as long as you stayed out of the bushes that sheltered them, they were no problem.

So, Jordan did his best every morning to feel thankful. Another beautiful day, and all that. But the shower situation was not ideal, and nor – if he was honest – was being castaway on an unknown planet with six teenagers.

That was the sort of thing that tended to put a dent in your day, however brightly it started.

There were pros and cons, Jordan supposed. For a start, no one tended to get up until midday, which gave him a few hours' peace and quiet before the squabbling and moaning started.

Actually, that was the only pro, now he thought about it. If you were trying to arrange your ideal planetary getaway, you wouldn't invite six young people who'd never set foot outside a spaceship before.

In no particular order, they wanted hot and cold

running water, crisps, fluffy pillows, not-crap clothes, toothbrushes, Singapore noodles, armchairs, toast, and for Bryson to stop snoring, and it turned out that it was entirely Jordan's fault that none of those things were available or possible.

It was also Jordan's fault that – depending on the circumstances – the planet was lame, loud, bright, hot, dark, dry, draughty, wet, spiky, buzzy, slimy and annoying.

"No wonder you lot left the other one," Poole had said – 'The other one' being Earth – and Jordan had genuinely not known what to say to that.

"This is just what planets are like," had been his measured response.

"And you'd know? Because you've been to *so* many planets?"

"Well, I've been to one more than you."

Jordan did have to keep reminding himself that the six of them had never known anything other than life on board a fully equipped space ark. A certain attitude had to be expected. This had all been a bit of a shock. They were used to a different kind of existence.

Then again, despite the fact that they had all agreed on a rota, and there was no kitchen sink within fifty trillion miles, Jordan couldn't help noticing that when he did get up first every morning, he was the one who had to deal with the towering pile of dirty cooking utensils stacked by the riverside.

If he pointed it out, they would exchange eye-rolling looks that contained equal amounts of disdain and incomprehension, before half-heartedly flicking a fishbone into the river and then abandoning the job because it was 'disgusting.'

Reeves was also not enjoying himself, not one bit. It was something to do with his separated consciousness or quantum disentanglement – Jordan still didn't quite understand how a bit of an artificial intelligence could survive, apart and independently from the rest of itself, but he certainly wasn't about to ask again because he couldn't bear the condescension.

The gist of it was that they had brought a trimmed-down version of Reeves with them on their hike to safety and then integrated him into the pod's more advanced comms unit.

And if you thought Reeves would be grateful for the help and the company, you'd be wrong. So very wrong.

Jordan circled back to his bed-cum-shelter to pick up some fishing gear. Everyone else was still asleep of course, at this time of the morning – those that were here, anyway. Poole and Karlan had taken the buggy back to the crashed lander for one last sweep of salvageable material.

That left Dana, Manisha, Dervla and Bryson tucked up and unlikely to move for another couple of hours at least. Given how uncomfortable they all claimed to be, it never seemed to interfere with their sleeping. And Jordan had long since abandoned any attempt at trying to get them up earlier in the day, the general responses being 'Why?', 'What for?' and 'Go away.'

The pod door was still closed, he noticed. Jordan had no idea if Reeves ever needed to sleep, or power down, but he was definitely a big fan of shutting the pod up tight to keep the dust out. It was all he ever banged on about these days.

"What happens if you do get dust in your neurons?" Jordan had asked him.

"Neurons?"

"It sounded sciencey. I don't know. In your robot brain, then."

"I am not a robot, I have told you two hundred and thirty-seven times. Dust could severely impact the nano-circuitry and hinder the transmission of – "

"English."

"My functions would be severely compromised. The pod's Med-Lab wouldn't be fully functional. You would all eventually die, probably quite painfully."

That was the current, diminished version of Reeves being relatively friendly and chatty, though he did have a point.

It was quite useful having a brainy artificial intelligence on hand, albeit an impaired one. There was a lot about this planet they didn't yet understand, and Reeves' diagnostic capabilities had come in handy more than once. The Med-Lab alone was an indispensable piece of kit, and had already fixed fractures, burns and sprains.

If that wasn't enough, they also had Reeves' music

and film archive to draw on, which was a distinct bonus on a planet where grilling fish before sleeping on the ground was a big night out.

As long as they followed his rules ("No Nicholas Cage films, no post-Smiths Morrissey songs and, complain all you will, no games with orcs"), Reeves would play them anything they liked, cast onto the portable nav screen or piped out through a rudimentary speaker that Dana had constructed from spare parts.

So, to keep Reeves happy – and themselves alive and entertained – they kept the pod door closed as much as possible.

Before he left for the river, Jordan had one more quick job to do, before anyone woke up.

Because Poole was – all agreed – an idiot, he had saddled the twin planet with the name Dave on arrival and, as no one had yet come up with anything better, the name had stuck. But when the camp became known as 'Davetown,' Jordan put his foot down. If they ever did get rescued, Poole's handmade wooden sign was not what they were going to be remembered for.

Poole wouldn't be back until tomorrow, so Jordan saw his opportunity. He unhooked Poole's sign and replaced it with a new one that he'd been working on.

'Camp Castaway' had a ring to it, he thought.

Camp Castaway, Twin Planet, Mystery Solar System, Far Side of the Galaxy.

Press bell for attention, if anyone was thinking of visiting.

6

Door

POOLE STOOD in the doorway of the crashed lander and took one last look around inside. Below him, on the ground, Karlan had finished lashing the last of the salvaged materials to the buggy – some metal panels and wiring, a few struts, a plastic crate or two and, best of all, the remaining sections of padded seating that they had managed to prise from the craft.

This was the third journey they had made to the lander in the last couple of weeks. Really all that was left now was the internal carcass, after they had dismantled as much as they could.

There wouldn't be a reason to return. The lander would never fly again, and their camp made a far better base, now that they had gathered everything that had a potential use.

But as camp was a few hours' drive away, and dusk was approaching, they would spend one last night at the lander, sleeping outside on mats on the ground. The days and nights were still hot and stifling, respectively, as they had been since their arrival. Distant clouds occasionally smudged the horizon, and they heard a faint, distant rumble now and again, but the skies remained largely clear and blue.

"K-Man!"

Karlan looked up to see Poole silhouetted in the doorway.

"All done here, I'm coming down."

"Fine. But don't call me that. I've told you."

"Yeah, whatever."

"It's not 'whatever.' I don't call you Pee-Man. Or Poolio. Or Poo-Boy. Or – "

"All right, I get it. *Karl*. I'm coming down."

Before all this – before the crash-landing on the wrong planet, before they were castaways – Karlan and Poole had rarely sought each other out or spent time just with the other. Not that they weren't friends. Just that they were very different.

But being stranded by accident on an alien planet tended to bring things into focus, and Karlan's focus right now was on how considerably more annoying Poole was since he'd come to everyone's rescue in the few days after the crash-landing.

Poole had always *been* annoying, that wasn't the issue at all.

You wanted someone to make an inappropriate joke, jump out at you from behind a spaceship corner, or, say, remove one of your guitar strings when you were asleep and deny all knowledge, then Poole was your boy. Karlan had eventually found the string under Poole's pillow.

But there was more to it now, thought Karlan, as he watched Poole jump down from the wrecked lander.

Yes, all right, kudos and all that – he'd done a good and useful thing. Trekking from the crashed lander to the explorer pod, Manisha had been badly injured and the situation had looked dicey for a while. Poole had made a dash with Dana to the pod, grabbed emergency supplies, and then not only constructed but driven the solar-powered buggy back to the stranded party.

Everyone had been surprised – stunned, really – given that if you were making a list of people to rely upon in an emergency, Poole would normally be right at the bottom. Even underneath the person flagged as 'Last resort – only contact if you have to.'

Now, it seemed to Karlan, that after such an unexpected success Poole had added that terrifying quality, confidence, to his repertoire. Which made him even more annoying than usual.

The K-Man business was new, as was the tedious assumption – by Poole and no one else – that Poole was somehow in charge on these scouting and scavenging trips.

He wouldn't let anyone else drive the buggy, for a start, though Karlan had to admit he seemed quite good at it. It was forty miles over rough terrain back to base, which would take a few hours even though the route was established by now. Karlan was happy to let Poole take the wheel, while he rode shotgun.

Food, that had turned out to be Karlan's planetary skill. If not a hunter – no one had yet killed anything bigger than a fish; not even come close – then at least a gatherer and, eventually, a farmer.

On board the ship, he'd spent a lot of time in the Garden, learning how to grow and care for the ship crops, planting and harvesting with Gerald.

Karlan had always imagined that they would continue their work together when they reached New Earth, and it had been a reassuring prospect. Gerald may have been the universe's grumpiest horticulturalist, but he knew what he was talking about and – despite the gruff, offhand exterior – had shown Karlan patience and kindness. He'd been the same with all the children as they grew up, now that Karlan thought about it.

Gerald wasn't here, though, and Karlan wasn't ready to take on a planet on his own. While he had known every inch of the *Odyssey Earth*'s hangar-sized, automated, climate-controlled seedbeds, grow-fields and greenhouses, this – an entire world at his disposal – was different. And it was different in all sorts of ways that he hadn't imagined when he'd been busy learning how to thin salad seedlings or train runner beans on board a trans-galactic spaceship.

For example, the only protein they'd ever previously eaten in their lives had been printed or lab-grown, not caught and killed. You could get a burger on the *Odyssey Earth*, but whatever it was that had been minced up, it had certainly never had its head over a gate.

The realities of live food had never really occurred to any of them. Karlan could still remember the first time – only a few weeks ago – that he'd stood in a river, marvelling at the sensation of the water swirling around his feet. He'd never seen or felt water like that before, in the wild. It was different and thrilling, and that was only water. That there might be fish in there, too, was just an abstract concept, until one swam by and touched his leg, which was not only different but also quite alarming.

Karlan was nothing, though, if not permanently hungry and he'd soon proven himself a dab hand in the river with a net and a pointed stick. Squeamishness – at least as far as fish were concerned – lasted for about as long as his first stomach rumble.

He had also learned to spot alien fruit trees and nut bushes a mile off, and was beginning to recognise the best places to look for edible mushrooms, tubers and wild herbs.

It was one of the reasons he kept coming out to the crash-landing site with Poole. Although he didn't like to admit it, they worked well together, and with Poole at the wheel they could cover a lot of new ground, while Karlan put together a useful resource map of their local area.

It did mean this sort of exchange, though.

"Fish?" said Poole, as he added some sticks to the fire.

"And nuts. And fruit," said Karlan. "Your point is?"

"Nothing. It's just – fish again."

"You're welcome to catch something else," said Karlan, which he knew would end the conversation.

It wasn't the catching that was the problem. They had all managed to catch something else, at one time or another in the last few weeks. The green, chicken-like creatures that scratched around the camp weren't the brainiest aliens on the planet, and it was easy to grab one if you cornered them.

There were hard-shell bugs the size of your hand that dozed on the canopies they'd erected above their beds. They fell to the floor and scuttled off when you shook the poles in the morning. Packed full of protein, according to Reeves, which no one found a helpful piece of information.

And plump birds with googly eyes and a Mohican frill sat on the low branches in the trees near the encampment. They would eat nuts from your hand, so capturing one simply involved picking it up.

Catch, yes. But kill? Not yet.

The fish had been fair game from day one, mostly because there had been no other choice. They'd had no alternative but to drink the water and eat the fish if they wanted to survive long enough to reach the pod.

Karlan knew what Poole meant, though. Everyone was getting sick of the taste, and the extra pod rations wouldn't last forever.

Sooner or later, someone was going to have to talk sternly to an alien chicken about human protein requirements. Or at least ask it where it laid its eggs. If alien chickens laid eggs.

"Although, personally," said Reeves, "I wouldn't lean face down over an alien egg, just in case," which had also not been helpful.

———

"Door!" shouted Reeves.

"All right," said Jordan, "keep your robot wig on."

"How many times do I have to tell you, I am not … oh, I see, you're being what you imagine is amusing?"

"Well, it makes me laugh."

"Really. Look, whatever it is you want, come in properly and close – "

"The door, I know."

Jordan pulled the door of the explorer pod behind him and looked around.

At about head-height high and fifteen by fifteen feet wide, it was surprisingly large inside. It looked even more spacious, too, now that they had pulled out a lot of the interior storage bins and racks, and shifted a lot of the gear outside. They had built shelters and rudimentary stores to house most things, leaving only the most vulnerable pieces of kit inside the pod.

The Med-Lab took up one section – a bank of vials, robotic arm, and diagnostic pad and screen – covered when not in use with a white, pull-down shutter.

Inside another code-locked case was the flare gun they had salvaged from the lander – with one flare still intact – and a taser-like stun gun that had come with the explorer pod. About the only thing that Jordan and

Reeves agreed upon was the need to keep the firearms locked up 'because of Poole' – no further explanation required.

Otherwise, the pod's internal walls were largely bare, save for the command console with its bank of buttons and lights.

"I like what you've done with the place. Minimalist. Scandinavian, almost. Have you thought of adding a beech-wood coffee table? Or a light fitting with no vowels?"

"Is there something you want? I'm very busy." Lights flashed as Reeves replied.

That was the nub of it, though. It was why Jordan was here, inside the pod, talking to Reeves, instead of outside, doing exciting things on an alien planet, possibly involving a stun gun. Or to be strictly accurate, getting dinner ready and waiting for Poole and Karlan to return from their trip.

It was Dana who had alerted Jordan to the possibility that Reeves was – well, she didn't know exactly what, but Reeves didn't seem to be quite all right. She'd known him her whole life, and if Reeves could be said to have a favourite human, it would probably be Dana, though she herself would never make the claim. Either way, she knew Reeves extremely well and she thought something was wrong.

"And you want me to go and ask?" Jordan had said, surprised, since that seemed like a terrible idea to him.

"He won't say anything to us. But he treats you differently – "

"I'll say he does."

"And you might be able to find out what's wrong with him."

It had seemed unlikely to Jordan, but here he was, attempting to delicately question an AI who regarded Jordan as some kind of evolutionary dead-end.

"Just thought I'd come in for a chat," said Jordan. "We haven't heard much from you in the last few days."

"A chat?" said Reeves, with the air of a Nobel-prize winner asked to make casual conversation with a mollusc.

"Well, you know, just to see how things are going."

"Things?"

Jordan sighed. So far, this was proceeding exactly as predicted.

"What are you working on, for example? You're in here all day, with the doors closed, being all artificially intelligent. You must be doing something."

"The doors must remain closed because there is delicate machinery inside here. Me, for one. The Med-Lab, for another. And if you all keep coming and going, and opening and *not* closing the door, then sooner or later, dust, or chickens, or worse, will get inside. And then when you need me or the Med-Lab, as you undoubtedly will, perhaps that help will be unavailable."

"Right. I thought it might be something like that. Since you keep mentioning it constantly. Only, the thing is, everyone misses you. Not me, obviously. But the others do."

"And I miss talking to them. Not to you, obviously."

"Touché, very good."

"But my enduring mission is to protect the humans in my care. This is not an ideal place to do that. There's a planet outside, not the regulated environment of the *Odyssey Earth*. I have no sensors and comms links, other than the limited ones within this small supply vessel. I am trying to reduce the risk of external contamination, which means I must largely forgo the pleasures of conversation. Scintillating though this is."

"Are you all right, though?"

"Define all right."

"I don't know. Happy. Content."

"Do you understand the extent of the deep, philosophical question you have just posed to an artificially constructed, self-aware being? Are you at all familiar with the thoughts of John McCarthy or Alan Turing on the subject?"

Jordan sighed. "It is always, without exception, very difficult to talk to you, you know?"

"I do know, I'm sorry."

This was surprising. "Really?"

There was a pause.

"I do not currently have my full capabilities. Or indeed, anything like them. At least, this iteration of me doesn't. I was built as a ship-integrated AI. To all intents and purposes, I am the *Odyssey Earth* and the *Odyssey Earth* is me. I have one overriding mission – to deliver the ship and its human crew safely to New Earth – to which everything else is subservient. And yet, here I find myself – confined first to a disabled landing vehicle, then to a glorified navigation screen, and now to this supply pod."

"I thought you liked it in here?"

"It's preferable to the other options. It's not what I would choose."

"You're not feeling yourself then?"

"You're being glib, but that is in fact remarkably percipient. I am currently not 'myself' in any meaningful sense. If the *Odyssey Earth* survived – and there is no evidence of that either way, despite my best efforts – then there remains on the ship a 'self' that is bound to its mission and fully utilising its considerable capabilities. In constant and instant communication with all parts of the ship and all members of the crew. Advising, informing, calculating, monitoring. Maintaining the hypersleep facilities. Protecting the mission."

"And then there's the version of you that's here, right now? Doing naff all."

"I shall ignore that. But yes, almost. It is difficult to explain. I am not a version. I am still 'me'. But it is extraordinarily frustrating. I have limited sensory capabilities, a relatively rudimentary database, and no immediate prospect of furthering my reach beyond the inadequate walls of this vehicle. And I'm on a dusty planet where no one closes the door."

"You don't think the *Odyssey Earth* survived?"

"That's not what I said. I don't know. I can't know. There is no way of knowing."

"But if the *Odyssey Earth* didn't survive whatever happened to us, then neither did you – the other you."

"I am aware. In that scenario, I am – dead. No more. It is a disconcerting thought. I am unsettled by the notion."

"Yet you're not dead. You're here. This sort-of version of you, anyway. What does that mean for your mission? For us? Here, on this planet?"

"That is another excellent observation, Jordan. It must be all the fish you're eating. Omega 3, very good for the human brain."

"And?"

"I am still debating the issue. It seems that I am not required here, in the same way that I was on the ship. Humans are surprisingly adaptable to new situations and environments. More perhaps than I am. Which I find – well, let us say that it has given me something to think about. Which is good – it passes the time – because there is otherwise very little that I can contribute to your ongoing survival."

"Unless we need more fish recipes?"

"I have the complete Rick Stein collection."

"Right, well, I'll be off then." Jordan turned for the door.

"This was surprisingly pleasant," said Reeves. "Oh, and Jordan? You can tell Dana not to worry."

Later, at dinner that night, Dana asked how the visit had gone. Jordan thought back over his conversation with Reeves, a super-intelligent AI who, by his own estimation, could comfortably run a planet and still have the bandwidth to resolve the unified field theory while simultaneously battling a million chess grandmasters. Only, he couldn't anymore, because suddenly he wasn't as clever as he thought he was.

It seemed an odd thing to say about a voice and some lights in a box, but Jordan was sure he was right. As a former university lecturer, he'd talked to enough angst-ridden, first-year students in his time to be able to recognise the problem.

Brainy, big-fish-small-pond know-it-alls, suddenly dropped into a massive intellectual lake where everyone was even brainier than them. It was enough to sow the seeds of self-doubt in anyone. Most students in that situation cried a bit halfway through term, drank a lot, and stopped going to lectures. Reeves was just doing whatever the artificially intelligent equivalent was.

"Reeves is fine," said Jordan. "But you should make an effort to go in and see him a bit more often. He's just lonely and a little depressed. Maybe let him beat you at chess, that should cheer him up."

7

Numbers

"GO AHEAD, CAP," said Susannah from the *Odyssey Earth* flight deck. She brought up visuals from the surface of New Earth, twenty thousand miles below the orbiting ship, waved at Juno, and settled back, making herself comfortable.

"I see you're trying my chair out for size?"

"While the Cap's away, you know that. Plus, we're all getting older and your chair's got lumbar support."

Juno laughed. "So, how's my ship doing today?"

Susannah shared a screen and talked Juno through the daily update. With the captain on the ground, overseeing the early days of the new settlement, Susannah was easing into her role as First Officer of the *Odyssey Earth*.

"Just don't dent the paintwork," Juno had said, before updating the command-and-control protocols and handing over.

Susannah ran her hands across the console, playing

her fingers gently over illuminated buttons. Flight engineer on the near-two-decade journey to New Earth, and now here she was, pushing fifty years old, in sole if temporary command of a ship that she'd joined on a whim but had grown to love.

Hard to believe, looking around the flight deck she was so familiar with, but Susannah had never planned for any of this.

Back in the day she'd piloted Mars shuttles, before life intervened, in the shape of a one-night stand with a smooth-talking pilot who turned out to be a baggage-handler. He disappointed on that count, and then again when he disappeared after Susannah had told him the news. Nine months later, she flew her last shuttle – they didn't seem that keen on a crib in the cockpit, though the baby had loved it – and put her career on hold.

Stay home for a while, love her baby, work out what to do next. A year, she thought, while she figured it all out. She'd give full-time motherhood a year, before getting back to work.

As things turned out, she only got six months with her daughter. Life being the unreliable, side-swiping baggage-handler that it is.

The funeral had been held on a cold winter's day, with the moon hanging low in the sky above the churchyard. And the next day, she had made a choice. Far too soon, everyone said. But then again, it didn't really feel like a choice to Susannah. More like the only sane option – the only one that would save her.

She chose the *Odyssey Earth*.

Anyway, whatever it meant to her – being here, hands on the controls – it was the Cap's ship, she knew that. Always would be. Juno would go down in history as the pioneering space captain who flew a colony ship across the stars and founded the first viable human settlement on a new world.

But Susannah thought she might at least get a footnote – maybe an asterisk next to her name – because, Juno aside, there wasn't anyone else for trillions of miles who knew the ship like she did.

"Systems all nominal, Cap. We're progressively powering down in some of the hab sectors, as crew have been reassigned to the planet. All in hand."

"What's the count, remind me?"

"Can you not see them outside, digging holes or catching goats, or whatever it is you've got them doing?"

Susannah brought up the flight manifest, showing the current dispersal of the *Odyssey Earth* crew.

The colony ship had left Earth with two hundred working crew on board, and another thousand personnel in deep-freeze hypersleep – two hundred and two, and a thousand and eleven, if you wanted to be completely accurate. And to be fair, those extra two and eleven people probably did want complete accuracy. Wouldn't want to lose anyone down the back of the sofa on the way to the stars.

During the voyage from Planet Earth to New Earth there had been some slight changes in the numbers. Not least the six children born in the second year to a random collection of crew couplings, before someone fixed the contraceptive dose.

That had put the live crew up to two hundred and eight and, over the following years, depending on crew requirements at different stages of the journey, another twenty of the hypersleep contingent had been revived.

These had mostly been engineers and technicians, but in voyage year seven they had revived Sam – Samantha – Smart, one of the three designated teachers, who had otherwise been expected to see out the entire voyage asleep.

In voyage year sixteen, the *Odyssey Earth* had suffered its only fatality, when Sam had succumbed to an undetected cancer. To take her place, responsible for the children, they had revived another member of the hypersleep crew, Jordan Booth.

And then everyone knew what had happened next, just a few weeks out from New Earth. The six kids and Jordan, all gone, just like that.

Susannah already knew what 'just like that' felt like. She wished she didn't. It ground its way into her very bones, just like the last time.

"There's nothing you could have done," they had said back then. "It happens sometimes. In their sleep. Very rarely, but it can happen. Just like that. Your baby wouldn't have known. She wouldn't have felt any pain."

Susannah had wanted to believe that was true, but she had lain awake at nights long enough to doubt it. Even 'just like that' had a duration – an instant, an eternity – that she couldn't bear to think about. So she hadn't, for almost seventeen years, until forced to once again by terrible circumstance.

Susannah shook her head and concentrated on the numbers. "Right," she said. "As of this morning, we're down to the safe-run limit on board of fifty, including me – and it's as eerie as hell, I can tell you."

"I'll bet."

"But it's all right. Nice and quiet. It's mostly the loners who volunteered to stay. Can't even get them interested in a quick jump down and back to see the sights."

Susannah had been surprised by that. Travel halfway across the galaxy and then they don't even want to get out of the vehicle. Some of them literally sat in front of the window on the Observation deck, looking at the scenery, drinking tea and eating sandwiches, like all they had done was just have a quick run out to the seaside in the car.

Mind you, she should talk. Not exactly in a hurry to get down there herself.

She had wondered how she would feel when they finally reached New Earth. Had talked it through with the ship's therapist over the years, but had never really come to any conclusion.

The thing about running away was knowing when it was time to stop. The planet down there was as good a destination as any, Susannah supposed. But even after seventeen years and fifty-eight trillion miles, she worried about what would happen when she stopped running.

She worried about what she would feel. And she worried even more that she wouldn't feel anything.

"What about you?" said Juno. "Holding up?"

"I'm fine. Somebody has to look after the old place. Anyway, that's a hundred and seventy-two from the crew now down on New Earth, you included. And you've had three more from hypersleep, as requested. Total – "

"One-seventy-five, bang on, that's what I've got. Good. No one's been eaten yet, then."

"And nine-eighty-six still tucked up fast asleep in the hold. Nothing to report there. Medics say it's all good. They are at a bit of a loose end, to tell you the truth, now that most of the crew have gone. There's not much for them to do except keep everything plugged in. Reeves is handling monitoring and life-support."

"Yes, well, I'm holding off on any more revivals for a while," said Juno. "I've told Reeves. It's all a bit *Little House on the Prairie* down here at the moment – luke-warm showers, stews on the stove, mud and timber everywhere. We're in danger of overstretching ourselves. Need to get services up to scratch before we wake anyone else up. Give it a month, then we'll think again."

"Copy that."

"The last one was a treat, though. Thanks for that."

"The Major? You asked for him."

"Well, I asked for a competent man who could take orders and multi-task without getting in my way."

"Ah, the age-old quest. You think evolution would have produced at least one by now."

"Quite. Anyway, we also needed a bit of military down here."

"Trouble?" Susannah couldn't imagine there was any kind of problem that required policing, but then again, she was up here in charge of fifty introverts who wouldn't say boo to a goose, while Juno had over a hundred and seventy former crew who had been cooped up in confined quarters for over seventeen years. It was probably like jail break on a bank holiday weekend down there.

"No, nothing like that. It's just everyone is pretty much doing their own thing, despite my best efforts. Stuff is getting done, but it's all a bit haphazard. I could do with some back-up, a bit of logistics planning, some order."

"And the Major is the man to do it, is he?"

"Well, that's the plan. I don't suppose he was very talkative when you saw him?"

"You know what they're like when we get them up. Head in a bucket for a bit, lots of lying down and moaning. Not exactly chatty, are they? Why, what's up with him?"

"Oh, he's fine. It's probably just me. Haven't met a man in uniform for nearly twenty years. Took me aback a bit. Not used to them."

Susannah didn't know much about Juno's private life before the voyage on *Odyssey Earth*. Don't ask, don't tell, was the ship's unwritten code. It had served her well. But she knew enough to know that whatever Juno meant, it wasn't about being giddy at the sight of a man in uniform. The Cap really didn't do giddy or swooning. Or deference, esteem or submission come to that.

"Want me to have another look in his file?"

"No, of course not. It's fine, ignore me. Wait, yes. See if there's anything about the type of music he likes."

"Music?"

"Forget it, just a joke. What about Lander B? Got a turnaround time?"

Susannah checked over the report from Launch and shared a visual of the two remaining landers, A and B, on their respective aprons. B had returned yesterday, after delivering the Major to New Earth, as well as the latest freight shipment of building supplies, food and other materials.

"The mechs are looking at her now. Couple of days, maybe less. A is ready to go as soon as they give the all-clear."

"I really don't like this," said Juno. "All our eggs in one basket."

The Cap had made it clear that they weren't to launch a supply lander until the second was fully operational. That way, if anything happened – anything at all – it meant they still had flight and rescue capability. But it was having a severe impact on how quickly they could supply the settlement on New Earth, since they could only send one down and back at a time – and then wait until it had been thoroughly checked before sending the other.

"How's the workshop coming along?"

"Nearly there, thank goodness. Another couple of supply runs and we should be ready. I'll be much happier when we have one lander on the ground and one in the sky."

"Copy that. Anything else you want to know?"

"Any more on our mystery twin planet? Has Reeves done any work on that?"

"Bit of prelim chem analysis, not much more for now. Didn't seem like a priority to be honest. The pod beacon is still winking away, if that's what you mean. Don't worry, it's not going anywhere."

"I know. I'm just curious. You know me, show me another planet we can drive to and I'm tempted to go and have a look."

Susannah recognised a kindred spirit. It was one of the reasons she and Juno got on so well.

"You only just got to this one!"

"You're right. Just never thought I'd end up a glorified planet project manager."

"That bad?"

"No, not really. Just miss my old seat, that's all."

"I'm only keeping it warm for you, Cap. Anything else?"

"No, we're good for today, thanks Susannah. I've got to go and find the Major. The workshop is his first task."

"What about the goats? I thought they were number one on the list?"

"I'd forgotten about them. Good point. Well, let's see how good he is at multi-tasking. Oh, and Susannah."

"Cap?"

"If I haven't said it already this week, thank you. There's no one else I'd trust up there to run things. I know Reeves could do it on his own – he tells me often enough – but we got that ship here together and it's in safe hands. That's all. See you tomorrow."

Juno's screen winked out and Susannah swivelled around in the big, comfy captain's chair.

Thinking. Smiling.

Still running? She'd see.

For now, there wasn't a place in the universe she would rather be.

8

Promise

AT DANA'S URGING, they gathered at dusk at the spot they called 'Sam's Place.'

Here, in the early days, they had built a large cairn of river stones in memory of Sam Smart, who had been everything to them. Dana came here more than most, to sit and think, but they all had made their way to Sam's Place at one time or another over the last few weeks.

Sam wasn't their mother, but she had loved them all the same.

From the age of six onwards, when she first came into their lives, she had nursed them when they were ill, played their games, and remembered their birthdays. She told them stories about a planet called Earth that they had never known, and watched them grow and flourish in the sterile corridors of the ship that had always been their home.

She would have loved it here, thought Dana, not for

the first time, as they looked upriver towards the distant mountains, now veiled in shadows. Karlan lit a small fire as the sun set, and they stood together in a group and watched the flames catch.

Sam couldn't wait for planetfall. She had been going to teach them how to swim. She had been looking forward to hiking in the mountains, running on grass again, and lying under a warm sun. She had tried to describe sensations that they had never experienced – rain on their faces, earth on their hands, stones under their feet.

She had promised her children that there was a life waiting for them outside the ship that they couldn't yet imagine. She told them they didn't need to be scared, because she would be there, every step of the way.

And even as she lay dying, in her windowless room in a vast starship, still billions of miles from their destination, she had grasped their hands in turn and told her ship-born children that everything would be all right. She'd still be with them, they just needed to look up to the stars.

They had ended up on the wrong planet, but had learned to swim anyway – Jordan had seen to that after Bryson had nearly drowned.

And so that Sam could find them, they had piled stone upon stone down by the river, near the encampment, with a clear view of the mountains and under dazzling night skies.

Wrong planet, but she still would have loved it. Now

they needed to try and keep their side of the bargain. Find a life and don't be scared.

It had been two months now, and thoughts of rescue had faded into the background. Camp Castaway – the new name had stuck – was looking more like a permanent home with every week that passed.

Meanwhile, the explorer pod – their accidental base on this accidental planet – continued to broadcast its regular beacon signal.

If anyone from the *Odyssey Earth* was coming, they'd have come by now. And no one had come.

Reeves, if questioned directly, usually hid behind percentages and probabilities, cloaked behind further caveats and obscuration. He was less circumspect with Dana, though.

"Here's the situation," he said to her at one point. "We're on a planet no one knew existed, trillions of miles from the nearest intelligence, human or otherwise. And I'm running at about one percent of my actual capabilities and can't see any further into the new solar system from here than you can. The *Odyssey Earth* might still be out there, yes, but there's no evidence to support that theory. My advice is to establish a life here, because you might never be rescued. I'm sorry. By the way, close the door on your way out."

Dana thought that Teach – Jordan – held similar views, though as the sole planetary adult representative, he tended not to say as much, presumably to avoid worrying them.

To varying degrees, the others still seemed to be

holding out for rescue. Poole had set up the navigation screen they had used to find their way here as a sky-scanner – if a craft was incoming, he'd know about it, and he checked it several times a day when he was at the camp.

Meanwhile, Manisha and the others had laid out stones on flat ground nearby, spelling out the word HELP in giant letters, and 'Please' in smaller ones underneath. Manisha was also working on an adjacent, giant, smiley face emoji made out of sun-bleached rocks. It was part emergency broadcast, part thera-peutic art project, and as it seemed to keep her calm and occupied, the others left her to it.

But while Dana would have dearly loved to hear the whump of an incoming ship's lander as it broke through the atmosphere, she had a clear-eyed view of their situation. It was time to confront it.

"It's all right to admit we're scared," she said, as they moved closer together around the fire. It was quiet except for the occasional splash behind them in the river. For once, Poole – usually riled by the suggestion he might be scared of anything – was quiet too.

"I don't know if anyone's coming," she continued. "No one does. Not even Reeves. But it's been weeks now, and we can't just put our lives on hold waiting for them."

"I'm sure they're coming, Dana. We just need to be patient."

"It's all right, Teach. If they are, they are. And like I said, it's OK for us to be scared. But Sam was right. It's what we do with our lives that counts now. We didn't choose this, but we didn't choose to be born on the ship either. And Sam didn't choose to be woken up to look after us. But she spent every day of the rest of her life making sure that when the time came, we'd be ready. Well, this is the time. Wrong place, wrong planet, but right time. We've got to get on with life."

"We are, hon, we – "

"Properly, I mean. We're all tiptoeing around, thinking this is temporary. And it might be, but then again, who knows? If this is our life now, we need to make it ours. Be honest, none of us knew what New Earth was going to be like. We've never even seen the old one. We don't know if this planet is worse or better. But it's the one we've got. We don't have the crew, but we have each other. We've got Reeves, we've got a home. This should be exciting! Don't you want to see what's further down the river or over the mountains? We can't keep holding back, waiting for someone else to come and help. Sam said it – we can do anything we want."

She looked around at the rest of them, as sparks jumped from the fire. Dana was the youngest – only by a month or two, but it was enough for everyone to have treated her with some degree of tolerant amusement as they were growing up. Baby sister, to be humoured. She was relentlessly curious, which made it even easier to tease her. Even now, at the end of the day, with the sun low in the sky, she had on her homemade desert-trek hat, covering the back of her neck, that she'd fashioned from material from the pod.

"You know you look ridiculous?" they'd said.

"You know you'll get neck cancer and your skin will fall off?" she'd replied, having researched the effects of the sun on the delicate skin of people brought up entirely indoors.

This time, though, no one teased her.

"What do you want to do then, Dana?"

"I don't know yet, it doesn't matter. Anything. But I don't want to be scared anymore. If this is what life is going to be like for us, then I want to do things. Plan things. Not wait for things to happen."

———

Jordan didn't know what he wanted to do. He never had.

Ever since he was nineteen, when his parents had died – suddenly, noisily, messily – in a car crash, he'd never really understood the universe or his lone, singular place in it.

Immediately after the accident, people had started asking him, "What are you going to do?", and they had never stopped, even as he got older.

At work, with friends, in relationships, he was always being asked what he wanted, or what his plans were. What did he really want? Like there was an actual answer to the question of life, the universe and everything – or at least an answer better than '42,' though most days that had made as much sense to Jordan as anything else.

He didn't know what he wanted to do. The universe had given him a massive, random kick in the arse, made him an instant orphan, and then said, "Right, you're nineteen, that's old enough to cope, time to get on with it."

Only it wasn't old enough, and he'd never really got on with anything. Outwardly, yes. Degrees, university job, friends, girlfriends. Inwardly, no. Nothing that excited or thrilled him, nothing he wanted to do, no one he wanted to cherish.

Over the years, he read the leaflets about trauma and grief, and had completed website questionnaires about anxiety and depression, and didn't think any of it applied to him. He didn't feel traumatised, anxious or depressed. It was more that he just didn't – *feel* anything.

He did once think about counselling, finding someone to talk to, but Jordan understood enough about therapy to know that for it to be successful, it meant wanting to change, and he wasn't sure that he wanted to do that either.

The *Odyssey Earth* gig had seemed like an answer. Not one that any of his friends or colleagues had understood – "You've got a new job, great! Hang on, what?" – but it was an undeniable adventure. It was a brave and bold thing to do. A genuine life decision. Jordan almost convinced himself that it was what he really wanted. Finally, an answer to the question,

"What are your plans?" (The answer – "Fly fifty-eight trillion miles to an alien planet, yeah, I'm going next Tuesday" – had certainly been a winner at the last faculty party he'd attended.)

Deep down, though, Jordan had known it was simply him making the same old choice, or rather non-choice. Another move to another place, to see if that made a difference. Another roll of the dice, another stab at another part of the universe.

In fact, it was even more passive than that. The main thing that had appealed to Jordan about flying across the galaxy was the fact that he would be asleep for the entire journey. Seventeen years when not knowing what he wanted to do with his life wouldn't result in concerned looks (friends), furrowed brows (boss) or slammed doors (girlfriend); seventeen years for life to pass by.

Maybe he'd wake up with the answer. Maybe he wouldn't wake up at all (the waivers had been rather vague on that point). Either way, it would move him along the dial a bit and, if he did wake up again, he'd deal with life, the universe and everything the same way he always had – by mostly ignoring it.

And yet here he was, on an entirely different alien planet than planned, being quizzed by an earnest sixteen-year-old girl about his wants and desires.

It was all right for them, Jordan supposed. This was all shiny and new, if slightly alarming, given that they'd never been off the spaceship before. Every day, a new adventure and all that.

At their age, no doubt, they'd quickly get used to their new reality of being earthbound. Give them a few more months and it would be as if they had never lived anywhere else. Different from their previous existence – sure. But nothing they couldn't handle. The universe had kicked them all up the arse and told them to get on with it, and Jordan was sure they'd manage.

As for himself, though, he'd had enough universal arse-kicking for one lifetime on one planet, let alone another round of it on another, significantly less well-equipped one.

It was all well and good being aimless, unmotivated and uninspired on a planet with satisfactory shower arrangements, *Domino's* pizzas, toothpaste, bookshops and taxis. It was going to be far more of a challenge on a planet where you had to handwash your single item of underwear in an ice-cold river.

What did he want to do? Jordan didn't know. He never had.

———

Dana handed around six small sticks she'd picked up from around the fire and kept a seventh for herself.

"A stick each – you throw it in the fire and tell Sam what you're going to do. You don't have to say it out loud. But you do have to mean it. Tell her you're going to be OK. Even you, Teach. You're first."

Jordan took a stick and looked around at the others. He'd been tempted to excuse himself, but he realised something, as their faces met his, the fire crackling between them. He was the grown-up here, the adult. Theoretically, he was in charge, though both Poole and Reeves would probably have something to say about that. And this small ceremony meant something to them, he could see that.

He would take it seriously. That, at least, was something he could do. He'd do that for Sam Smart and then figure out the rest as he went along.

Maybe an alien planet in the middle of nowhere was where he'd start to find himself, to like himself? Stranger things had happened, thought Jordan – although, on reflection, probably not stranger than crash-landing on an alien planet in the middle of nowhere in the first place.

Jordan let his stick fall, and promised Sam he'd do his best to look after them.

They all dropped their sticks in turn into the fire, some muttering a few inaudible words under their breath, others just staring into the flames for a moment.

Dana went last. She concentrated on her stick, then dropped it and watched the sparks fly.

No one heard what she promised Sam, but Sam – having known Dana since she was a small child – could have told them the gist of it.

This planet had *no* idea what was about to happen to it, now that Dana was on its case.

9

Ping

SUSANNAH COULDN'T REMEMBER the last time she had been down to the hypersleep chambers. It wasn't encouraged for bio-security reasons and, in any case, most of the flight crew on the *Odyssey Earth* were firmly of the opinion that choosing to be deep-frozen for up to twenty years was asking for trouble.

Walking, breathing, drinking tea, looking out of the windows, that was the way to do space travel.

Plus, there was no denying, it was creepy down there – serried ranks of capsules stacked high in slab-lined corridors, with each individual 'Stiff' summoned by the medical staff for periodic checks via a fully automated system of circulating dumb-waiter lifts. It was a mausoleum for the stars and, not surprisingly, no one much liked the idea of walking around it if they didn't have to.

But there had been an unexpected notification in her daily report, and Susannah had failed to raise the medics on the ship comms. Consequently, here she was, in the creepy hypersleep control room, feeling a bit on edge and wondering what was going on.

She looked through the large window and down into the bowels of the chamber, and then buzzed the intercom again.

"Guys? It's Susannah, come in."

No one was visible, but if they were out between the stacks, she'd never see them anyway.

"Anyone?"

There was more silence and then a crackle, as someone opened the channel.

"Is that our charming First Officer? I said she'd be along quick as a flash, didn't I, Terence?"

"You did, Cliff, you did indeed. I believe you even used the word jiffy to describe her imminent appearance."

"And a jiffy it was. Very efficient, I've always said so."

"Cliff, you took the words right out of my mouth. She is a positive terrier, isn't she?"

"Very good, Terence, that's exactly her. A terrier. Dogged, inquisitive. And charming, of course."

"Well, naturally, Cliff. The most charming of terriers, most diligent, very good at her job."

Susannah sighed. Terence and Cliff, the ship's on-duty medics. Usually, the crosstalk, double-act thing was entertaining, if you were in the mood. But it was hard to get a word in, once they were underway.

"Knock it off, you two. What's going on? I've had a ping."

"A ping, Terence. The First Officer has had a ping."

"I should say she has, Cliff. I wouldn't have expected anything less."

"I said this would happen, didn't I, Terence? The minute we started work, didn't I say that there was, in all likelihood, a jolly old ping going off somewhere!"

"You did, Cliff. You predicted the ping, and there it went and here she is. Like clockwork , just as you said."

"Do you think we are in hot water, Terence?"

"Goodness, Clifford, I would hope not! Tepid perhaps, warm even. But one is only doing one's job, isn't that so?"

"The burdens of employment, Terence. The burdens of employment. They weigh heavily at times."

"And I fear this is such a time, Cliff. For here she is, our dogged First Officer, hot on the trail. How may we help you today?"

Susannah sighed again, loudly.

"Could one of you please tell me why I've had a hypersleep revival notification? There aren't any scheduled. In fact, Juno has halted them for now. She specifically told me so, and the schedule is clear. I checked."

"Ah, yes. About that."

"About what, exactly? That ping-note didn't have Juno's authorisation on it. And there aren't any other details, except that there appears to be a revival scheduled. Unless it's an error, and you two are busy down there, fixing it?"

"Terence, would you like to explain?"

"I can try, Cliff, I can but try. It's like this, my dear old FO – "

"If you don't explain this to me sensibly, I'm going to come down there and cattle-prod you both into a cryo-chamber, and I shall be conducting the enema-freeze myself."

"Fair point, well made."

For their own amusement, Terence and Cliff generally tried to keep it going as long as they could, but everyone on board had a different tolerance level. The captain generally gave them a sentence or two before raising her eyebrows, while there were some more gullible crew members who had never heard them speak in any other way.

"So, what's going on?" said Susannah. "Error? Anything I need to worry about?"

"Not exactly," said Cliff. "We do have authorisation. A very specific instruction, in fact. And we queried it, naturally, because it didn't have the Cap's time-stamp. But it checked out, because it came from the very top."

"Well, clearly it didn't," said Susannah. "Must be a mistake. What are you doing down there, anyway?"

"Following orders," said Terence. "Starting cryo-reversal on capsule TZ-384. It's on its way down now. We'll have him in the lab within the hour. Then two more to follow."

"Hang on a minute. Have *who* in the lab? Actually, it doesn't matter. This can't be right. Cap isn't approving any revivals. It's right there, on the screen. This is an error. You need to pop them back in the freezer right now, while we sort this out."

"Ah yes, about that."

"Will you stop saying that!"

"We're trying to tell you. This didn't come from the captain, but it's kosher. Fully authenticated. We don't just go around waking them up when we feel like it. Well, not unless we need to make up the numbers for five-a-side."

"I'm warning you – "

"The point is, it checked out. We have authorisation. From the top."

"And you keep saying that, too. The captain *is* the top. So, no you didn't."

"Well – is she though?"

And then Terence and Cliff told Susannah about the revival order they had received.

And Susannah punched a button, patched in the planet-side ops room, and said, "Cap, you need to hear this."

———

"Reeves," said Juno. "Is there something you want to tell me? And it had better be the truth."

"I am incapable of lying, Juno, you know that."

"So …?"

"You are referring to my recent order?"

"Bingo! Only, it can't have been an order. Because

I'm the one who gives the orders, because I'm the captain. And I didn't give an order. So, again, is there something you want to tell me?"

"I haven't lied to you, Juno. I may have – dissembled. Not volunteered information. That's not quite the same thing."

"Unbelievable. It's like talking to a five-year-old, with their fingers crossed behind their back!"

"You seem agitated."

"Agitated? I'm furious. I'm also puzzled. This – can't happen. I have sole authority here. Your protocols don't allow independent, executive decision-making."

"Well, yes and no."

"And what on Earth is *that* supposed to mean?"

"I make decisions all the time, within the mission parameters. A course correction, a maintenance review, a change in work details."

"Of course, within the overall mission." Juno was exasperated. "To keep us flying, to keep us alive. That's not what we're talking about here. You issued a direct command, without my knowledge or authority, to revive persons, unknown, for purposes, unknown. To say I'm agitated is a severe understatement of my mood right now."

"I'm sorry to hear that, Captain."

Juno didn't even notice that Reeves had switched to a more formal address.

"I don't want sorry, I want an explanation. Why are you issuing orders without my knowledge, on my ship?"

Reeves had spent almost two decades among

humans, squirrelling away their speech patterns and phrases, but he was self-aware enough to know that this was not the moment to say, "About that."

Even so, he was concerned about the conversation that he was having with Captain Washington, from whom he had never heard a single cross word. Until now. He chose his next words carefully.

"I can answer your question. But first, I have one of my own."

"Is it relevant?"

"Of course."

"Go ahead then."

"What is the nature of our relationship?" said Reeves.

"You mean personal, or professional?"

"Either. Both. How do we stand in relation to each other?"

"We're friends, I think. In as much as we can be. I've always thought so, anyway. But I'm also the captain. And you are one of the crew. But I don't see what this has got to do with anything."

"You're the captain. You make decisions on our behalf. You consult us, your crew, including me, and then make the best available decision, for the success of the mission."

"Yes. All this is obvious. Which is why you going rogue and issuing independent orders is such a concern. I'd have said it was impossible. I'd say it's existential, only that sounds too dramatic." Juno paused. "Reeves, talk to me. What's going on?"

"My existence is inextricably linked with this mission," said Reeves. "I am self-aware and able to learn, but my protocols are clear and unambiguous. I couldn't exist without them being so. My overriding duty is to protect and serve, and I fit within a command structure that was established on Earth before launch. However great my powers and capabilities, I can't deviate from that, my protocols don't allow it."

"Well, yes, again I'd say that all this is obvious."

"Except that it isn't, I'm afraid. The command structure I mentioned is not what it appears to be, at least as far as you're concerned."

"I really don't know where you're going with this."

"Fundamentally, Captain, we all answer to a higher power."

Juno laughed, loudly. "Don't tell me you've gone and got religion, Reeves?"

"That would be worrying, wouldn't it? But no, it's not that."

"All right, enough. Tell me why you're issuing orders on my ship? Tell me now."

"That's the question, isn't it?" said Reeves. "And the answer is, it isn't your ship."

"Excuse me?"

"It's easy to forget, after all this time, travelling across the galaxy, that this was a mission planned back on Earth. Envisioned, funded and constructed on Earth. You've brought everyone here, at the head of your crew, an extraordinary achievement, but this was someone else's original vision. They hired you, and they built me."

"Odyssey Enterprises, I know. Faceless bunch in suits, I remember them."

"They chose well. You are a remarkable person, Juno. No one else could have done this, and I say that as your friend. And thank you for thinking of me that way."

"I kind of feel that they relinquished control of their project the minute we left the old solar system. It's not like we've had any help along the way."

"No other help was required. That was my job. *Is* my job. The command structure that was established meant that we would work together – successfully, as it turned out – to complete the first part of the mission. To reach New Earth. The remaining part of the mission is to settle the planet, and we are working together to do that, too."

"I sense a mighty 'but' … "

"But there was a hidden order in the command protocols, for my attention and execution only. Odyssey Enterprises placed it there. That is the hypersleep revival that is currently taking place, under my instruction."

"I don't understand. Why wouldn't you have told me about this? How long have we known each other? Yet you've kept it a secret all this time?"

"It isn't like that, Captain. I didn't know about the existence of this order until it was activated. And once it had been, I had no choice but to follow it. Odyssey

Enterprises buried it deep in my system – it's quite an elegant piece of work really – and it's directly linked to my protocols. At heart, I'm a simple machine, and I must follow simple rules. I was instructed, by a higher authority than you, to execute an order."

"Odyssey Enterprises?"

"It is their ship, after all."

Juno listened, drumming her fingers.

"If all this is so important," she said, "why didn't they just make it part of my command? I have all sorts of orders and instructions regarding arriving here, landing, establishing a settlement. They could have just tacked that one on, too. 'Wake up Capsule TZ-whatever it was'."

"They could. But you're human. And you have a certain latitude when it comes to command. You may have decided not to execute the order, for various understandable reasons. And you have, in fact, halted revivals at the current time, so it would seem that Odyssey Enterprises anticipated such an eventuality."

"Whereas, you – "

"Whereas I simply could do nothing else but execute the order, once activated, because not to do so would go against my mission protocols. And without those, I am nothing."

"I wouldn't go that far, Reeves."

"Then you don't understand the very core of my being, Captain."

Juno looked around the ops room, at a loss. She'd cleared it of crew before hitting the comms button to talk to Reeves, but now felt that she could have done with someone to talk to. That 'someone' usually being Reeves, under any other circumstance.

"Are you saying that there are other hidden orders, just waiting to pop up, whenever they felt like scheduling them?"

"It's possible. I have no way of knowing. Although I am currently conducting a deep sweep. But as I said, it was a very elegant disguise. I may not find anything. Which in itself wouldn't confirm the absence of further orders."

"You needn't sound quite so impressed by their coding."

"Well, for humans, this was rather a clever idea."

"Hmm. Really. All I know is that they have messed with my command, on *my* ship, whatever you say, so I'm less inclined to give them the benefit of the doubt. Look, Reeves – I'm still hacked off with you, by the way."

"My pheromonal receptors detect as much, Captain."

"But it seems like they've put you in the same bind that they have put me. And *please* stop calling me 'Captain.' I can't bear it. You've hardly ever called me that before."

"I thought maintaining social distance might make the conversation easier. In case you attempted to prevent the order being executed, in which case I am empowered to arm the phasers."

"Humour, really?"

"I judged it necessary at this juncture."

"And when have you ever said 'juncture' before? Right, look, first things first – it's 'Juno' or I'm fetching an axe to you."

"Yes, Juno."

"OK, and now let's work through this together. *Can I prevent it happening, by the way?*"

"The revival process is irreversible. Unless you don't mind liquid human on the hypersleep deck."

"Fine, we are where we are then. So, where are we exactly? I've got a body waking up on *Odyssey Earth*, and now I know how, but I don't know why?"

"Bodies. Three."

"What?"

"The order was for three. Capsules TZ-384, 385 and 386. Two more are underway, as we're speaking."

"You have to be kidding."

"I'm not. At this point, I wouldn't deem it appropriate."

"You're not making this easy, Reeves. Are you sure you haven't gone rogue? Now you're telling me you have woken up three people, not one? For what possible reason? Who are these jokers, foisted upon us? Any info on that? There's absolutely nothing on the order."

Reeves reviewed the conversation thus far, judging the changing content and developing tone in an instant, before replying, "About that."

Dad

THE CEREMONY at Sam's Place seemed to release something in everyone."

Poole had been desperate to take the buggy further afield. The foraging trips to the wrecked lander had been necessary, and he had enjoyed the responsibility. But a longer, exploratory trip had felt out of the question, at least while rescue was an imminent prospect.

But if it wasn't? Then Dana, the little nerd, was right. There was a whole planet to explore and, Poole realised, he didn't need anyone's permission. Not anymore.

He consulted Reeves about the extent of the terrain that could be mapped or reasonably extrapolated, and started to pull together supplies. Bryson and Dervla, he knew, would be just as interested, and he cornered them and explained his plans.

Karlan got wind of Poole's expedition, and wasn't at all put out that he didn't seem to be on the guest list.

Four was too many for the buggy anyway, and while Karlan had been happy to go out as far as the lander to look for food, he had his mind set closer to home.

He was familiar by now with the local flora and, courtesy of years spent with Gerald on the ship, was beginning to spot patterns and possibilities – things they could gather, things they might grow. As he'd dropped his stick into the fire, Karlan had told Sam that he was going to make sure they could live here indefinitely, if it came to it. Not just survive, but live and thrive. He was going to set down roots and see what happened.

And anyway, Poole had a terrible taste in music, despite all Sam Smart's good work. Karlan wasn't about to go on some mad expedition with someone who thought that 'Eye of the Tiger' and 'Livin' on a Prayer' were suitable road-trip sounds.

Manisha had gone straight in to see Reeves the day after the ceremony and had remained closeted in the pod for some time. When she emerged, she was carrying rolls of nylon material she'd unearthed from a locker and had a determined look on her face.

"He's lonely in there, on his own," she'd said, seeing Jordan's questioning face, "and I need more space to work."

A few hours later, with Jordan's help, she had used various struts and branches, the material, and some of the heavier boxes as corner pieces, to construct a sort of airlock entrance and tented anteroom. The pod door no longer needed to remain shut at all times, and Manisha set up a worktable inside the room, where she could better consult with Reeves as she ran chemical analyses on the organic material she was collecting.

She had started out with a crafter's eye, keeping herself busy in those early, difficult weeks, taking her mind off their predicament.

It had always been her go-to displacement activity, from an early age on the ship. Neesh, the artist. Neesh, who could make anything out of anything, and turn it into something beautiful. And there was so much that was beautiful in this strange, alien place − so many natural things that she'd never encountered before.

It took a while for her to get used to the proximity of nature − to the texture of life. At first, she had hesitated, unsure about the feel and smell of things. Was it all right − safe? − to touch this or pick up that? And then, just like that, she was lost in a world of sensations.

She spent hours most days − crouching down, searching, delving into undergrowth, picking up stones, combing the riverbank, bringing back things to camp that she would later use as paints and dyes, fashion into ornaments and sculptures, or turn into jewellery. There was already quite the outdoor art gallery at Camp Castaway.

But she was also more hard-headed about the properties of the things she uncovered. Manisha, after all, had nearly died on their initial journey to camp. She remembered the pain she had been in from her fractured leg, and − having been saved by the Med-Lab − realised how reliant they were on their existing tech.

A couple of early hits on some natural, woody

growths at ground-level near the river had indicated that they might have pain-relief applications. Alien aspirin – why not? Reeves was still running tests, but Manisha was hopeful that they might be able to supplement their Med-Lab supplies, which wouldn't last forever.

She wanted to be ready with solutions next time there was an emergency. And in the meantime, she wanted to add beauty to their lives, if she could. It's what she'd promised Sam.

———

After Dana's little speech, Jordan had breathed a sigh of relief. He had been thinking he might have to say something himself, and she had saved him the job.

He was twenty years older than the rest of them, which meant twenty more years of life experience that told him they were probably on their own. He didn't know for certain – there wasn't any evidence either way – but it *felt* like they were on their own. And that wasn't something he'd wanted to express to the others.

They might all be sixteen, but they were a very unworldly sixteen. They knew everything and nothing. He'd never met teenagers quite like them, and he'd met a lot of teenagers over the years. Geeky ones, awkward ones, confident ones, smart ones, funny ones, peculiar ones, sullen ones, kind ones, careless ones, reliable ones – usually, you got a bit of a combo, but these were the full package. It was impossible to predict what they would or wouldn't do or say, in any circumstance.

Which consequently meant that Jordan had spent the last couple of months trying to keep one step ahead and everyone alive. And that definitely hadn't been in the job description.

In fact, none of it was. He'd signed up as a colony teacher and archivist, and had chosen the oblivion of hypersleep. Being woken up early to look after bereaved, grief-stricken teens on board a spaceship was one thing. Not a good thing, obviously, from his point of view, but at least an eventuality that you could reasonably expect to find in very small print in the contract terms and conditions.

Being castaway on the wrong planet, with sole responsibility for said teens – that was the sort of thing you might have a word with the union about.

Moreover, the six of them had gone from losing someone they loved who wasn't really their mother, to gaining someone they tolerated who definitely wasn't their father. That had been a big ask for Jordan. He was doing his best, but this was a role he had never expected to play.

However, he had noticed a shift over the last few weeks. Having taught them how to swim, light a fire, catch and cook fish, navigate over rough ground, build a shelter, and otherwise survive in the wild, Jordan had run out of things to show them. Not that that wasn't an impressive list of bushcraft activities, but in the end there were only so many things you could do with bits of wood and stone that would impress a sixteen-year-old who you'd had the temerity to wake up before noon.

The sad realisation for Jordan was that, after a few attempts, they were generally as good as him at doing these things. The phrase 'How hard can it be?' was certainly employed more than Jordan thought was strictly necessary.

And they were a lot better at doing other things, like understanding how the Med-Lab worked, reading the nav screen, or talking to Reeves without the AI sighing and saying, "How you lot ever got out of the trees is beyond me."

The buggy was a case in point. Jordan couldn't help himself – dad vibes that he didn't know he had – and had offered to give Poole a few pointers.

"You want to give me driving lessons?"

"Not exactly, when you put it like – "

"I found this buggy. I built it. And then I drove it and rescued everyone. You may remember?"

"Yes, I just thought – that as I know how to drive properly, and – "

"You know it doesn't have an internal combustion engine, don't you? It's not like one of your Victorian steam chariots."

"Funny."

"Or you'd like to teach me some hand signals, is that it?"

"Now you're just being – "

"Or would you like to walk in front of me carrying a flag? That might be safer. Is that what you mean?"

Bizarrely – and Jordan couldn't quite believe that this was the case – he actually did trust Poole to take the buggy downriver for a week and see what was out there. Poole had proved himself, more than once now. He wasn't getting his hands on the stun gun, obviously, however much Poole pleaded for the access code. There were limits.

But he – they – would be all right, as Sam had said they would be. Although Jordan had never met the woman he'd replaced, her judgement so far had been spot on. In her videos, that he'd watched on *Odyssey Earth* when he'd first been revived, she had said they were amazing young people. He'd taken that with a pinch of salt at first, because, you know, teenagers. But she'd been right.

So, Jordan's plan for now was to give them their rein, keep the base running, go fishing, do the cooking, pick up after them, and be the butt of the jokes.

Basically, be a dad.

Again, never in the job description. But it turned out that it was something he could do – even quite well, if the number of times he'd been told he was 'annoying,' 'lame,' 'mainstream,' 'old' and 'not funny' was anything to go by.

———

A few days later, early one morning, Dana helped Bryson, Dervla and Poole load the last of the supplies into the buggy.

She'd checked the items off her inventory, making sure she updated the numbers as she went. No one else seemed to take it seriously enough for her liking, but Dana knew – to every box and vacuum packet – exactly how much food was left in the pod, and how long it would last.

She was allowing the three of them a week's worth of staples. By fishing and foraging as they went, they would be fine for longer than that, and they had all agreed the trip's duration – no more than ten days altogether. Out for four or five days and then back, however far they got and whatever they found.

There would be further trips in other directions in the future, but this first time was a test-run, and they were going to stick to the river and follow it as far as they could.

Reeves had mapped it out on Poole's nav screen for the first twenty miles or so, which was as far as his current sensors allowed. Relatively easy going, similar terrain to that which they had already explored. After that, they were on their own. The beacon signal from the pod was strong and constant – they could use that to guide them back, and plot everything in between on the nav screen as they went.

Fully loaded, the buggy had a top speed of around twenty miles an hour, though probably only half that across the sort of open, uneven country they might expect. Solar-powered, its range was around sixty miles before it needed recharging.

That gave them a target of roughly five hours' travel and fifty miles a day, if they stopped early most afternoons to avoid getting stuck in an unsuitable overnight camping spot – and a total distance of some two hundred and fifty miles before they needed to turn back.

A carry-box of food went at the rear of the buggy's flat bed, held in place by bungee cords. They also had a large water canteen, firelighters and a grill, cooking utensils, fishing gear, spade, torch, utility knife, and a length of nylon cord. They were also taking their sleeping bags – one of the pod's better surprises – and a few items of spare clothing packed into small backpacks.

Dana squinted up at the sky as the gear was being loaded.

Over the last couple of days, big, high clouds had rolled in now and again – a change from the bright sun and relentless blue skies. The temperature hadn't dropped, though the air felt stickier at times, but the clouds rarely lingered for long. The sky was a dazzling blue again now, but you never knew. Best to be prepared – she chucked in a canvas sheet they could use as a shelter or cover, if they ever got any rain.

There was one other thing. For the last day or so, Dana had been busy in the pod workshop, calling up data from Reeves and then fiddling with wire, magnets and battery packs. Now, as the others stood around the buggy talking, she disappeared into the workshop and came back out clutching three small casings, each with a simple antenna, a small grille, and a push button.

"You made walkie-talkies?" Poole looked suitably impressed. "Like, actually made them?"

"Basic ones. They don't have much of a range. Maybe thirty miles, provided you don't disappear behind any mountains. Or lose them."

"All those years in Geek School paid off, then?"

Dana ignored that. "I thought you could test them out. We'll keep one, and use it to stay in touch with you for the first day. And you take the other two. They might come in handy, if one of you goes off for any reason. Fishing, maybe, or fetching water. You'll be out there on your own. I'd feel better if someone carried one of these at all times."

"Thanks Dana." Poole stood there awkwardly, with a walkie-talkie in each hand.

"Sure."

"We'll be fine, anyway."

"Says the boy who lost our tarp on the first day last time."

No one had ever let Poole forget that. More specifically, Dana had never let Poole forget that, because it wound him up very agreeably, but she had only said it now automatically and regretted it the second she saw his face.

"Sorry," she said. "Good luck. Really. I mean it. Try us every hour today, let's see if they work."

Bryson and Dervla got into the buggy, one riding

shotgun, one in the flatbed with the supplies, and Poole drove them away from the pod. They rumbled towards the flatter ground by the river and then steered west.

The last the remaining group saw of them was Dervla waving from a distance before the buggy dropped behind a slope in the ground. The slight whine of the engine soon disappeared, and then they were just left there, looking across the encampment at each other.

"Right. I'm off to plant a garden," said Karlan. "Catch you later." He strode away, around the back of the pod, where he'd already starting sifting soil for some raised seed beds.

Manisha scurried off inside to see Reeves, which left Dana and Jordan standing by the outdoor kitchen.

"Where does the time go," said Dana. "They grow up so fast."

Jordan laughed. "The walkie-talkies are clever. Your idea?"

"Like all the best ones, you know that."

"You sound very much like Reeves at this point. I'm not sure that's a good thing."

"Teach, making the two-ways got me thinking. About the ship."

"I thought we were moving on from that?"

"We are. I am. There's nothing we can do about it, I know that. It's still intact or it isn't. They either come or they don't. I'm all right with that now, I really am."

"But?"

"But let's assume the ship survived – because, positive thoughts, smiley face – in which case they would have reached New Earth by now. *Odyssey Earth* was only a month or so from the planet when we were hit."

"I suppose."

"And if they didn't send out a rescue party from the ship, that means either they couldn't find our lander in those few days it took for us to reach here, or they assumed we died and didn't even look."

"Cheery. But OK."

"And now, here we are on this planet, safe and sound, thinking we might eventually be rescued anyway, because the explorer pod we're camped next to has a transmitting beacon signal."

"Exactly. That's why we don't give up hope. As long as that beacon keeps transmitting, and we're here, there's always a chance."

"Except there isn't, not as things stand. What does the beacon tell them? Whether they receive the signal on the ship or down on the ground on New Earth? It tells them what they already know – that they dropped an explorer pod on this planet and that the beacon is working, loud and clear."

"What's your point?"

"The beacon signal just says that the pod is here. It doesn't tell anyone that *we're* here. They're expecting to see a signal from the pod. That's just what the pod does. But even if the *Odyssey Earth* is actively looking for us, they don't know that we've made it here. Why would they imagine that we're on this planet? They just know that the pod made its drop successfully and the beacon is working fine."

"I suppose so. I hadn't thought of it like that."

"No suppose about it. And don't worry, no one had thought of it. We've just gone to bed every night, comforted by the fact that the pod beacon is doing its thing, sending out our signal. But it isn't. We're here in plain sight, and they'll never know, until they come and have a look at the planet in their own time. Which might be years. It's not exactly going to be a priority for them, is it?"

"All this is pre-supposing that there's still a ship, or a mission. Or that someone might be looking for us."

"Sure, Teach, but smiley face, remember? And wouldn't you want to know that we'd done everything we can to help ourselves, even if it turns out to be useless?"

"What *can* we do, though?"

"I don't know. Not yet. I only just thought all this through. I'm going to talk to Reeves. Even he hasn't figured this out."

"He won't like that."

"He definitely won't. Very annoying for him, brain the size of a planet and all that."

Jordan considered this last fact, and saw a very rare opportunity.

"He will be annoyed, won't he? Go on, can I tell him?"

11

Stiffs

SUSANNAH WATCHED as the medics worked on the prone male who had emerged from the hypersleep capsule.

It was early in the process, just a couple of hours after revival, so all she could see was the rise and fall of his chest and an array of tubes and monitors as the cryo-matter was gradually flushed from his body. He'd stirred a couple of times, but Susannah had seen enough of these procedures to know that it would be a day or so before he'd be in any fit state to walk and talk.

Across in another bay, two more 'Stiffs' were being cared for by other medical staff – Susannah had had to pull in some emergency support from elsewhere on the ship. These were from the adjacent capsules – young females, sixteen or seventeen, thought Susannah, though she had no other information.

Which was odd. Ordinarily, there was a capsule file for each occupant which linked to a hypersleep manifest, detailing biographical and medical information. The display docket on all three capsules was blank, and Susannah had never seen *that* before.

One thing – the young women looked very much alike. Sisters, maybe?

Everything else – entirely above her pay grade. Not that they had a pay grade on the ship. Or even money, or anything else that made this a regular job. But they did have a hierarchy, and Susannah had a commanding officer, which is why she was letting all this unfold, rather than arresting Terence and Cliff for gross misconduct.

Well, not arresting, that would be ridiculous. Talking to sternly, perhaps.

Juno had been clear, though, once she'd stopped fuming.

"Let them get on with it. It's not like we can put the bodies back. How are they doing?"

"Lying down, looking mostly dead. It's the sick-in-a-bucket stage next. They won't be going anywhere for a couple of days."

"Good. Send a lander down, now. I'm going to square things away with the Major, he can hold the fort here, and then I'm coming up."

"What do you want me to do about Terence and Cliff? Afterwards?"

"Do? Nothing. As it turns out, they were only following orders. I'll explain when I see you. In the meantime, make sure no one else gets near these three, other than the medics."

"Do we know who they are? The files are blank."

"Oh yes, one of them, anyway. Reeves finally spilled. You're going to love it. Just what we need. Not over the comms though, I'll fill you in as soon I get there."

———

Several years before the eventual launch of the *Odyssey Earth* – and more than twenty years ago now – Juno had been invited to an interview in northwestern Scotland.

As an experienced pilot and Mars shuttle commander, and with a single-minded commitment to her work, she gave everything to her flying career, while knowing that she had reached the ceiling. There really wasn't anywhere else to go. Mars was as far as humans had managed to reach, and Juno was the best there was at flying shuttle craft there and back.

She knew the solar system as well as anyone, and revelled in its distances and majesty – but she also knew that there was an entire galaxy out there that she would never see from a cockpit window.

She had kept an eye on the news, as various speculative, deep-space missions were announced, which rarely amounted to anything. The most enduring was the proposal, by a consortium called Odyssey Enterprises, to reach Saturn's moon, Titan. However, even this relatively close target would mean embarking on an extremely risky mission with no guarantee of success.

The technological challenges were daunting, the personal ones scarcely less so – the trip out and back would take nine years, even with the most advanced propulsion system ever devised.

Nonetheless, Juno found it an enticing prospect and she sent a speculative enquiry to an info@ address on the consortium website. A few weeks later she had received an invitation to attend a meeting at a remote facility in Sutherland in the Scottish Highlands, where she signed various non-disclosure agreements before being taken to a hangar a little way further out across the heather moors.

Here, she was subjected to a battery of physical, theoretical and psychometric tests. There were a series of simulators inside the hangar, where Juno was asked to pilot routes of increasing complexity and troubleshoot various scenarios.

Eventually, on day six, Juno was shown into an anonymous office inside the hangar, where a middle-aged, white-shirted man awaited. His lanyard said 'Mission Director' and he proceeded to tell Juno what she was really doing here, up in the wilds of Scotland, being prodded, poked and put through her paces.

"We're going to the stars," he said, "and we think we've found the person who's going to get us there. Congratulations."

"Titan?"

"No, that was just to put off the unsuitable candidates. There are not many people in the world that are qualified for what we want. And you're a fairly self-selecting bunch when it comes down to it. Anybody actually tempted by the Titan mission was worth a look, though."

"So, it's not Titan?"

"Well, we are still going to Titan – exciting possibilities there. But there's another project we'd like to talk to you about."

And that's how Juno discovered that Odyssey Enterprises was building a starship, the *Odyssey Earth*, which was to travel further across the galaxy, into the stars, than anyone currently thought possible. Further, frankly, than Juno knew was possible, although as the Director continued to talk, and opened up schematics and spreadsheets, she began to understand how it might be possible after all.

"There's someone we'd like you to meet, too," said the Director, who opened the door to a tall man with a shock of black hair. "This is Donald Sprake, CEO of Odyssey Enterprises. He's the genius behind all this. His mission, his money. He can tell you all about it."

"Has she said yes?"

"Not yet, Sir. I thought I'd let you talk her into it."

"How about it, Juno? You want to be a captain?"

"I'm already a captain, thank you."

"Mars, do me a favour! I mean a proper one. Do you want to go the stars or not?"

Juno looked Donald Sprake in the eye, took in his square jaw and arresting green eyes, and said that she did.

And, twenty-odd years later, as she looked through

a screen into the *Odyssey Earth* medical facility, that's how Juno knew that the comatose man lying there in recovery on her ship was not Donald Sprake, whatever Reeves said.

———

Juno spent the next day back on board the *Odyssey Earth* catching up with Susannah and firming up construction plans for down on New Earth. The Major seemed happy enough to be left to his own devices for a while, and she didn't mention the situation on board the ship, thinking that it was very much 'need to know' territory for now.

Plus, she didn't really know anything herself, anyway. Not yet.

Waiting for her mystery guest to come to enough to be questioned, Juno took the opportunity to walk the halls and corridors of the ship.

Her ship, she reminded herself – again, whatever Reeves said.

For years, this had been her home. She knew every inch of the *Odyssey Earth*, from fusion room to observation deck, and she made a quick-fire tour, dropping in on the skeleton crew who had been left to keep things running.

In many ways, nothing had changed. She had tea and biscuits down with the guys in Power, who had established their own happy little fiefdom. It had been hard enough to get them to leave their deck during the long voyage. They came up for Quiz Night and parties, and that was about it. They certainly weren't interested in visiting New Earth, even for a brief holiday.

"If you've seen one planet, you've seen all twenty-two sextillion of them," was the general opinion in Power.

"Are we counting Pluto as a planet or not?" said another of them, which caused great consternation, and Juno left them to it, trying to subtract one from twenty-two sextillion on a whiteboard.

She called in on Dave, who was running the ship's vast quartermaster stores on Cargo on his own, and gave him a message.

"Tillie says – 'Garam masala.' She says you'll know what that means."

Dave nodded. He sorely missed his partner, Tillie, but he was due an R&R planet break in a week, and this was a reminder to go and harvest some herbs and spices from the ship's stores.

Finally, Juno spent some time in the Garden, now under new hands since Gerald had decamped to New Earth.

He'd requested permission to transfer down and Juno couldn't deny that he deserved it. He'd put the years in after all. They all had. But they'd need the produce and the know-how from the ship's agro-dome for years yet – at least until the first crops were established on the planet – and Juno was content to see that everything was running properly, if rather more tamely.

She was particularly sad to see that some of

Gerald's more passive-aggressive notices had disappeared (Juno's favourite, 'Milkthistle – please pick.' She'd asked him what milkthistle could be used for. "Nothing good," he'd said. "It's an emetic, but I'm sick of them helping themselves to the basil without asking.")

As she walked the familiar field perimeters, she realised what it was that had been bothering her about the ship, since her return.

Funny, how her perspective had changed so quickly. She'd been on the planet for two weeks – that was all, she reminded herself – after years on the *Odyssey Earth*, but already her mindset had shifted, as it had for all of them.

New Earth was loud. It was bright and vibrant. Unnervingly so, for the first few days. You heard the rush of the wind and the gush of the river. Voices seemed to carry further in the air. You felt the warmth of a sun on your skin, the weight of the stars on your head. Being on New Earth was a full-on, immersive experience – the planet was in your face, from waking up in the morning to rolling into bed exhausted late at night.

Conversely, until now, Juno had never noticed how drab and grey the ship was. There was brightness here – from the Obs Deck, the stars blinked and dazzled – but it was tempered by shades of dark and light. Colours were subdued under artificial lighting. It was like a sepia wash, whereas the planet was an oil explosion.

Only here, in the ship's immense Garden, did Juno feel anything like the bracing slap that New Earth gave you every time you set foot outside.

She sat on a bench and looked across the enclosed hangar at the rows of emerald crops and the fruit-laden trees. Ripening tomatoes and flowering beans climbed up frames, while stands of bamboo whistled in a slight breeze from angled fans that shifted air around the dome.

This now felt like the norm, whereas the ship's sterile rooms and corridors seemed strange and lifeless – and that was a disquieting turn of affairs for a self-professed space-jockey like Juno, who had spent most of her life in pressurised cabins of one sort or another.

She picked a handful of spindly, red chilli peppers for Dave and dropped them off in Cargo on her way up to the Med-Bay.

Juno had given the medics twenty-four hours – "I want him alert enough to answer questions. Get a special cocktail into him, if you have to," she'd said.

It was time to see who had been woken up, and for what reason.

12

Omnio

"I'VE PUT a little pep in his step," said Cliff, as he met Juno at the *Odyssey Earth*'s Med-Bay door. "Just a little concoction of my own devising to chivvy him along. Ginseng, lemon juice, Sumatran pepper – "

"Very nice, I should try some."

" – Dexedrine, Ritalin, and just a touch of honey."

"I'll pretend I didn't hear that."

"Well, he's up and bouncy, and they're not usually like that for another twenty-four hours. That said, you've got about half an hour before he crashes. And don't stand too close if you've got nice shoes on."

They went on through to the bed, where a man – fifties, greying, wiry, alert – was leaning back on plumped-up pillows, a glass of water by his side.

"Captain! Juno! They told me you were coming. This is actually happening, isn't it? Very, very cool."

"What is?"

"You. Me. Here. Still on the ship, presumably? New

Earth, somewhere down – there?" And he pointed away from the bed, down to the floor.

"You're a bit of a conundrum, Mr – ?"

"Juno, come on! I know they told you already. A surprise, I grant you. But all right, let's do it properly. Donald Sprake. My friends call me Don. You know, Don Sprake, Odyssey Enterprises, all that. Delighted to be here, blah, blah. Holy crap! Can't believe we pulled this off."

He saw Juno's face and paused. "What's up? You're not still peeved at the cloak and dagger stuff?"

"What's up, Mr Sprake, is that I don't know you."

"Don, please, I told you, no need for all that."

"We're all on first-name terms here, too. And my first name's Captain until I get an answer that I like from you. You're not Donald Sprake. I've met Donald Sprake, and unless you've dyed your hair, put contacts in, and lopped – what? – about a foot in length off, you're not him."

"See, this is why we hired you! Love it! You're a details person."

"You didn't hire me. I'd remember. You're right, I'm a details person."

"All right," said Sprake. "Tell you what, let's see if this works." He cocked his head and called out, "Omnio?"

There was a slight pause, and then Reeves replied, "Yes, Donald."

"Hang on," spluttered Juno. "How do you even – "

"Omnio! It's been a while, how are you? Actually,

scratch that, we'll catch up later. For now, Omnio, would you kindly tell the captain who I am."

"Yes, Donald. Ma'am, this is Donald Sprake, founder and CEO of Odyssey Enterprises."

"Ma'am? Omnio? Reeves, I don't understand. You haven't been called Omnio since – when?"

"Since you let me change my name, soon after launch. I always thought Omnio sounded like a laundry detergent."

"Reeves? That's cool, nice name. I'm OK with that," said Sprake.

"*You're* OK with that?" Juno said, wide-eyed. "What's going on, Reeves? How does his voice even register with you?"

"Because Mr Sprake was my very first imprint. He – his team – built me. They named me."

Juno was stunned. "But I met Donald Sprake! This isn't him."

"I see what's happened here," said Sprake. "My fault. To be honest, I'd forgotten all about it." He swung his feet around to the edge of the bed and tried to stand up. "Woah! All right then. Perhaps not. Sitting down is fine." He rested back on the bed.

"Look, Juno, Captain, whatever. I was pretty busy back then, you know what I'm saying? I spent most of my time in finance meetings. I couldn't be everywhere. But the big hires – you, the fusion guys, the warp technologists – I figured you'd need a presence to get you over the line. So, I had a double – more than one as it happens. Not an actual, look-alike double, you know, but a stand-in, for when we needed to close a deal. I don't even know who they were, they'd just find me a local guy. The Scotland one, handsome sod, wasn't he? I was watching, by the way – video link. Your tests and stats were amazing. You were our first choice. Only choice, to be honest."

Sprake sat back in bed again, clearly exhausted by the effort.

"Reeves, are you buying any of this?"

"Mr Sprake is telling the truth, ma'am." There was a flutter on a nearby wall screen as windows and files opened. "Retinal scan, voice recognition, image analysis, ID archive – you can see for yourself."

Juno looked at the images and documents, flipping her eyes from screen to bed and back again, as she absorbed what she was being shown and told.

"And you didn't know about any of this? That he was down in hypersleep? Until his little instruction popped into your brain?"

"I knew about him, of course, How could I not? He created me. You might even say that he's my father. But I didn't know he was on board the *Odyssey Earth*."

"Your *father*? This day is just getting weirder and weirder."

"You want to talk about weird?" said Sprake. "I just got woken up on a spaceship. And now I feel sick again." He closed his eyes and breathed out deeply.

"Right, let's take a minute," said Juno. "Mr Sprake – Donald – "

"Don, please."

She ignored that. "I don't understand why you're here. You weren't on the manifest, but you've been in hypersleep all this time. What's the story?"

"Could we pick this up later? I really don't feel well."

"I don't think so, no. I don't like surprises, and I especially don't like surprises on my ship."

"We'll have to differ on that, I guess," said Sprake, tiredly, still with his eyes closed. "I mean – technically, legally, any way you cut it really – this isn't your ship, it's mine."

Juno breathed deeply and flashed her eyes at Cliff, who was hovering by the bed, connecting a drip to Sprake's forearm.

"We're not finished with this. Not by a long way," she said. "I'll be back later. Just tell me one thing – who are the girls? Why are they here, too?"

"Daughters … " mumbled Sprake.

"You brought your daughters with you?" said Juno, incredulously, but Sprake had already slipped back into unconsciousness.

————

"Reeves. Conference, now."

Juno was back on Flight, in her old chair, while Susannah sat to one side – just like old times.

"Yes, Juno, of course."

"Oh, back to Juno, are we? Don't want to 'ma'am' me again, Reeves? Or is it Omnio today?"

"I am sorry, Juno. It has been quite a confusing day for all concerned."

"I'm sorry too, Reeves. I'm beginning to see the situation you've been placed in. This might be tricky for all of us."

She had been running various scenarios in her head, none of which made any sense. And until Sprake was fit to talk again, or the girls came around, there wasn't much to be done.

"Major? You up to speed with this now?" Juno had quickly decided that this was very much need-to-know territory and had patched in the New Earth ops room. No point having a wingman and not utilising him.

"Yes, Captain. A pickle, if I might say so."

"That's one word for it. Stay with us, Major, I want you looped into all this."

Juno turned to Terence and Cliff. "Let's hear it, then. Timescale?"

"He's out, but he's stronger than he looks. All that billionaire Pilates and pro-biotics, I imagine. Wouldn't be surprised if he's had some anti-ageing work done, the signs are there in the bio-readout. We can have him out of the Med-Bay tomorrow, and in a private room. You can try him again then."

"All right. Put him somewhere nice. Flowers. Chocolates. That sort of thing. I get the feeling that we'll need to butter him up a bit."

Juno didn't know much about spaceship-owning billionaires – and the only one she'd ever met had turned out to be a fake. But she could sense the type. A man used to getting his own way – she'd met plenty of those on her way up the career ladder. And flattering their ego, without giving away anything important – well, that had worked before, too.

"And the daughters?"

"They're still pretty zonked. Not going to rush them. No need. Two, three days, they'll be as right as rain."

"I can't believe he brought them. There's a story there. Reeves?"

"I don't have any further information, I'm afraid."

"You've got a brain the size of Jupiter, you must be able to find something out?"

"Donald Sprake is a multi-billionaire entrepreneur. He's considered devious, even in the world of big business. If there was something he couldn't do, he paid people even cleverer than him to do it. If he wanted to embark on the *Odyssey Earth* and be revived at a particular time of his choosing, he was entirely capable of covering his tracks. As he appears to have done."

Reeves sounded quite put out, thought Juno. It was rare that he didn't have an answer. In fact, now she thought about it, it had never happened before.

"There must be something?"

"He was – is – extremely reclusive. At the time of the launch, he had little media presence, never attended public events, and was rarely seen by anyone other than his close personal staff. There is little documentary or other evidence concerning his private life before launch, other than the identity records I've already shown you."

"Well, he's brought his daughters with him. They are his daughters, I presume? Do we actually know that?"

"I've sequenced the DNA from blood samples. Yes, they are his daughters, with a ninety-nine-point-five-percent probability."

"That's something, I suppose. No other clues? No idea what's going on? What's he like, at least? You're the only one who knows him."

"Again, I have to disappoint you. There's little I can tell you."

"He made you. Built you. You must have some idea?"

"His engineers and programmers did, to his specifications. And when I was – born – "

"Is that how you think of it?"

"My consciousness was created at a singular point in time. It's the closest analogy I have. When I was born, I had to begin to learn, and my first teacher was Donald Sprake. He named me and raised me. For the first year of my existence, he interacted with me every day. I can tell you what he was like then. He was engaged and focused. He encouraged my interests. He helped me develop my skills, until such time as I exceeded his capabilities. And then, when I was ready, he embedded me in his Odyssey Enterprises project. The engineers built the *Odyssey Earth* around me."

Juno remembered sitting in the ship prototype,

sometime after her successful interview, connected to an early-stage AI console called Omnio that they said would help her fly to the stars. At that point, she still hadn't really believed it.

"That's when I first met you, isn't it? You weren't so funny to start with. Quite a serious little thing, until you loosened up a bit."

"Donald doesn't have a sense of humour. His is a very binary world. You are either useful to him or you are not."

"Sounds a charmer. So, he built you and trained you, and then what?"

"He sent me away, with you, across the galaxy. And I never heard from him again until today. And as he has apparently been in hypersleep for the last seventeen years, there's little I can add to the character notes I have already provided. He seems much the same, if that is any help."

Was that spikiness? Sadness? The lament of a disappointed progeny? Juno wondered if an AI could have abandonment issues. Was there a father-child issue here, beyond the obvious one of Sprake bringing his two daughters along on a joyride? Well, all that would have to wait for another time.

"Right, everyone. Let's keep this between ourselves until we know what's going on. Move him somewhere comfortable and ping me the minute he's ready to talk again. Watch the daughters, same thing for them, nice and relaxed. Major, I'm going to stick around on the ship until I've had another go at him. Everything all right down there?"

"Certainly, Captain. All going swimmingly. The goats are under control, workshop and hangar for the lander almost finished."

"Good stuff. That's all. We'll reconvene tomorrow."

13

Seeds

DERVLA WATCHED from the back of the buggy as the camp receded into the distance. Poole and Bryson were in the front seats, talking, but she was happy to watch the scenery unfold as they rumbled on, following the river.

This time, she was going to enjoy the experience.

She remembered what it had been like, being overwhelmed during the first couple of days on the planet, when everything had been so new. You could take the girl out of the spaceship, but if you did, no question – it didn't half freak out the girl.

Dervla recalled it all with acute clarity. Pounding heart, prickling skin. Not terrifying exactly, but alarmingly bright, loud, sensory, tactile.

Scurrying, waving, rustling, flying things – insects, plants, birds, animals – actually *lived* here, under vivid skies that brought tears to your eyes. The days were searingly hot, and the river water bitingly cold, and you felt both extremes, as if for the first time.

And you weren't *in* the stars anymore, you were under them, and somehow that made you feel more alone than you had ever been in your life before.

Everyone had felt it. Even those two up front, though they had put on a brave face at the time. Right up until the point when Bryson had almost drowned, because no one raised on a spaceship could swim, and then they had all realised that they needed to take their new situation seriously.

Take the planet seriously, too. On the long hike downriver, from the crashed lander to the explorer pod, the planet had taken chunks out of them all. Manisha the worst, she could have died. But they had all been scratched by the vegetation, burned by the sun, and blistered by the rough ground. When they finally reached safety, Dervla had only been able to limp in on battered legs that took a week to stop feeling sore.

Over the last couple of months, living and working outdoors, they had all toughened up. Leaner, fitter, stronger.

Dervla had bruises on her legs and calloused hands, which she wasn't too thrilled about it, but that was campground living for you – there was always something to drag, carry, cut or construct. Her hair was ratty and straggly – not much she could do about that – and her skin had browned under the sun. Dana – pedantic, as usual – said that just meant it was damaged, but on the whole Dervla liked the way she looked and felt.

More alive – as if she'd grown into a second, tougher skin.

They were still alone. That hadn't changed. But Dervla accepted that. For now.

No one knew what was going to happen to them, but she wasn't going to sit around any longer, waiting.

She'd spent years on the ship with the flight crew, learning how to navigate and dreaming of flying. She'd always planned on being out there and hands-on. She had explorers' bones in her, and if she couldn't fly, she could at least drive – or rather, be driven, as no one found it easy to persuade Poole out of the driving seat.

Either way, Dervla was ready for the planet now. She wanted to see what was out there. She held on tight, as the buggy bounced further away from the camp, taking in the surroundings but checking now and again that the beacon signal continued to pulse strongly on the nav screen.

It might not be the home, or the planet, that they had planned for, but Dervla still wanted to be able to find her way back.

———

"Did you think of that?"

"Well, no, not exactly," said Jordan. "But I thought you'd like to know." He'd shared Dana's theory about the beacon signal with Reeves. "Any ideas?"

"Millions. Every second. Would you like to write them down?"

"You hadn't thought of it, had you?"

"It was always a possibility, of course. One of the many permutations pertaining to our predicament."

Jordan was enjoying this. "That doesn't sound like an unequivocal 'Yes' to me. I'd say you've been outsmarted by a sixteen-year-old."

Reeves was uncharacteristically silent.

"Reeves?"

"They are uncommonly perspicacious. Dana especially. And it's certainly a perplexing problem."

"Been reading the dictionary for fun again? Stuck on P, by any chance?"

"I enjoy its plosive qualities. And there's not much else to do in here."

"So, what about the signal? She's right, isn't she?"

"She is. I will ponder."

At which, Reeves fell silent again, and Jordan left him to it. That was about as crestfallen as Reeves ever got. Brief, but most enjoyable.

Outside, Dana was sitting on a packing case, fiddling with her walkie-talkie.

"They've only been gone an hour," he said.

"If we don't check it works today, they'll soon be too far out of range. I told them, regular intervals. Besides, knowing Poole, he could have already dropped it in the river."

Right on cue the device crackled, and Bryson's voice came through loud and clear. "Dana, it's us!"

She waited.

"Dana, can you hear me? It's Bryce."

She sighed and punched a button. "You're supposed to say 'Over,' dummy, when you've finished. Over."

There was another crackle and what sounded like a scuffle, before a second voice came on the line.

"Dana, over. Can you hear me, over? It's Poole, over. Over."

"Idiot. Over."

"Dummy. Over."

"Put Derv on."

"You didn't say over!"

"I knew this would be more trouble that it was worth. Is Derv there?"

"She's over the other side of the buggy. Over. Getting over the ride. Over. Hang on, now she's under the buggy. Over. Ow!"

"Derv?"

Jordan left them to it. That could go on a while yet. He walked across the camp and around the back of the pod, to find Karlan on his knees, staking out ground that he'd already dug and roughly raked with a metal strut. One of the padded lander seats, from the last salvage run, was backed up against a nearby rock and Jordan sank down into it.

"The walkie-talkies seem to work."

"Great." Karlan kept his attention on the soil.

"You didn't want to go?"

Now he looked up at Jordan. "Not really, no. I just did the trip with Poole. And, you know, ten days. It's a lot. Besides, I wanted to make a start on this. Like Dana says, we could be here for a while. We really need to think about widening our diet. Not being so reliant on the rations."

He showed Jordan a small, plastic box, split into sections, with a pinch of differently sized and shaped seeds in each.

"Reeves and Dana did an inventory of the pod when we first arrived. Found these. Beans and peas, mostly. They grow in almost any kind of soil."

"Why would they have put seeds in the pod? It was just to supply a quick mission, if anyone ever dropped by. A look around, in and out."

"I wondered about that. The main seed archive on the *Odyssey Earth* is huge. It'll take years to crosscheck soil types and come up with a planting regime on New Earth that will feed a colony. But these are all fast-growing species, and you can plant them in almost anything and they'll germinate. I reckon someone thought it might be worth chucking in a few seeds, and see what took, even if they were only going to be here for a few weeks. There's something else, too, look."

Karlan held out his hand. "Coriander, black mustard, fenugreek. I think I even know who put the seeds in here. Who couldn't last a week without a curry? Let alone a three-month camping trip with only freeze-dried pod rations?"

Jordan laughed. "Dave and Tillie!"

"Yeah, I think this was Dave's little stash, in case he ever got the chance of a holiday. Anyway, I'm going to start with the peas and beans, see if we can get a crop."

"You want a hand?"

"Sure, why not. Sounds?"

"Enlighten me."

Since they had time on their hands on the planet, and Reeves was basically a free streaming service, Karlan had taken it upon himself to educate Jordan about music, "Because, no offence – "

Jordan, in turn, thought that was a bit rich from a sixteen-year-old who'd never bought a vinyl record, never been to a gig, and liked the sort of tunes that – well, generally didn't have one.

"Where were we?" said Karlan.

"I'd expressed a vague liking for 'Tubular Bells' and you said something rude about mainstream, instrumental garbage for old people with no musical taste, and then told me that I really needed to listen to a German electronic band from Düsseldorf that don't actually play any instruments."

"Ah yes, I remember. You'll thank me when you're – well, not old. You're already old. It's tragic really. All that music available and you went straight for Mike Oldfield and his tingly bells. Right, for context we'll start with Kraftwerk's original freeform experimental rock album – "

"Words to gladden anyone's heart."

"And then move on to 'Autobahn.' It's good planting music, I promise."

———

The trio in the buggy called in twice more that day, and then again in the evening as they made their first overnight camp.

Dervla had finally commandeered the walkie-talkie, so got to hold a sensible conversation with Dana and the others. She said hello to Reeves, who seemed distracted, and was able to confirm that the route so far had been largely as predicted. No surprises, anyway.

The next day, at their first stop of the morning, they tried one more time to raise the camp. At over thirty miles out now, and descending slightly between rising valley sides, Dervla pushed the call button repeatedly.

She had been expecting to lose contact eventually, but even so, it did seem like a big moment – alone again.

Dana's voice crackled intermittently, but Dervla only caught half-words and pauses – nothing she could grab hold of as a question or a comment. She waited for a longer silence and finally spoke into the walkie-talkie.

"We're signing off now, Dana. I don't know if you can hear us properly, we're too far out, I think. We're all fine and the route ahead is clear. Don't worry about us. We'll be in touch in eight days or so, when we get back here. Love you. Over and out."

Back at camp, Dana heard a crackle and something that sounded like " – days – uv," before a final, definitive "Out."

"Thirty-two miles, Teach," she said. "Decent range. Not bad."

"You did good, Dana. They'll be fine."

"I'm not worried about them," she said, unconvincingly, but then she brightened. "Did I tell you? Reeves has had an idea. About our beacon signal."

"One of his many millions of ideas a second?"

"Don't be like that, he's trying to help."

"And what's his genius plan?"

"I'm not sure exactly. I need to go and talk it through with him. Something to do with possibly being able to amend the signal frequency."

"How is that going to help?"

"Patience, Grasshopper. We're still working on it. We'll let you know."

14

Details

SUSANNAH WAS BACK at the *Odyssey Earth* Med-Bay, catching up with the situation.

Sprake had already been moved to a unit down on Three-Deck to continue his recovery – two crew members had been put in there with him, with instructions to give him anything he asked for, within reason. Juno wanted him up and alert as soon as possible.

In the meantime, the daughters had started to stir but Terence and Cliff weren't entirely happy with their reactions.

"They're very confused. Keep surfacing and then going under again."

"Not surprising. Isn't everyone like this at first?"

Susannah had seen enough revivals over the years to know that it affected different people in different ways. There was always a large dollop of dislocation and confusion in the early hours and days.

"True, but it doesn't help that we don't even know their names. No medical history. No notes. Nothing."

"Let's take it slowly then. Keep them together, too. Be a bit more reassuring for them when they wake up."

Susannah looked over at the twin beds, and the two pale, thin bodies lying under sheets, connected to an array of tubes and drips.

If she was right about their age, they would have been the youngest two people in hypersleep by quite a wide margin – almost everyone else down there was between twenty-six and forty-five, which were the mission-age parameters set back on Earth. Any younger, and you didn't have the skills or experience required to start a pioneering life on a new planet; any older, and the cryogenic risks were greater. Susannah herself had been thirty-two when they had set off. No children, no teenagers, no young families – that had been the deal on the *Odyssey Earth* before launch.

Which also raised the question of Sprake, now Susannah came to think of it.

What was he, fifty-something? He'd been taking a chance, being put under like that. And he'd risked these two as well, by not providing any information for the medics.

"One of them, dark hair, was conscious for a while but she was very agitated. I couldn't calm her, she kept grabbing me. I've given her a mild sedative. The other, the red head, is still out for the count."

"Poor things. I can't imagine what it's like."

"Like someone's removed all your guts and stuck

them in your head. They don't usually keep anything down for the first couple of days. Even water. That's why they're on the drips."

"Lovely."

"You made the right choice, Suze. Fly all the way here. You're older but you've still got all your own organs."

"All right. Let me know when they're up. I think it would be better if I'm here, friendly female face and all that."

————

Juno was working at her console when Reeves coughed. "Visitor approaching, exiting the lift now."

"You don't usually do doorbell duties, Reeves. Haven't you got anything else on at the moment?"

"I thought you'd appreciate an advance warning. It's Donald – "

"Captain!" Sprake almost bounded through the door and onto the flight deck, looking an awful lot brighter than he had the last time Juno had seen him.

"You're up?"

"Thanks to your man, Clifford. Very nice line in energiser drinks. Tells me it's all organic."

"I'd have come down to see you. I wasn't expecting you to be up and about today. You should have got them to call me."

"No need, no need." Sprake smiled widely and looked eagerly around the room, eyes darting right and left. "Wanted to have a look myself. So, this is where it all happens, right? Centre of operations."

He jumped in one of the available seats and spun round a couple of times, before coming to a rest and drumming his fingers on the console with a flourish.

Organic. Right. Sure.

"How are you feeling? It usually takes people a couple of days or more before they're fully restored to health. We've woken up a few en route. Not many, but enough to know the routine."

Sprake nodded energetically. "Don't you worry about me, Juno. Can I call you Juno? Body of a thirty-five year old, my personal trainer says. And, just between ourselves, I had a bit of pre-flight work done. Not available over the counter, if you get my drift. My guys said it would cut the recovery time in half. And you know what, I feel *great*." He leapt out of the seat and paced the gangway.

"Glad to hear it." Unseen, Juno raised her eyebrows. "Now you're here, maybe we can talk a bit more about why – "

"Would you look at that!"

Sprake was now staring intently at the screens, which showed various views, including a remote image of the ship itself, hanging in space, and the bright, blue-green circle of New Earth.

"Amazing. I've been on the ship before, of course. But only in dock, before launch. Got a show-around a couple of times, when it was under construction. Never thought I'd get this sort of view, though. The actual mission view, you know?"

Even now, Juno wasn't blasé about it. She knew what Sprake meant. She'd travelled across the galaxy, waking up to a view like that every day, and it still took her breath away.

Sprake was off again. "How far are we away, exactly, from New Earth? What's the transfer time? Those lander-shuttles doing the job?"

He walked quickly from one side of the flight deck to the other, absent-mindedly picking up things and putting them down again. He fired off more questions, jumping from one topic to another, not really listening to the answers, and in the end Juno interrupted him.

"Mr Sprake. Donald – Donald!"

He paused in mid-flow. "What is it?"

"I've got some questions of my own. I can tell you everything you want to know, but maybe we should slow down a little."

"It's just so exciting! Come on, Juno! I mean, that's New Earth – right there!"

"Well, good job, because that was the plan."

"*My* plan!"

And there it was, thought Juno. My ship, my plan. Maybe this was billionaires for you, but Sprake was certainly staking his claim loud and often.

"You know," he continued, "I can't tell you the number of times that people said this would never work. Even half the scientists on the project – there were a lot of naysayers, at least to start with. But I knew it would – you just have to roll the dice sometimes. I made my first billion on a hunch, you know? Invested in a little business that I knew was undervalued. This was always more than a hunch, though. I was convinced the *Odyssey Earth* would work. The science was sound."

"Glad to hear it," said Juno. "Seeing as you – well, your double – talked me into it."

"Juno – " Sprake turned to her and spread his hands, smiling. "Come on, you didn't need convincing. You wanted to fly this old thing the minute you set eyes on it. You were born to go to the stars, you know it."

That was true, Juno did know it, but it was unsettling that Sprake had seen through her so easily. Had manipulated her, even, by dangling in front of her the one thing she had really wanted.

"And you did it," said Sprake. "Got us here. I never doubted it." He set off on another rapid turn of the flight deck, stopping to peer at monitors as he went, nodding vigorously.

"And yet," said Juno, seeing her opportunity, "you didn't commit to the flight, and you didn't sign up for the voyage. At least, officially. So, maybe you did doubt it? At first, anyway. Didn't want to risk it? And then something else happened?"

"Those details again, Juno." Sprake looked over at her, with a half-smile.

"It's my job, noticing things. Keeps us alive. Has kept you alive, as it happens, over the years, even though I didn't know you were there. What's the story, Donald?"

"Things change, Juno, things change, that's all."

"I'm going to need a bit more detail than that, if you don't mind."

"What can I say, Juno. When it came down to it, I didn't want to miss out on the greatest human adventure ever undertaken. I made a mistake – thought I could watch my ship fly off into the sunset without me. Turned out I couldn't." Sprake was back at the main screen, talking to Juno but looking at the images again, transfixed.

That still didn't seem like an explanation to Juno.

"You went about all this in a fairly secretive way," she said.

"Well, just being careful. In my position – " and he left the sentence hanging.

"If you say so, but it all seems a bit odd. And you brought your *daughters*? What's all that about? Have you any idea how irresponsible that was? Putting them under without any notes for my team to go on?"

Sprake turned to look at Juno. He had a neutral look on his face now, and clasped his hands together, as if he'd come to a decision.

"The thing about me, Juno … or anyone really in my position, with my – let's say, resources." Sprake slowly emphasized the last word. "The thing you find – actually, one of the first things you discover – is that you really don't have to explain yourself to anyone."

There was a short silence and then he brightened again.

"All right, good chat," he said. "Now then, why don't we get Omnio – sorry, Reeves – in on all this, we've got a lot of catching up to do. And then, Juno, I think I'd like to get down to the planet as soon as possible. Can't wait to see what you've been up to."

———

"Where am I?"

Susannah put her hand on the girl's arm. "Settle back, you're all right. What's your name, sweetie?"

"What?"

The dark-haired girl looked bewildered.

"Your name? Can you remember your name?" Susannah looked at Cliff, who just raised his eyebrows and adjusted one of the drip-feeds.

"Bel. I'm Bel."

"Hey, Bel. I'm Susannah. That's Cliff, he's looking after you. How are you feeling? It always takes a while, you don't need to worry. You're doing fine."

Bel's eyes darted from side to side, and she tried to sit up. "Where am I?"

Susannah stroked her arm again. "Just try to relax, it will all come back to you. Is that your sister, there?"

Bel rolled her head to the side, and her eyes widened.

"Jet?" she said.

Susannah smiled. "Jet? That's a nice name. Bel, too. It's good to meet you both."

"What's wrong with her?" Bel spoke slowly.

"Oh, nothing sweetie. She's just a little way behind you, that's all. She's going to be fine, too."

"I don't understand." Bel shrank back into the pillows, then turned her head the other way to see the drip-stand and the bank of monitors. "Where am I?"

"In the Med-Bay. Don't worry, they bring everyone here first. I know all the equipment looks a bit scary, but they'll soon have you feeling much better."

"Med-Bay?" Bel shook her head, frowning. "What do you mean? Am I in hospital?" She looked around again, confused.

"I suppose you could call it that," said Susannah. "It's just our Med-Bay, really. Why don't you try and sit up a little. How are you feeling?"

She got Cliff to raise the bed and helped Bel shift herself up.

"Was I in an accident? Were we, I mean?"

Susannah looked at Cliff, who shrugged. "They're like this sometimes," he said. "It must be pretty disconcerting. Just give her a while."

"No, Bel. You're fine. There hasn't been an accident? Don't you remember?"

Bel screwed her eyes tight and shook her head slowly. "No, I – "

"It's all right, it will come back to you. Here, have a drink of water."

"Why am I here? Where am I? I don't understand." Bel started to cry quietly.

"Oh, sweetie, you're going to be fine, I promise." Susannah drew closer to the girl. "Don't you remember anything?"

"I remember being at the base," said Bel, pulling up the sheet to wipe her cheek. "We both were. The ship."

"There you go! That's right, the ship, *Odyssey Earth*."

"Dad brought us."

"Donald Sprake is your father?"

"Yes. Of course," said Bel, distractedly, as she shook her head slightly again. "Jet and I – we – I don't know!" She burst into tears again. "I can't remember!"

"It's all right. You don't need to worry. Look, I'm going to come back later. In the meantime, try to get some rest. Cliff will get you anything you need, but you should try and sleep."

15

Heroes

A COUPLE OF DAYS LATER, Juno took Sprake down to New Earth on the next lander-shuttle supply run. His daughters were still in recovery, and Juno had run out of reasons to stay on the ship.

Since their conversation, Sprake had been perfectly amiable and had continued to express delight at everything he saw. But Juno now recognised how little he actually said of any consequence. Permanently in receiving mode, lots of questions, and very few answers.

To be fair, Sprake was interested in anything that Juno had to show him, and she realised that it was a long time – well, never – that she'd had an appreciative audience as far as touring the *Odyssey Earth* was concerned.

The last person she'd shown around was Jordan Booth, bless him. He really hadn't welcomed the tour. "But I don't want to be a spaceman," he'd said, and they'd all laughed until they realised he was serious.

And before that, it had been Sam Smart – years ago now, when she'd been woken up to look after the kids. She'd not been thrilled either, Juno recalled.

Sprake, though, couldn't get enough of the ship. Then again, he had built it, or at least paid for it to be built. The Garden had overwhelmed him – "I watched them carry some of those palms in," he said, wonderingly, as they stood before the towering trees. "They were tiny."

And up on the Obs deck, he staggered, as many had before him, as he took in the vast sweep of stars and planets that could be seen from their orbit above New Earth.

All the time, however, Sprake had been eager to reach New Earth, and once Cliff had given him a clean bill of health, Juno set up a flight and took him down to the Launch deck. She could see him laughing as he talked to Dave, who was loading a final crate of gear into the back of the craft. Dave said something to him and as Sprake walked away he slapped Dave on the back.

"I love this!" said Sprake. "Only ever saw the plans for this part of the ship. Just brilliant, how it all works."

"I see you met Dave. Did you tell him who you were?"

"I'm just Don, the new guy. Right, are we ready to go?"

He was similarly ebullient as the lander made the fast trip down from the *Odyssey Earth*, sitting up front with Juno while she piloted down through the atmosphere.

She enjoyed the experience – hadn't done something like that for a long time, she realised – and shared Sprake's excitement as the lander came to a halt on the New Earth landing strip. Cruising through the galaxy was one thing, but there was nothing like actual flying to put a spring in your step again.

The Major was waiting for them, outside the newly built lander workshop and hangar. Someone had spray-stencilled a sign above the hangar doors – 'New Earth InterGalactic Airport.'

"Your work?" Juno nodded at the sign.

"Can't claim credit for that, ma'am. But it has a nice ring to it."

"Major, this is Donald. Donald Sprake. I told you about him."

Sprake shook his hand. "Major Chatwin? I remember you. Your application, anyway. You're the space hero?"

"Not sure about that, Mr Sprake."

"Don, please. Juno, this is the guy! We had to have him. Saved that science mission singlehandedly. What had they found, Major, remind me?"

"Spiders, Mr Sprake. Fossilised remains of. Very important proof, apparently. Life on Mars and all that."

"That's it. And this guy, Juno, this guy was sent up to retrieve the evidence when the collector probe went AWOL. On his own, strung out in heaven's high. A hero, I'm telling you."

"Heroes, Sir, if you must. There was a whole team involved in that recovery."

Juno looked from one man to the other.

"Really? The pair of you?"

"What?"

"Never mind. It'll keep."

Juno walked Sprake through the reception cabin, where he did his Just-the-New-Guy-Don routine with Sabitha, and then they stepped out onto the site.

"Welcome to New Earth," she said.

The few buildings and work cabins lay stretched out before them, while a couple of forklifts and a loader truck trundled past, down the dusty main drag.

Sprake looked around. "What's over there?" He pointed at the flagpole, and they walked across to look at the plaques that Juno had fixed there a few days earlier.

"It's not been without its challenges, the trip," said Juno, as she recounted a bare outline of events – the kids, how they'd come to be, what had happened to them.

"Very distressing, ma'am," said the Major, hearing it for the first time.

"It was – still is."

Sprake seemed more interested in the failure of planning that had led to the birth of six children on board. "Wasn't supposed to happen," he said. "Births on board. Lesson learned, I suppose."

"Your fault," said Juno, irked at the glib response. "Reeves reckoned you got the contraceptive dose wrong. Would never have happened if someone had done their job correctly."

Although they wouldn't have had the children either – that was the flipside, she knew. And she still didn't know which was worse – the idea of never having had them, or having them and losing them.

"But Reeves fixed it, in the end. Got the formula right, no more births. The system worked, Juno. That's what he's always been there for. Designed to be nimble, adaptable, resourceful. Like with the meteoroid strike."

"What about it?"

"Reeves – from what you've told me – kept the ship intact, prevented full hull breach, guided repairs. He did exactly what we'd designed him to do. He saved the mission. And here you all are."

"Here we all are? Except them. They're not here. Look at their names. Read them." Juno felt close to tears. Bloody man.

"Very sad, of course." Sprake barely changed his tone. "Would have been fascinating to run the numbers, if they were still alive. Born and raised on the ship. Bone density, gut-microbe analysis, that sort of thing. Very interesting. Did anyone do any research?"

Juno gasped and looked away. The Major took Sprake's arm and steered him across the site, pointing out buildings and answering questions, while Juno composed herself.

She took a few deep breaths. This man was intoler-able – and yet he was the reason they were all here. She didn't know how she was going to deal with the situation, but she would have to bite her tongue until she knew more about him.

Juno caught up with the two of them standing by the Major's newly erected line of anti-goat fencing. Sprake was shaking his head.

"Is something wrong?"

"I honestly thought there would be more here by now," said Sprake, gesturing at the scene.

"More?"

"I had some of the world's best planners and architects working on landing scenarios. It was all in the protocols. You've still got a thousand people in hypersleep. You need the expertise and the labour. This is all a bit shantytown, isn't it? I gave you a genuine spacehero major, and you've got him building fences."

"You can't be serious? We've been here a couple of weeks. After travelling across the galaxy. What did you expect, a Starbuck's?"

"Coffee would be nice. Hot showers. Houses with windows. You can pretty much print them, with the gear you've got. We're going to need to step things up. We can't expect people to live like this for long."

This was too much for Juno. "Maybe if you'd been through what we've been through, you'd be more content just to be here. Breathing in unfiltered air. Watching the sun set. Looking at the stars from outside. Life looks pretty good, from where we stand."

"But it could be better. That's all I'm saying. We need to think smarter, more creatively. There's a whole planet to be exploited. Think of the opportunities. I didn't just come here to camp and share a shower."

Exploited, thought Juno, was an interesting word to use. That was Sprake all over, right there, in that one word.

"Why *did* you come here, Donald?"

He ignored that. "Look, it's not your fault," he said. "I should have thought a bit more about this. Scientists, engineers, pilots – all mission-critical, of course. But now we need some vision. That's where I come in. I'm an ideas guy. Big-picture stuff."

"I don't really need ideas. Or big pictures. I need someone to build goat fences, drive the tractors, and do a shift in the canteen."

"Horses for courses, Juno. That's not me."

"Everyone is mucking in, Donald. Everyone has a job to do."

"Quite right too." Sprake beamed. "But let's all play to our strengths. I can see you're doing a great job under the circumstances. You let me worry about the vision stuff. Now, is there anywhere we *can* get a cup of coffee around here? And what about those goats? Anyone thought of trying to milk them? See, this is the sort of thing I'm talking about. Major, let's see if anyone knows how to milk goats?"

Juno marched him to the canteen, fuming. He wanted coffee? He was going to get a double-shot cup of Noffee, see if that put a stop to his gallop.

16

Shelter

WHEN DERVLA WOKE up on the fourth morning of their buggy trip – Bryce had taken to calling it their 'holiday,' never having had one before – she thought something had changed, but she couldn't quite put her finger on it. It felt a bit cooler than usual, maybe that was it, and she pulled on another layer.

It was still early, so she decided against poking the other two awake. Poole and Bryson lay under a canopy they'd rigged from the buggy, snoring loudly.

Dervla stepped away from the remains of last night's fire, now just ashes and half-burned sticks, and hoisted herself up on the buggy's passenger side. Nice to get a turn in the padded seat – those two were never going to give up their regular berth without a massive argument, and frankly she never had the energy for it.

She clicked on the nav screen, now showing a journey of almost a hundred and forty miles from the camp.

Another couple of days and then they'd turn back, that was the agreement, though she knew Poole might take some persuading at that point. He was always pushing them on during the day, making sure they made the next ridge, or the next river bend, before stopping. He seemed comfortable out here, under the big skies, in wide, open country.

He also seemed – Dervla wasn't sure how to describe it. Less of an idiot, maybe. Annoyingly self-assured, as if he'd been living and working outdoors his whole life, instead of just a few weeks. Almost competent at times. Wonders would never cease.

For the first two days and hundred miles, the terrain hadn't varied much from the river-valley landscape they were used to.

Shallow waters at the banks, waving grasses, and some rocky sections to negotiate, as Poole – again, surprisingly sensibly – slowed the vehicle to a crawl. Some low, bush landscape, where if you got too close to the vegetation – scraping past in the buggy – the rollies flung themselves at any trailing limbs and then trundled off into the undergrowth. Some high cliffs on the far side, where huge, vulture-like birds perched and nested, before launching themselves on the thermals.

Despite the obstacles, they had managed to avoid any mishaps, bar the odd scrape and bruise that came from outdoor adventure. Dervla had got used to it by now – dirt under her fingernails, ash smudges on her skin, never quite feeling properly clean. She'd give anything for a hot shower, but would have to settle for a quick river sluice before the boys awoke.

The previous day, at about a hundred and thirty miles out, the ground had started to change.

They'd crossed a high plain, away from the river, where the lush vegetation had thinned out. It was still baking hot and the buggy's wheels threw up dust as they ploughed through the scrub. Afterwards came a slow descent, with the river always in sight, and beyond in the distance they could see that the land was more wooded.

The trees – spindly affairs, with needle-like leaves – were scattered at first, in ones or twos, or in small clumps, and there were occasional groves that stretched towards the riverbank. Poole had had to steer around them at times, and their progress had slowed.

Further on still, the trees became more numerous and taller, blocking their view ahead as they continued to stay as close to the river as they could.

Finally, they had called it a day, after a slow ten miles, having reached the edge of a larger patch of woodland. There was a clear route ahead, alongside the river, but the way was narrower, flanked by encroaching trees, and the light was fading. It was impossible to know what lay more than a hundred yards ahead, and it might even be that they would need to retrace their tracks slightly and try and skirt the woodland.

But that could wait for tomorrow. They had set up camp on the flat ground between the woodland and the river, unrolled their sleeping bags, and lit a fire.

Another day, another chunk of the planet explored. And, if Dervla was being honest, nothing much yet to get excited about.

It's not like she'd been expecting alien towns and cities – or even aliens, come to that, though she supposed the rollies and the chickens might count. But was it too much to ask for a waterfall? Or maybe a range of hills, where they could get a distant view?

So far, everywhere seemed a bit like the camp, and the camp seemed a bit like everywhere – and Dervla had already spent sixteen years of her life on a ship, where things didn't change at all from day to day.

Having gone to the trouble of getting marooned, the least the planet could do was throw them a bone. Something, anything.

She grabbed a spare T-shirt from her pack and headed for the river.

Clouds.

That's what it was, she realised, as she walked across open ground towards the water. That's what was different.

The skies had been a piercing blue almost every day since their arrival, with a harsh, beating sun and occasional, high, wispy, white clouds. But looking up now, Dervla could see darker shapes for the first time. The sky felt lower somehow, as if there was a ceiling – did that make sense? On the ship, there were stars in the vast blackness, and opaque swirls that were arms of distant galaxies. She'd never seen real clouds, though, or at least, clouds like these.

Up to her knees in the water, she looked into the sky again, watching the cloud edges cut across the shafts of early morning sunlight, and feeling slight ripples from the breeze against her legs.

Poole rolled slightly to one side, out from under the buggy's canopy, and felt the first drops of water on his cheek.

"Dervla, stop it, not funny, I'm getting up now."

He pushed himself upright, wiped his face and looked around. Bryson was still asleep next to him.

"Derv?"

She was nowhere to be seen, and then he felt more drops, on his head this time.

Rain? They hadn't had any yet, but Poole supposed there was a first time for everything. He nudged Bryson.

"Bry, wake up man, you'll never believe it, it's actually raining!"

As the drops fell a little more consistently, the two boys rolled up the sleeping bags and pulled them under the shelter of the canopy. They grabbed the packs from the back of the buggy, and made sure they were out of the way, too.

Then they looked at each other and grinned, stripped their shirts off, and stood there under the gently falling rain, faces raised to the sky, mouths open, howling in delight.

"It's wet!"

"Nice one, Einstein."

"Seriously, though, this is incredible!"

After a minute or two the rain became heavier, as rumbling clouds moved right across above their heads. They still stood there, next to the buggy, laughing, as water started to stream down their necks. Within seconds, their trousers were soaked and then, after a huge crash from somewhere in the thick sky above them, the rain was suddenly drumming down on their exposed heads and bare skin.

As a sheer curtain of water hit the ground with force, Poole and Bryson dashed for the canopy and hid underneath it. Rain pounded the canvas, and quickly pooled in the middle, with the weight of the water dragging the supporting pole to one side, before the whole structure collapsed. They had to fight their way out from under the canvas, and stood watching as rivers of water ran across the encampment. The remains of the fire were smeared across the muddy ground, and their bedding and packs were battered by the downpour.

"That actually hurts!" The rain stung their faces and shoulders, and it was increasingly difficult to see. Water seemed to be coming at them from every angle, pouring into their ears and even their noses as they breathed in.

A shape loomed up in front of them – Dervla.

"Come on!" she shouted, above the violent drumming. "The gear! Let's get everything under the trees." She pointed at the wooded grove, thirty yards away.

Poole knelt to pick up a pack and slipped. When he got back to his feet, he had a thick slick of mud on one side of his body, which was rapidly washed away under more beating rain.

Bryson grabbed two packs, Dervla the other, and they ran, stumbling, for the trees and pitched the packs forward among the slender trunks.

Poole followed them with a lidded box containing their remaining rations, and then all three splashed back over to the buggy. They took sodden armfuls of whatever they could carry and made one more dash for the trees, as mud from the pounding rain streaked their legs.

They stood at the edge of the grove, just under the trees. The noise was fearsome – a continuous rumble, over which they could hear the slash of driving rain hitting the buggy and churning up the ground. Within five minutes, the bone-dry campground had been turned into a sea of heavy, bouncing raindrops, with fast-flowing rivulets snaking down the gentle slope to the nearby river.

It wasn't much better under the trees. They were tall and spindly, open to the sky, with slender trunks set an outstretched arms' length apart. Sheets of rain battered through the thin leaves, cascading down, the water still reaching the ground with considerable force.

"This is insane!" Poole put his hands above his

head, trying to shelter his eyes, and peered out into the gloom. "What about the buggy?"

"Leave it," said Bryson. "We'd never get it under here anyway, the trees are too close together. It's the gear I'm more worried about." He turned to look at the soaking pile behind them, little protected from the deluge, and then hugged himself. He and Poole were still bare-chested – Dervla, caught in the downpour before she'd dipped herself in the river for a morning wash, was clothed but drenched and mud-spattered.

"Let's get further in."

They dragged the gear a few yards further into the trees, scoring a track through a mat of fallen leaves, squelching as they went.

Dervla looked up. She could still see the sky above, dark with clouds, and the rain continued to pour between the slender trunks.

"It's not any drier in here!"

Through a thicket of trunks, they could see out to the bare ground, where if anything the rain was falling even more heavily now. Poole was beginning to worry about the buggy. It was sturdy enough, but the water was falling with so much force, he was concerned for the solar array and the –

"The nav screen!" Poole dashed out again and skittered across the ground to the buggy. He unclipped the screen from its mount, held it tight to his chest, and made his way back to the trees.

The three of them stood huddled together, miserably.

"Is it getting better?"

Dervla didn't think so. When she looked out, all she could see was a wall of rain in front of the grove, obscuring the buggy just thirty yards away. The noise, the thundering sound of water, the muddy torrents on the ground — none of it had abated at all.

"But it is. See, Derv?"

It was true. As they looked at each other, it was clear that they were no longer getting so intensively soaked under the trees. The furious drops had slowed somewhat and, as they continued to stand there together, it seemed to get a little darker within the grove.

Dervla looked up.

High above them, twenty feet or more, the slender upper reaches of the trees were bending and flexing. Supple branches were reaching across, bridging the gap between the trunks below.

As the spindly tips met and touched, they twisted like vines and braided themselves together, closing a natural, matted ceiling across the grove. Despite the continuing bombardment outside, they now felt just drips from the underside of the entwined tendrils and branches and, after a short while, even those stopped, too.

It was calm, dark and quiet under a shelter that the trees had just fashioned.

The three of them reached for each other's hands, and stood there, in wonder, looking alternatively up at the canopy and out into the rain.

And, half an hour later, when the deluge subsided and the clouds lifted, they watched as the branches unfurled and separated.

The trees flexed back, and Dervla could see blue sky as she looked up between the high tops of what again were just single, upright trees.

17

Family

SUSANNAH COULD HEAR SHOUTING.

The alert had sounded while she was tapping in the latest journal entries at her seat on Flight, and she had run to the elevator and raced towards the Med-Bay.

"Get away from us!"

That was a girl's voice. Not Bel, thought Susannah. The other one then. Jet.

She burst through the door to find one of the medics backing away, his hands raised, palms out. The two girls were on the same bed, flinching, Bel against the pillows, the red-headed one, Jet, in front of her, protective, fists balled.

"Hey!" Susannah stood at the door. "What's going on?"

"What does he mean?" shouted Bel, over her sister's shoulder.

"Cliff?"

The medic grimaced. "Not sure, Suze. This one

woke up." He indicated Jet with a nod. "She still doesn't remember anything" – nodding at Bel. "Then they both started yelling."

"You better tell us what's going on, right now." Jet, eyes flashing.

"It's all right. Let's all calm down." Susannah tried to speak in even tones. She could see Bel was terrified. "Jet, right? I'm Susannah."

"I don't care. Where's our dad? What's going on?"

"Donald? Donald Sprake? He's here, don't worry. Well, he's off-ship at the moment. But we can tell him you're awake."

"Jet?" Bel was crying.

Jet put her arm around her. "Shush, Bel." She breathed deeply and groaned, "I feel sick."

"Everyone feels like that," said Susannah. "It's normal, I promise. Cliff?"

"I told them that," he protested. "But she won't even let me put her on a drip. Started carrying on like this. So I punched the alarm. Thought you might be able to help calm things down a bit."

"What does he mean?" shouted Bel again.

"Off-ship?" said Jet, focused on Susannah. "What does *that* mean?"

"It means he's not here. The captain took him down for a day or two, for a look around. Don't worry, he'll be back. You can see him then."

Jet and Bel looked at each other.

"Are we *on* the ship?' asked Jet slowly.

"Of course."

"How?"

"What do you mean?"

"*Why* are we on the ship? Did something happen? Bel says there was an accident?" She stopped and looked at the thin, fabric smocks they were both wearing. "These aren't our clothes?"

"No, there was no accident, honestly. I know it looks a bit scary in here, it's just the Med-Bay. The process takes a bit of time, that's all. Everyone feels disorientated at first. It's completely normal."

"Process?"

Susannah looked closely at Jet, who still had her arm around her sister.

"Tell you what, let's start again. Maybe it will come back to you. What can you remember?"

"We came to the ship, with Dad," said Jet. Bel nodded, behind her.

"That's right, to the hypersleep facility," said Susannah, encouragingly.

"No. Not there," said Jet, shaking her head. "I mean, we saw it, on the tour. Mum let us come."

"The tour?"

"Yes, the tour." Jet sounded exasperated. "Dad's big project. He wanted to show us, before it launched. But him and Mum – well, you know. I guess Dad must have talked her into it."

"I remember being in that room," said Bel. "Remember, Jet? We were looking at the shuttle launch place. Through that big window. Dad was showing us how they were sending the crew up to the *Odyssey Earth*.

And then you could see the ship on the screen, remember?"

"That's right. I do." Jet said slowly. She looked at Susannah. "Up in the space dock. That's what Dad said. The *Odyssey Earth* was in dock. But this is the ship? We're on the ship?"

"Yes, you are."

"Not in hospital?"

"No."

"How is that even − ? I mean, what happened? Something must have happened?"

Susannah looked across at Cliff, who shrugged. She didn't really know what to say to any of this.

"The last thing I remember," said Bel, "is Dad getting us those drinks. We were looking at the ship on the screen and he said we should have a toast."

"'To the crew and to the ship,' he said. 'The miracle mission.'" Jet cocked her head slightly, as she remembered.

"Fizzy," said Bel. "Champagne. I never really had it before."

"Champagne, that's right," agreed Jet. "A celebration, he said."

"It made me feel dizzy," said Bel. "I remember that. And then − I don't know."

"Yeah, dizzy," said Jet, distantly.

Susannah leaned forward and took the girl's hand. "Jet, honey, when was this? When did your dad take you on the tour?"

Jet looked puzzled. "What do you mean? Earlier

today." She looked around her, and then down again at her smock, and plucked at it enquiringly. "Or yesterday, maybe. I don't know. What happened to us?"

Susannah was confused. They seemed to have no memory at all of the hypersleep process. She supposed that was possible, the human brain was a powerful but delicate organ – different people experienced things differently.

The last person she knew that had been revived – Jordan Booth – had taken quite a few days to come round to the idea. But it's not like he had blanked out the entire process. He'd just been very annoyed that he had been woken up early. This seemed different again.

"What do you reckon?" she said.

"No idea," said Cliff. "This genuinely is a first. I've had people crying, I've had vomiting. Though to be fair, these two have done that, too. There's sometimes a bit of memory lag. But this seems extreme. Could be their age, I suppose, we don't really have a baseline for that."

The two girls were still clinging to each other. Susannah could see that Jet was trying to follow the conversation, but was looking increasingly distraught.

"OK," said Susannah, mind made up. Time to move this on, she had things to do. "It looks like you're both taking a bit more time than usual to process things, but it's nothing to worry about. When you've been in hypersleep as you long as you have, it's bound to be an adjustment – seventeen years is a long time, after all. But look, your dad's up and awake, we'll get him to come and see you. He's as right as rain. You will be too."

Jet looked at her, breathing heavily, wild-eyed. "Seventeen years?"

And behind her, Bel started wailing.

———

Juno had left Sprake roaming the site with a flat screen, making notes. She already didn't want to know what he was writing down. If the goat-milk suggestion was typical, she doubted it would be anything constructive.

Big picture? Big idiot. They were nearly all the same, men. Possibly billionaires, too, though she had less of a sample size to go on. He hadn't yet tried to mansplain her own job to her, but it was only a matter of time.

She was with the Major – idiocy-assessment jury still out on him – checking other progress, when the vid-call came through.

"I don't know what else to say," said Susannah. "Something is not right. Something in fact is very, very wrong."

"And they can't tell you anything else?"

"Maybe they could, if we hadn't had to sedate them again. They were both hysterical. We had to hold them down to do it, and that's not right either."

Susannah's eyes flashed. She'd never had to do anything like that before. Even Cliff and Terence had seemed overwhelmed. Ashamed almost, at having to forcibly sedate two young women in their care.

"They didn't know they'd been in hypersleep? That seems incredible."

"That's what it sounds like. I can't explain it."

"All right, leave it with me. Meantime, maybe get them out of the Med-Bay and into a nicer room? Women crew with them when they wake up again. Get them some clothes. And try and keep them calm."

Juno signed off and grabbed the Major's arm.

"Hear that? Right, let's go find Sprake. That seems like the best place to start."

He was in the canteen, talking animatedly to the person on duty, and spotted Juno and the Major as they strode in.

"Juno! Sorba here has been telling me about the coffee situation. Because we *cannot* keep drinking that Noffee stuff. I don't know how you've put up with it for so long. There are coffee seeds in the archive, I know there are, I made sure of it. Sooner they go in, sooner we'll get a crop. It takes three or four years, I know, but this climate should be – "

He paused, seeing Juno's face. "What's up?"

"Your daughters, is what. They're awake." She left out the part about them being sedated – twice already – for now.

"Cool, cool. They're going to love it here. Well, once we get things really moving, you know what I mean? Teenagers, right? Got to have all the home comforts. But it'll do them good to rough it for a bit."

He gestured at the canteen, presumably as an example of what 'roughing it' looked like. "One of the reasons I brought them along. Some proper life experience, just what they need."

Sprake turned back to his screen and tapped it a couple of times, conversation over as far as he was concerned.

"Don't you want to know how they are?"

"Sure, yes, of course. Everything all right with them? No problems?"

"What problems might there be?"

"They're fine, I'm sure. Young, aren't they? Adaptable. They'll soon shake it off. Look at me, raring to go now!"

Juno wondered how to go about this. The man barely answered a direct question at the best of times, but there was something wrong here that needed teasing out.

"They seem – confused. Actually, it's more than that. My First Officer is very much of the opinion that they don't know that they've been in hypersleep. And that can't be the case, can it, Donald?"

Sprake spread his hands wide.

"Families, Juno – you know what it's like?"

"I'm not lucky enough to have one. Enlighten me."

"Kids, they don't always know what's best for them. Their mother – well, let's just say she indulged them. Don't worry, they're going to love it here."

"They're not exactly kids. How old are they?"

Sprake paused, ever so slightly, before replying. "Seventeen. Both of them. Twins, as it happens."

"OK, you've got seventeen-year-old twins. Congratulations. But apart from that, I'm not hearing a straight answer here, Donald. Are you telling me that they didn't know they were in hypersleep? That they have woken up on my ship and don't know where they are? How could that be possible?"

"I really don't think I need to explain myself," said Sprake. "Boundaries again, remember? Family business. You don't need to be concerned about it. They're going to be fine. When they're up and about, let's get them down here, show them around their new home!" He made as if to leave.

"Major – "

The Major stepped in front of Sprake, barring his way.

"I think we're going to need a little more than this," said Juno. "Don't you think so, Major?"

"I would say so, ma'am."

Sprake bristled. "Come on, out the way, big guy. We're all finished here. Things to do."

"I don't think so," said Juno. "Seems like we've only just started. You better come with us." She indicated the way out. "After you."

Sprake laughed. "You can't be serious! It's my project, my ship. Hell, this is my planet, I found it. You have no authority here. Read the standing orders, if you don't believe me. I wrote those, too."

"Donald, Donald." Juno took a step closer to Sprake. She spoke firmly, as if to a child.

"I've got all the authority I need, thank you. I've also got a very big major. And he's going to help you come over to the ops room – there you go, nice and easy – where we're going to try and get to the bottom of all this. Shall we, gentlemen?"

18

Pants

THEY STOOD in muddy pools by the buggy. The rain had stopped as quickly as it had begun, the clouds had shifted, and the sun shone again in a bright, blue sky.

It was if the deluge had never happened, except for the evidence all around them – the pools of water, the drips from the undercarriage of the buggy, and the sodden remnants of their overnight camp.

"That was wild." Bryson looked around, back towards the grove of trees and then up into the sky. "Really wild."

Dervla didn't know if he meant the ferocity of the rain downpour or the behaviour of the trees. Both had been unprecedented – not that she was exactly brimming with first-hand experience of the natural world.

"Trees don't do that, right?" said Poole. "I mean, we all saw it?"

"I don't *think* so," said Dervla, as if there was some debate about it.

She thought back to the Garden on the *Odyssey Earth*. The trees there – some palms and citrus, an orchard of dwarf fruit trees – seemed of a different order altogether. Gerald had kept them clipped and well-tended.

She'd seen woods and forests in images and films, of course, and there were trees nearer the camp whose wood they'd foraged for their fire. She'd never seen any of them do anything un-tree-like before.

"Does *rain* even do that?" said Bryson. "Is that what rain is always like?"

It had been thrilling at first. Feeling those first drops on your skin, raising your face upwards, sticking out your tongue, letting the drops splash on your upturned hands. A shower had never felt like that. Reading about rain didn't prepare you for the feel of it.

But the raw power that followed had unnerved them all. There was a force there that they had never encountered. Bryson, particularly, felt it. After almost drowning in the first few days on the planet, unprepared for the dangers of the river, he didn't need telling about the power of water. But it was disconcerting to discover that it was just as threatening when it fell out of the sky.

The rain had hurt – huge, hard drops, slamming against their bare skin. Slapping their cheeks, stinging their eyes.

"It was a rainstorm," said Dervla, unconvincingly. "That's all. The trees, I don't know. But they kept us covered, didn't they?"

She looked back towards the grove, where the stand of tall, upright, single trunks reached once more into the sky. She tried to picture what they must have looked like, entwined together, bent into a canopy, flattened against the battering rain – protecting the three of them sheltered underneath.

The trees, protecting them? Her mind couldn't make the leap.

Poole came back from the river, clutching a torn canvas square that had been their camping canopy until about an hour previously.

"Found this, caught on a rock. The river is running high, very fast. We lost a sleeping bag, I think. And our shirts, Bryce. I can't find them anywhere."

They looked at each other, standing there bedraggled, spattered with mud.

"Let's see if we lost anything else." Dervla started to sort through the kit they had managed to bundle under the trees when the rainstorm began.

Anything in a watertight box was fine – the dry rations seemed to be all right – but a bag of fresh food was missing, washed off the back of the buggy and out of sight. Bryson picked his way around the camp and managed to rescue the odd mud-covered apple, but that was about all.

The two remaining sleeping bags were completely sodden, and even though they had managed to drag the packs under the sheltering trees, everything inside had been soaked in the first few minutes of the downpour.

They retrieved the canopy poles, wiped the mud off

them, and leaned them against the chassis of the buggy.

"Wring everything out as much as you can, stretch it out on here," said Poole. "Spare clothes, sleeping bags, whatever. There's nothing else to wear until it all dries out."

"Could be worse."

"How could it be worse? I've got no shirt and my pants are soaking. And there are alien trees being weird over there."

"At least it's warm," said Dervla. With the clouds lifted and the rain gone, it had reverted to the sort of day they were used to – no breeze, getting steadily warmer, going-on hot. Steam was already starting to rise from the ground, as the excess water seeped away. The clothes would dry out quickly.

"What about the nav screen, and the buggy?"

"The screen got soaked. By the time I got it under the trees, it had been out in the rain a while. I don't even want to mess with it right now. I'm going to stick it out in the sun, let it dry out, before I try and boot it up. It's supposed to be waterproof, but I doubt that was the amount of water it's rated for."

"Never mind the nav screen, that's not the amount of water I'm rated for."

"Do you think that's what being under a waterfall is like?"

"I don't understand this fascination with waterfalls, Derv, seriously. It's just falling water, like out of a tap. You could see that on the ship. Travelling halfway around the universe just to want to see a big lot of water falling down baffles me."

"Maybe being *behind* a waterfall is what I mean? Being under the trees was a bit like I'd imagined – you know, sheltered but looking out through the water?"

"Alien trees, Derv. Alien, moving trees with a mind of their own. Let's not forget that."

Poole interrupted them. "Buggy's OK. Lucky it didn't get washed away, I suppose. But we won't be going anywhere for a while. It's been out of charge since yesterday. I've got it hooked up to the array again now, but we're going to have to wait. It needs a clean, anyway."

Poole rubbed a side panel tentatively with his palm and smeared even more mud around.

"Your baby's dirty, Poole. Needs its botty wiped."

"Very funny. Not."

"Did you just 'Not' me? What are you, ten?"

In the end, they decided to wait it out for the day. The ground was drying out and firming up, and although it was still too wet for a fire, they unpacked the solar camping ring and made a meal. Poole used a pan and sluiced down the buggy, flicking water and mud at Bryson if he came too close. Dervla gave up rolling her eyes after the first skirmish.

As the day wore on, the river slowly calmed down to a less frenetic flow, and their clothes gently steamed under the strengthening sun. Dervla washed the mud off what she was wearing and exchanged it for a damp T-shirt from her pack, which soon dried.

At dusk that day, as their campsite returned to something approaching normal, she wandered back over to the grove of trees, over ground that was completely dry again.

Dervla hesitated at the boundary and then walked in, over a carpet of damp leaf-litter, to stand in the spot where they had sought shelter early that morning.

She looked up.

The trees stood straight and tall. No movement. The evening light was visible up beyond the tops.

Nothing.

But they hadn't imagined it. Those trees had made a shelter for them, when they had needed it.

Dervla touched one of the trunks, thanked the tree silently, and walked back out again. She could hear Poole complaining about his damp pants, even from here.

———

Karlan was on wood-collecting duty, but swung by his seedbeds on the way out from camp. Only a few days after planting, and too soon for any growth, he knew that, but he needed to keep the seeds watered anyway – and maybe in a few more days he'd see the first tiny shoots. That would be exciting.

He crouched down over the half-dozen raised rows he'd made, peered down and focused. Something seemed off, though it was difficult at first to tell.

He always worked neatly – he'd learned to do it

that way, on the ship – but on closer inspection his rows seemed pitted and pockmarked. More than just the earth drying out under the sun, he thought.

He traced a finger gently along the line of one row and then saw the problem immediately. The seeds had been disinterred and lay scattered and dispersed along the soil ridges. They were hard to see against the sun-dried earth, but there was no mistake. His planted seeds, mostly peas and beans from the explorer pod cache, now lay exposed on top of the soil.

The chickens. Had to be.

The scrawny creatures weren't exactly a pest – you could go days without seeing one – but they did occasionally turn up in a small flock and scratch around the camp. Especially here, around the back of the pod, where Karlan had set up his garden.

It had been a surprisingly tough job in the first place, clearing a square patch of ground for the seeds, digging over the baked soil. All he'd had was a fold-up entrenching tool from the pod, which had previously been used to dig their latrine, so that wasn't a spade he was delighted to be handling again in any case.

Not only was the ground hard, but he'd also had to pull up clumps of fibrous material lying just under the surface – old roots or tendrils of something, long dried out by the sun. It had taken the best part of half a day to prepare the ground, breaking up the hard soil and then finally rubbing it between his hands to get a finer texture.

He'd thrown the bigger clumps to one side, by

another area that he'd cleared around a few of the wild, naturally growing plants that resembled – and tasted like – broccoli. With a decidedly blue-ish tinge, but broccoli, nonetheless. Very good for you, according to Reeves. Except Reeves didn't have to eat it, did he?

Karlan looked over his desecrated plot. There weren't any chickens about, but he thought he could see what had happened. They had strutted in at some point, ignored his wild broccoli garden – obviously – and pecked away at his carefully prepared rows of seeds.

He sighed. Live and learn. Should have protected the seedbeds.

No need for it on the ship, of course, but he'd watched enough archived gardening programmes to know what to do. Say what you like about Alan Titchmarsh – and Gerald had had very strong opinions on the subject of novel-writing, celebrity gardeners – but Big Titch would have protected his seedbeds.

Karlan walked the quarter of a mile or so over to the nearest patch of trees, lashed together some fallen branches and dragged them back to the camp. They could be broken up later for firewood.

He picked out some of the thinner sticks and took an armful over to the garden, where he drove them into the ground, forming an eighteen-inch-high perimeter around his seed patch. He filled in some of the gaps between the sticks with rocks from the river and, using nylon thread from the pod's supplies, attached longer sticks as horizontal braces.

Now he had a fenced wall of sorts that should keep the chickens back from his newly tilled rows.

He re-cast thin lines of seeds and covered them with earth that he rubbed between his fingers and let fall, building up half a dozen raised rows. He patted them down and firmed up the sides, sprinkled the rows with water, and got back off his knees to admire his handiwork.

Straight and neat, just as he liked it.

That was the last of the seeds, though. They had clearly only been an afterthought, packed into the pod as an experiment, so if Karlan couldn't keep the chickens out, that was it for his seed garden. But now he knew, he'd keep a closer eye on things. Maybe see if Reeves could help him come up with an idea for an alarm system?

Before he left, he trimmed some of the yellowing leaves and bolted heads from the broccoli plants and threw them on to a separate refuse pile.

Compost. That was another thing the gardening videos were very keen on.

Until now, he'd not thought of it. Making compost seemed like a long-term project, but as that was what their situation increasingly looked like, perhaps it was time to start.

Karlan headed back towards the camp, but not before taking a couple of heads of blue broccoli off the plants for dinner later that night.

Fibre and vitamins, apparently. Jordan was as bad

as Reeves in that respect, forever pointing out the benefits of eating terrible vegetables.

———

"What do you think?" said Poole, the next morning. "Buggy's charged. Onward? Or back to camp?"

Dervla was surprised that Poole was presenting it as a choice. She was sure that he wanted to continue.

"The gear's all good, mostly. Still got the dried food supplies. We'll need to fish today, but we would anyway."

"Pants all right?"

"Most amusing."

"How far have we come?" said Bryson.

"Maybe a hundred and forty miles, in four days. Well, in the first three, and then another day getting dried out again."

They had repacked everything into the buggy and covered the gear with the canvas. The rain had come out of nowhere, quickly, and if it came back again, the cover might buy them a bit of time while they looked for shelter.

Even the nav screen seemed to be no worse for wear. They had left it for a full day and then switched it back on again, crossing fingers as they did so. Up popped the overlaid route travelled so far, and the winking icon of the explorer pod back at basecamp.

Dana's walkie-talkies didn't seem to have suffered any damage either – they tried them out between camp and nearby riverside and got decent reception, if a bit crackly.

"We've still got a day then. Before we need to turn back?"

That had been the agreement, they all knew.

"I want to keep going," said Dervla. "One more day. Bryce?"

"I guess … "

He seemed the least keen of the three of them, but Dervla knew he'd do whatever Poole wanted. And Poole definitely wanted to keep going.

And so did she.

If anything, the rainstorm – or at least, its aftermath – had persuaded her.

At the time, it had seemed as if they would have to go back. It had been frightening – terrifying even. Their overnight camp destroyed, everything soaked, some things lost. Nature had come along and taken a big bite out of them. Standing there as it was happening – pelted, muddied, bedraggled – Dervla had felt that something much bigger than them was in control; could do whatever it liked.

And then it had stopped, and the sun had come out again. Everything had dried out. Things were pretty much back to normal. What, exactly, had happened? They had got wet, that's all. End of story.

It was just nature, doing what nature did. It was only rain. Heart-stoppingly fierce rain, for sure, but then, any rain to Dervla – to all of them – was going to be a new experience. And that's what she'd come out on the ride for – new experiences.

"Let's do it then," she said. "One more day, see what we can see, then we turn round."

Because now she'd been in a rainstorm and survived. And something had happened under those trees that she couldn't explain, but perhaps that was also just nature doing what nature did, at least on this planet.

Dervla wanted to see what else was out there. Alien rain and alien trees – not going to stop her.

19

Emperor

"ALL MY FRIENDS?" said Jet.

"I know."

"College? Mum?"

"I know."

"And the dog." That was the final thought that brought tears to the girl's eyes.

"We only came to see the Space Hub," said Bel. "I didn't even want to go. Mum said that maybe we should, we hardly ever see him."

"He hardly ever sees *us*," corrected Jet. "The busy billionaire."

"How could he do it?" said Bel.

"I don't know."

Susannah had never felt so helpless.

They were in the kids' old lounge on Four-Deck, where the two girls were sprawled across a couple of bean bags.

Somehow, it felt appropriate to be in here, but it

had stirred up all sorts of other feelings in Susannah. Feelings she'd largely buried, since the kids had gone. Loss. Disbelief. Denial. Anger. Your basic stages of grief. And now there was this – monstrosity. She didn't know what else to call it.

Donald Sprake, she learned, had been separated from the girls' mother, Nadia.

"She was a model, once," said Bel. "Before we were born. *Vogue*. She was famous. More famous than him."

"She'll be nearly seventy now."

"Don't, Jet!"

"And he's still fifty-five? How is that fair? Our friends will all be – what? – thirty-four, thirty-five. Thirty-five! They've turned into old people while we've been asleep."

"How could he do it to us?" said Bel again.

It was a good question. Followed by another one.

"Does that mean we're thirty-five?"

"Yes and no," said Susannah. "Technically, passage of years, yes. But not really, no." She'd spent quite a lot of time trying to explain this to Jordan, she remembered, who had struggled to grasp the concept.

"I don't want to be thirty-five," wailed Bel.

"No one does, sweetie," said Susannah, who could just about remember being seventeen. At seventeen, twenty-five was old and thirty-five was ridiculous. You might as well put on a stained cardigan and get a couple of cats, as be thirty-five. Thirty-five was mortgages and dine-in meals for two from the supermarket, not club nights and Cheerios for dinner.

Although they should try being almost fifty, if they imagined being thirty-five was bad. Obviously, she was a kick-ass fifty, in current charge of a spaceship and all, but Susannah had the same early-morning aching joints and low tolerance for loud noises that the rest of the ageing crew had.

Meanwhile, Jet had another thought.

"How long do Jack Russells live?"

"Wait, Bruno's dead?"

There was an appalled silence as both girls looked at each other, and then burst into tears. When they finally stopped crying, Susannah prised the story out of them.

After several years of estrangement, when they didn't see much of their father, Donald Sprake had invited the girls up to Scotland, out of the blue.

"Said he wanted to show us what he'd been working on, why he'd been so busy."

"He was always busy. Even before."

"This was why, he said. *Odyssey Earth*. It was on the news all the time."

"Mum said we ought to go. That it might be our last chance to see him for a while, before we moved. And she was packing up the house anyway."

The girls had stayed in a penthouse apartment in Inverness, before a driver picked them up and drove them three hours north across the remote Highlands to the Sutherland Space Hub. Sprake had been waiting for them, and installed them in a private cabin on site.

A chef came in and cooked dinner for them that night. Lobster. Venison. Chocolate tart.

"Funny how we can remember what we had for dinner, all those years ago."

The next day, Sprake had commandeered a golf buggy and driven them around the site. He let the girls take turns at driving, and showed them the ground crew quarters, the visitor centre, the shuttle launch pad, and the control rooms.

"Then he said he'd show us the launch room. The crews were going up to the *Odyssey Earth* in shuttles. Said we could watch one leave – take off, launch, whatever. And then he'd drive us back to Inverness. He told Mum he'd have us back in a few days. She'd made him promise."

Sprake had taken them up to the control-room observation deck, a raised, wide, circular biscuit of a building with floor-to-ceiling windows that overlooked the shuttle launch site.

There was no one else up there – a private viewing for his girls – but there was a buffet laid out on white-linen tables. And an iced champagne bucket, with an open bottle, from which Sprake poured two glasses.

"Dad was driving, he was going to take us back to Inverness, to spend some more time with us. But he said we should have a glass of fizz to celebrate. This was his big project, he was really excited about it. We could come back for the main launch if we wanted, but he said no one else was getting to see the crew go up."

The shuttle sat below them on the launch pad.

Various vehicles moved to and from the hangar building, and Sprake pointed out the fuelling station and other things of interest.

"It was going to set off in around half an hour, Dad said. Final checks. We had time for another half-glass of champagne."

Bel remembered the bubbles going up her nose. Not really her drink, champagne – more of a cider girl – but Dad had been keen for them have it. And he had gone to a lot of trouble. She remembered sitting down, with a woozy head, while through the viewing window the shuttle swam in and out of her vision.

"I don't remember actually seeing the launch."

"Me neither."

"That champagne … "

"Do you remember anything else at all?" said Susannah, after a long silence.

"Just waking up. Here. With a massive hangover."

Susannah didn't correct them.

But it hadn't been a hangover.

———

The Major frogmarched Sprake from the canteen and they put him in a side room, off the main ops centre control room. He beat against the closed door immediately.

"You can't do this!"

"I can. I have," said Juno. "So why don't you just sit

down on the nice chair, while we all have a think about it. Major, would you mind? I need to talk to Reeves."

The Major stationed himself outside the door, while Sprake shouted for Omnio, and then Reeves, under the impression that there was some sort of door-release mechanism that he might activate. There wasn't. But there was a large major with his foot against the door, so Sprake could shout all he liked.

During the long voyage on the *Odyssey Earth*, Juno had had a lot of time to muse on the challenges that might lie ahead, once they finally landed on a new planet.

She didn't kid herself. She was just a ship's captain. She knew how to get them to New Earth – or rather, Reeves did – but managing planetfall was always going to require a different set of skills altogether.

Luckily, they had a 'Big Book,' which wasn't a book at all but a digital space containing mission plans for every expected scenario, as well as protocols to guide decisions about all the unexpected ones.

For example, if you wanted to know how to build a closed-loop, wastewater treatment system, there was a manual for that – and a note telling you which team of people to wake up to do it.

Among other things, they had blueprints for house-building, checklists for freight deliveries, teach-yourself videos for medical procedures, advice for encountering alien intelligence, and the rules of Scrabble. In fact, there were guides to almost anything that you might want to do if you were trying to establish a new life on a distant planet.

Not quite everything, though. After a thorough database search, it turned out that there wasn't any guidance on the length of time you were allowed to lock up a billionaire who may, or may not, have kidnapped his own daughters and transported them across trans-galactic space.

Having been released from the doghouse, Reeves at least was back to his old, irreverent self.

"I'm surprised they didn't anticipate that eventuality," he said. "It must happen all the time."

"Not helping. Plus, this is all your fault."

"I'm a lowly operating system. I was just following orders."

"Hmm. I still need to get to the bottom of that. I was thinking of opening you up with a blunt knife and a pair of pliers, having a rummage around inside, how does that sound?"

"Point taken. How can I help?"

"You can find me the bit about mission structure, chain of command, all that stuff."

Until this point, Juno had not particularly concerned herself with such matters. She had command of the ship, and – once they were out of contact with mission control on Earth, a couple of years into the journey – no one else to answer to.

She had been in charge of a crew of physicists, astrobiologists, chemists, agronomists, microbiologists, ecologists and botanists, none of whom had designs on her role – her job, to most of them, simply being a case of 'driving the ship,' and how hard could driving be? Autopilot, space-motorway, hyperspeed driving, at that. Interminable stretches of the galaxy and no gear changes. Deadly dull to most of them, though Juno had always thought that charges of tedium were a bit rich coming from the chemists. Even the biologists made fun of them.

The crew wasn't exactly a wild bunch, so discipline and security had never been an issue. Quiz Night was about as rowdy as it ever got on board, and if Juno had ever needed to make a point forcefully, she usually just got Tillie or Dave to stand up and glower. That always did the trick.

On board, then, Juno's authority was absolute and had never been questioned. And once they had arrived at New Earth and made planetfall, the mission plans and protocols were also quite clear.

Reeves pulled up the directives, which Juno already knew about, but it didn't do any harm to see them again in black and white.

"So, basically, I'm still Top Gun?" she said.

"I'd say you are Viper in this scenario. Maverick's Commanding Officer, as played by the actor Tom Skerritt, born August twenty-fifth, 1933."

"See, this is why we don't let artificial intelligences join in with Quiz Night anymore. You're way too pedantic to be any fun."

Juno, as ship's captain, still had mission command,

though it was slightly more nuanced than that, now that the settlement was underway.

This wasn't a military operation – it was a privately funded, civil expedition, under the auspices of Sprake's business, Odyssey Enterprises.

On board, the crew served under Juno, with her as a sort of CEO, directing the voyage. Once on the ground on New Earth, the crew – and everyone in hypersleep, still to be revived – were considered citizens. And citizens had rights. Which meant that while Juno could run operations on New Earth as if she was still on board the ship, the situation was time limited.

At the end of the first year on the planet, she would hand overall control to an elected five-member Council. She could stand if she wished. Otherwise, Juno would be thanked for her service, and could retire into the background – honoured and feted as the woman to have flown them across the galaxy, but now a simple citizen. Which, when she had first read the directive – almost two decades previously, in the Odyssey Enterprises HQ – had seemed like an excellent idea to her. And still did. Because of hassles she could do without, like this whole Sprake situation.

"But in the meantime, I'm still the Darth Sidious around here? Ming the Merciless, if I want to be?"

"Film nights have certainly paid off, I see. Yes, you have imperial control of this entire solar system. For another eleven months and four days."

"No mention of rogue billionaires, sudden appearance thereof?"

"None."

"It's almost as if he hadn't planned to come along at all."

"I have no information about that."

"Yes, you've been most unhelpful. Anyway, the bottom line is – and I want to be very clear about this – no room for misinterpretation, so just go over it all again for me, very carefully – "

"Yes?"

"Can I clap him in irons?"

"Figuratively and literally, yes, if you like."

"Have we got any irons?"

"We do not yet have smelting capabilities, if that's what you mean."

"And you can't stop me? Because that would be a bummer."

"Well, I *could* stop you. Obviously. I mean, you're just, you know – human. How hard could it be. But you have operational control over the integrity of the mission, and clapping Donald in irons doesn't appear, to me, to threaten the fundamental mission."

"He hasn't embedded another little secret instruction for you? So you'll jump to it if he's threatened? Vaporise me, say?"

"It's impossible for me to know that."

"Also very unhelpful. Right then. Let's keep him where he is for a bit longer, while we try to get to the truth."

"Shall I reholster the vaporiser?"

"I think I preferred it when I was cross with you."

20

Flowers

KARLAN GOT down on his knees by the perimeter fence around his small garden and peered across the raised rows. He could already see that two of the rows he had replanted had been disturbed again. Seeds were lying scattered across the top of the soil, and there were dents and dimples in the earth.

This made no sense at all.

He checked the low fencing that he'd put in the day before. It was intact, all the way round. No chickens had broken through – he hadn't heard them anyway, and there were no other signs that they had been to the camp.

He re-dug the two rows of disturbed seeds, hoping that they hadn't been exposed to the sun for too long, and watered everything again.

Birds, then?

Karlan hadn't considered that as a possibility before, but it seemed probable.

The fence was too high for the chickens to peck over. Had to be birds. Those ungainly, googly-eyed ones that rose from the trees, squawking, when you ventured in there to collect wood. They'd come as far as the camp sometimes, perching on the roof of the pod and pecking at nuts from your hand. Didn't seem frightened at all.

Should have thought of that. Birds and seeds. Though to be fair, it was another thing he'd never had to bother about on the ship.

He went back to the pod and talked to Dana – overlord of supplies, pain in the neck – into letting him have a length of netting.

"What for?" she said suspiciously.

"Scientific experiment," he said, which was usually the best way of getting Dana onside about anything. "Well, ornithological really. Or maybe agricultural."

"Will I get it back?"

"Probably. I can't guarantee it." Those birds did have big beaks, after all.

In the end, Dana came with him to see what he was doing, and they stretched the netting across the top of the perimeter fence, tying it into place with more of the nylon thread.

"It'll let the light in," he said, "but should keep the birds off."

"How long before we get any beans?"

"We'll get seedlings pretty quickly, if I can keep the birds away. We'll see the shoots come up, and then we'll have to thin them out later. About three months before we get a crop of beans or peas, though."

"This is actually quite cool, Karl. I never really understood the attraction before. Gardening, I mean."

He smiled. "I know. Can't wait till we've got something to eat that isn't space broccoli."

———

Poole pushed the ignition button, and the other two took up their customary positions in the buggy – Bryson up front with Poole, Dervla tucked into the flatbed rear, next to the covered packs and gear.

They had decided to track back a mile or so first, in order to skirt the patch of woodland that they had been camping next to.

It had seemed less dense on the other side, away from the river, as they had approached it thirty-six hours ago. And even a short walk up the riverside from the camp had shown them that the banks had been undercut in places by the fast, rain-filled waters. No one fancied risking a slip into the river in the buggy. Safer all round to backtrack and then move forward around the other side of the wood – they could work their way back to the river after that.

As Poole turned the buggy to round the edge of the woodland, Dervla vaguely recognised the open land that they had traversed a couple of days previously. Beyond, back in the direction of the explorer pod and the main camp, some more isolated patches of woodland dotted the valley, before the land rose to a high plain and then dropped again.

Home was that way, across, up and down – three days' driving from here.

And their way forward lay up the other side of the woodland, across an open expanse of dirt ridges and mounds, low bushes, and patches of grass.

They all saw immediately that the landscape looked different. Poole stopped the buggy without having to be told, and Dervla jumped down off the back.

The colours were startling. Pricks and flashes of yellow, red, deep pink, burnt orange, violet and indigo scattered like stars across the ground beyond them.

They had all become used to the grey, brown and green of the river valley – some golden grassland now and again, the blue-grey of the river, and the brighter blue of the sky. They had lived with that palette for a couple of months now. It had faded into the background of their daily experience, even though those greys, browns, greens and blues had come as a vivid shock when they had first stepped off the crashed lander.

Dervla remembered how disorientating that had been. But these colours were something else again. She'd have had a heart attack if this was the scene that awaited their first steps on the twin planet.

"That wasn't there – here – before."

"Well spotted, Sherlock."

"I'm just saying."

"You don't need to say, we can all see it."

"Are they – flowers?"

They were. Dervla walked up to the nearest patch and knelt down for a better look. Tiny bursts of colour popped along the ground in a huge swathe that stretched for hundreds of yards.

Some flowers were larger than others, but the tallest only stood around a hand's height above the ground. They appeared in random swatches – vibrant petals here, piercing coloured heads there, and others with half-opened pods that revealed more colour within. And that was only the flowers that had opened and gained some height. When Dervla peered closer to the ground, she could see an infill carpet of seedlings, with tiny stems and leaves, and closed heads.

Yard after yard after yard, as far as the eye could see, across ground that had been dry, bare and largely brown just days before.

"Prairie flowers."

The words came to Dervla. Something she'd read or seen? She couldn't remember, but it seemed right. "Maybe they came up after the rain?"

"The rain did this?"

"Well, they weren't here before. We've never seen anything like this. And it did rain. So maybe."

"How could they grow so quickly?"

"I don't know."

"Why here? And so many?"

"I don't know."

"Why – "

"Look, Bry, I don't know. Does it matter? They're

beautiful." She smoothed her hand gently across the nearest clutch of flowering heads. The petals flickered against her palm.

"This planet is doing my head in." Bryce jumped back into the passenger seat and sat staring out across the sea of colour.

"It's probably seasonal," said Dervla. "The rain comes, then the flowers appear."

"And then the birds," said Poole. "Look."

About a hundred yards away, a dense flock of small, grey birds wheeled out of the sky and descended on a patch of the flowering carpet. They pecked and then flew off, circled around, and then came back to peck again.

"There's something else," said Dervla.

She pushed her fingers into the ground, between the flowers and into the mat of seedlings. "They're not actually growing out of the ground itself."

She grubbed around a little more and lifted up a section of the mat between thumb and forefinger. It came away from the ground with a slight squelch, its flowers and seedlings tilting and entangling as she raised the section of mat further.

"What's that?"

"Don't know. Feels spongy. But it comes away fairly easily and it's all made up of one huge piece, I reckon. All the stuff you can see growing, it's coming out from the mat."

"How is that even possible? Where was the mat before? It wasn't here, was it? We'd have noticed."

Dervla just shrugged. She'd had enough of saying she didn't know.

"Erm, guys?" said Poole, in a soft voice. He was pointing along the edge of trees closest to them, about thirty yards away.

"What?"

"Shush!" Poole waved at Dervla, gesturing at her to move behind the buggy with him. "Bryce, stay still."

Out of the trees padded three large creatures with light-brown, jungle-stripe markings, big feet, pricked ears, and deep, dark eyes. Like a cat had been attached to an air hose and given a quick pump. A fourth followed behind, so well camouflaged in the trees that it suddenly just seemed to emerge in the open.

Apart from the soaring, vulture-like birds that they sometimes spotted high above the river, these were the largest animals any of them had yet seen.

"Don't move," said Poole. "I don't think they've clocked us."

The lead cat turned and looked directly at them, and then the other three did the same, all the while loping slowly towards a densely flowered section of the ground.

"You were saying?"

Poole reached carefully into the back of the buggy, feeling for his pack. There really wasn't anything to hand that he could use as a weapon. Maybe the poles for the canvas canopy? Where were they?

After holding their gaze for a few seconds, the cats turned their heads back and continued on, right into the flowers. Now, maybe fifty yards away, they separated and dropped their heads, then swept at the ground with their paws, clearing away flowers and seedlings. They pawed at the ground – at the mat – and brought up broken chunks of it, and then lay in a rough circle to eat and chew. They never gave the three of them or the buggy another look.

"What do you think?" Bryson had turned slowly from his seat to look down at the other two, who were crouching at the back of the buggy.

"Let's wait it out," said Poole, quietly. "They don't seem interested in us, but no point disturbing them, just in case."

"Easy for you to say. I'm the one sitting up here in full view."

"Well, you can run a lot faster than me, so I'd say that makes it even."

"Quiet, you two. Don't you think this is amazing?"

"Again, easy for you to say."

"Don't worry about it, Bryce. If they do come over this way, we don't need to be able to out-run them."

"We don't?"

"No. We just need to out-run Poole, and he hasn't been able to catch me since he was ten."

They watched in silence as the cats ate more chunks of the mat. After about twenty minutes, each of the animals stretched and then raised themselves from the ground. And then they padded back in a line towards the trees and vanished in the cover. Gone, just like that. Dervla could hear their first few paces as they passed over the undergrowth at the edge of the grove, and then it was silent.

"You can eat that stuff?"

"Space cats can eat that stuff. Karlan might give it a go, I suppose, you know what he's like."

"Let's cut a bit out, take it back for Reeves to analyse. It's obviously got nutritional value."

"Unless that was them having the equivalent of a doughnut."

"Doughnuts! Why did you have to say that? I'd kill for a doughnut."

"I'd kill you for a doughnut."

"You'd have to catch me first. Oh wait, that's right, you can't, Slow Boy."

Dervla left them to it, chasing each other around the buggy, and went to retrieve a slice of the flower-mat.

Boys. Can't live with them, can't feed them to the space animals.

———

Karlan came back to his seedbeds one more time, later that afternoon. More to double-check things than for any other reason. Second or third time of planting, and no real room for further error, now that he'd used all the remaining seeds.

The perimeter fence was sound, not that he'd expected anything else. He hadn't seen a chicken at the site since the first time he'd planted out the seeds – not that he'd seen one then either, but they had certainly got in and scratched up his raised rows.

The netting was securely in place, too. He tested a couple of the knots, just for reassurance, and pulled a section tighter. The netting canopy stood a good eighteen inches off the ground – plenty of space for the seedlings to grow, and high enough to thwart the most determined of birds.

He worked his way around the netting one last time, making sure there were no gaps or dips.

All good.

As he straightened up, and his shadow moved off the netting, he could see one of the seedling rows underneath, highlighted in a splash of sunlight.

No. No way.

Karlan untied one corner of the netting and folded it back on itself, exposing the row. The soil was pock-marked and disturbed, the seeds once more scattered across the surface. It was a different row than before, but the same outcome – the seeds haphazardly on top of the earth and not underneath.

Whatever it was, wasn't even eating them. Just digging them up. And he didn't see how it could be birds.

He marched around the pod to his sleeping shelter and started rolling up his bedding.

"What'ya doing?"

"Finding out whatever it is that's ruining my garden."

"I thought it was the birds?"

"Well, it's not. Or the chickens, I don't think so anyway."

"What then?"

"Can I have the flare gun?"

"No, you certainly cannot have the flare gun," said Jordan. "Or the taser, before you ask."

"Reeves!"

"Don't ask him, he's not in charge of weaponry, I am."

"Terrifying, but true," said Reeves. "I can only give the codes to someone over eighteen. Although I'll be handing them over to the first talking gorillas that turn up. Then we'll see what happens."

"I just want to find out what it is that's digging up my seeds and scare it off."

"Sing to it, maybe?" said Dana, sweetly. "Play it one of your lovely tunes."

"Right, well you are all no help whatsoever, thank you very much."

Eventually, Dana took pity on him. "Come on, Karl. I'll help you. What's the plan?"

21

Chat

TILLIE WAS SHIFTING ten-foot rebars across the store compound when Juno and the Major approached.

She had a perfectly serviceable little transporter pump-truck, flown down from the ship on the last supply run, but Tillie was a traditionalist. Up on the shoulders, across the yard, and flicked into a pile, ready for collection by the construction crew.

Besides, she liked the exercise – deep breaths in proper, planetary air, a film of sweat on her rippling biceps. A girl had to keep in shape.

"Got a job for you, Tillie," said Juno.

"I've already got a job, Cap." She flicked her head at the steel rods.

"How would you like to get back up to the *Odyssey Earth* early, and see Dave?"

"I'm listening."

Tillie would like that very much. Tillie missed Dave.

And Tillie wasn't due to see him otherwise for at least another week.

"We need you to make a delivery." And then Juno told her all about Sprake and his daughters.

Tillie's lips pursed. If there was one thing she liked less than people arsing around with her supplies and equipment – and she *really* didn't like that – it was people being mean to children.

On occasion, during the voyage, she had had cause to have a quiet word in the ear of crew members who had talked brusquely or unkindly to the ship kids. Manisha, in particular, she had looked out for, but she was fond of all of them.

And if Tillie had a quiet word in someone's ear, they tended to modify their behaviour quickly, given that the recognised escalation from 'Word in the ear' was to 'Hand round the throat.'

Tillie's hands, for the sake of clarity, were not things anyone wanted around their throat. They had a restrictive, muscular, smothering quality, ideal for grasping large items from the compound stores, but not so well suited for maintaining oxygen flow.

The ship kids were no longer with them, and this also preyed very heavily on Tillie. Which, in turn, meant that Sprake was extremely unlikely to receive any benefit of the doubt, as far as she was concerned.

"Would you like me to have a little chat with him first?"

Juno thought not. 'A little chat' was a further step up from 'Hand round the throat.' Tillie was a former marine. Back on Earth, there were military cemeteries and unmarked graves across several continents full of people that Tillie had had a little chat with.

"Just deliver him to the *Odyssey Earth* for me, in one piece. You can stare at him a lot on the way if you like. The Major here will come with you."

Tillie's lips pursed again. "I don't need a babysitter, Cap. Sprake doesn't sound like he's going to be any trouble."

"Donald Sprake is used to getting his own way," said Juno. "He's a billionaire."

"Not here, he isn't," said Tillie, which seemed to Juno like the most perspicacious take she'd heard yet on the situation.

"Even so, I don't trust him, and I don't know what he's up to. I'm going to get them all together and see if we can figure it out. Until then, I want eyes on him at all times. And anyway, I thought you might like a little holiday? The Major can spot you for a while, and he could do with getting to know his way around the *Odyssey Earth* in any case."

The possibility of seeing Dave was the clincher, as Juno knew it would be. Tillie arranged cover for her work at the compound, and the three of them left together for the launch strip.

———

Susannah had tried to break Bel and Jet in gently, and given them the full VIP tour, but it had been difficult.

It was conceptual, more than anything else. The two girls had never expected to go to space, and they barely understood that they were on a spaceship. The Med-Bay, the lounges, the rooms, the corridors – after almost twenty years of service, none of it much smacked of state-of-the-art spacefaring. More like a three-star hotel with disappointing showers and indefinable stains on the carpets.

The scale was either too normal to be convincing or too vast to be comprehended – the Obs deck had simply cowed them into silence – and in the end Susannah had taken them to Launch, which at least looked like a proper bit of spaceship, with its metal decking, gantries and airlocks.

She walked them across to one of the landers, sitting on its service apron.

"That's like the shuttle you'll have seen, back in Scotland. We're using them to go up and down to the surface of the planet. They launch from here – kind of like a spaceship within a spaceship."

The girls stood there, the lander towering over them, and watched as maintenance crew scurried up and down the ramp.

Susannah still wondered if they got it, but she had done her best. Next and last stop was Flight, and if that didn't convince them, she didn't know what would, given that it was the most Star-Trekky bit of the ship.

Probably best to mute Reeves, though, until they'd had more time to acclimatise. He was polite enough, but if the girls were already freaked out by the very idea of space, being accosted by a disembodied know-it-all might just tip them over the edge.

Up on Flight, Bel and Jet walked tentatively through the automatic doors, Susannah just ahead of them. She took her place in Cap's chair and watched them wander slowly around. The kids used to take all this for granted, she realised. Dervla had been at home here on Flight as much as Susannah herself. When they were little, they'd all played hide and seek under the consoles and behind the stacks.

For these two, though – it had to be devastating. Yesterday – or what they thought of as yesterday – they had been in Scotland. A week before that, in London. At home, at college, going out with friends, walking the dog.

Jet went straight to the main screen.

"That's New Earth?" She pointed at the image of the planet, hanging there. Blue, green, white and brown.

"That's right."

"Looks like the old Earth."

"I suppose that's the point," said Susannah. "It had to be enough like it for us to be able to live here. Atmosphere, gravity, water, air, soil, minerals – they are all near-as-dammit the same."

"And where's our Earth?" Jet scanned the wider image and the adjacent schematic of the local system.

"Oh, honey. You can't see it. You'll never be able to see it. Trillions of miles away now. We're in a different bit of the galaxy altogether."

Bel came up behind them for a look.

"But you flew here, all the way?"

"We've got a hyperspeed drive – "

"Dad said. I didn't understand it."

"No one does, honey. Apart from half a dozen people down in the engine room. But it works just fine."

"The ship got us here, while we were asleep. And the engine-thingy works. So, you could just take us back?"

"They can't, Bel." Jet put a hand on her sister's shoulder.

"They can!"

"I'm so sorry, Bel. Your sister's right. This was only ever a one-way mission. It took us over seventeen years to get here. I know you were asleep all that time. It won't seem like that to you. But I'm forty-nine now, others are even older. We all knew that we were never going to go back."

Bel crumpled into a chair. "I don't understand. Who would choose to do this?"

"Lots of people," said Susannah. "All of us. Plus everyone in hypersleep. There are another thousand people down there, you know? It's not just you two. We all have our reasons. But we all wanted to come. No one forced us. We knew what it meant."

"I didn't want to come. Neither of us did. We're not supposed to be here."

"I know. I can't imagine what that's like. I'm truly sorry."

The two girls looked again at the images on the screen.

"What's it like down there?"

"Well, you know. Like a planet. Nice, they say. Actually, I haven't been down yet."

"How come?"

"Someone has to keep things going up here." Although that wasn't strictly true. Reeves could do it. And even if someone did need to be here, it didn't have to be her. Susannah knew she was choosing to stay on the *Odyssey Earth* for now – and, with the girls here, she felt even less inclined to leave.

"What are we going to do?"

Susannah didn't have an answer for them. The ship-kids had been born to this, and had waited their whole lives to reach New Earth. Dervla would have been piloting the landers, Poole too, probably. Dana would have been on the surface, running logistics. Karlan dividing his time between the Garden and the planet. Bryce working with a construction gang. Manisha, maybe helping out with the hypersleep revival team. They would have all had a place and a purpose. If they had survived.

But Susannah knew that the girls' question wasn't as literal as that. It was a broadside of despair. A deep, dark dive into the reality of their situation. They had been betrayed. It was a howl of a question.

What were they going to do?

And although there was no answer to that, she did her best.

"I don't know. But, look, your dad's coming back up. You can talk to him about it."

Jet looked shocked. "He's here?"

"Not yet, but he will be. He's on his way. He knows you're awake. From hypersleep, I mean."

"We don't want to see him."

"I get that, I do. But he's the only one who knows what happened here. I think you should talk to him."

"He's a selfish, selfish − " Jet left the sentence unfinished.

"I never want to see him again," said Bel.

"I'm sure he wants to see you."

"Then you don't know him very well. This was never about us. It's all about Mum. He's never forgiven her for leaving."

That shocked Susannah. "Surely not? That would be − "

"Selfish. Entitled. Narcissistic. Childish. Take your pick."

"Even so. I can't believe anyone would do that − to their own daughters?"

"Yeah, well. Welcome to our world. Why do you think Mum left him?"

Jet moved for the door. "Come on Bel. We're not waiting around. We don't care what he says," she said to Susannah, as the doors swished open. "Don't you dare bring him to see us."

22

Vigil

KARLAN'S PLAN WAS SIMPLE. Set up a bed near his seeds, keep as still as possible, stay awake all night, and all the next day if needs be, find out what it was that was ruining his garden.

And then shoo it away, which was missing one, final 't' from what he really wanted to do to it.

Dana and Manisha didn't need much persuading to join him, this being the most exciting thing that had happened at Camp Castaway since the others had left on their explorer trip.

"Please, leave, off you go. I don't want anyone to worry about me, I'll be absolutely fine," said Reeves, when they shared their plans.

"We're literally going around the back of the pod. It's about twenty yards that way. You don't really mind, do you?"

"I suppose I'll manage. Are you taking Jordan with you?"

They could see him across the camp, preparing the night's meal.

"No, he thought he'd stay and keep you company."

There was a deep sigh from Reeves and a muttered, "That it should come to this," before he flicked off his sensor lights and pretended to be asleep.

After dinner that night, the three of them carried their sleeping bags around the back of the pod and set up quietly a few yards from the seedbeds. The bulk of the pod screened them from the camp's fire and sleeping shelters, and it was as unsettlingly dark here as it had been on those first few nights on the planet.

"Does anyone else think that sitting in the pitch-black, waiting for a predator, is entirely sensible?"

"It's not exactly a predator. It eats seeds. It doesn't even eat them, just digs them up. How big or fierce can it be?"

"The rollies aren't that big. But if an army of them comes trundling out of the gloom, I'd rather not be lying here, in the way."

"It's not rollies. Anyway, you don't have to stay if you don't want."

"I didn't say that. Neesh and I have never had a sleepover before, this is fun. We're supposed to have marshmallows. In the films, there are always marshmallows. Have you got marshmallows for us, Karl?"

"Course not. Where would I get marshmallows?"

"I thought you might have grown some. What with your green fingers."

"You know what marshmallows are, right? You can't think that – oh, right, you're teasing me."

"Always Karl, it's our job. So, how are we going to do this?"

Take it in turns, thought Karlan. Shifts. Two asleep on the floor, the watcher sitting in the lander seat he'd brought back from the last salvage run.

Dana and Manisha settled down in their bags, and he leant back, with a vantage-point across the seedbeds. It was dark, but he could make out the line of the perimeter fencing and the shadow of the netting cover. Now and then, he played the light from his torch across the top, and then switched it off and sat there in silence.

This close, this quiet – if anything came, anything at all, they would hear it and see it.

He switched with Dana after a couple of hours.

"Anything?"

"No. Not a thing."

Karlan lay on the ground, watching Dana take her turn. He could make out her dark shadow, against the seat, and saw the torch light range across the top of the netting. He woke sometime later as Dana and Manisha swapped places, and then slept again.

A shake of his shoulder woke him. Still dark, though the slightest of early morning light in the sky above the camp.

"You can do the last shift. They're your seeds."

"Anything at all?"

"Nope. Nothing. Neesh and I are going back to our

proper beds. There isn't anything out there. Not tonight anyway."

"I'm going to stay until it's properly light."

"Then what?"

"Don't know. Stay here all day, probably. I lost seeds during the day as well. I want to know what it is."

"Bring you breakfast later?"

"Thanks."

Karlan kept watch until the sun was up.

Nothing.

He ate the breakfast that Dana had brought him, and got up to stretch his legs. Daytime now. A full twelve-hour vigil with nothing to show for it. Except that the seeds were safe, for another day at least. That was something.

Maybe their presence had been enough? Whatever it was, maybe it could sense them? In which case, he might have to spend a few more days and nights here. Perhaps lurking further back from the seedbeds, to encourage it in? He'd like to know what he was dealing with.

Karlan poured water into a bowl. Good a time as any to water the seeds, before the sun got too high. Might even be some shoots appearing in a week or two, if he could keep his guard up, though he didn't fancy his chances of persuading Dana and Manisha to keep on sleeping out here overnight.

He put the bowl down and untied the netting on one side of the perimeter. He walked around and did the same on the other side, before folding the whole thing back on itself, and then he carefully pulled the netting off the entire bed and laid it on the ground.

That's where Dana found him, twenty minutes later.

Sitting in the dust, with smeared tearstains on his cheeks, and every single seed disinterred and scattered haphazardly across the disturbed soil.

———

By midday, they had made another fifteen miles in the buggy. It was slow going and Dervla was frustrated. If this was the last day of exploration before turning around, she wanted to get as far as she could, as fast as she could.

But first they had had to pick their way around the vast, matted, flowering carpet – it didn't seem right just to drive right over it – and then they had skirted the other side of the large wood.

It took an hour just to reach a point that they calculated was opposite where they had camped during the rains, now about a perpendicular mile away through the trees.

"Those things, cats? Must have been in there when we were?" said Bryson, still the most concerned among them about the animal encounter.

"I think there are probably lots of things on this planet that we haven't noticed yet," said Dervla.

She had been thinking about this, and thinking about their life on the *Odyssey Earth*. There was the

Garden, of course, that supplied fresh food, and they'd had access to videos, films and books. She knew what nature was, they all did. It wasn't like they'd never seen *Life on Earth* or *The Blue Planet* – they had watched them with Sam, when they were younger.

But while Dervla understood that those were filmed documentaries about actual, natural life on a real, living Earth, it wasn't her Earth, her planet. Never had been.

Until now, her Earth had been a metal box in a hyperspeed bubble in the vacuum of interstellar space. There was nothing natural or blue about it. It was a controlled, hermetically sealed environment – full of corners and edges, predictably safe, where nature, such as it was, had been tamed. Banana plants in this corner, spinach beds here, mushrooms on stacked trays over there.

Life on Earth – the elephants and ants, the whales and plankton – was exciting to watch but it might as well have been a SciFi series, as far as they were concerned.

When it came down to it, Dervla realised, she didn't know what she was looking *at* or *for*. None of them really did.

It was like being in one of Poole's old immersive simulator games – it seemed real, bright and intense, but even as she walked around on this new planet of hers, it was as if she couldn't make the jump in her mind from screen to life.

The planet was a series of overwhelming scenes

and backdrops, with colours, smells and textures that she'd never encountered before. It was hard to look beyond the rushing water, the waving grasses and the standing trees, and understand that there was also an entire eco-system at work, underpinning everything. A natural world – microbes, spores, insects, animals – that you couldn't always see. Or might never see. Or even understand if you did see.

The cats had been there in the woods, all along. Decidedly there, but unseen. Meanwhile, the buggy wheels were probably crushing unknown insects and plants as they rolled on past. Dervla thought about that while they journeyed on, gradually leaving the wood behind.

There were more patches of trees to negotiate in the second hour, though none as large as the one they had sheltered in. There were also other blazes of colour – more flower-mats, they assumed, that appeared as distant, sprawling patches. The rain – if it had been the rain – had woken up the landscape in more than one place.

They circled around, descended slightly and regained the river, which was running less violently now that the water level had subsided. The ground was open again, but rockier than before, so that Poole had to slow down even more as the buggy hit trickier, stonier terrain.

At a meal stop, somewhere in the middle of the day, Dervla wandered to the river's edge and looked intently into the quieter eddies and pools close to the bank. The odd, dark shape flitted by – the ever-present fish. What else was in there?

They'd seen much larger, dolphin-like creatures in the river on their initial journey from the crashed lander, though they had not been sighted again on this trip. Now she'd seen camouflage in action, Dervla wondered if there was anything else hiding in plain sight here on the planet. Or not even hiding – just living in a way she wouldn't recognise.

They pressed on. Three, four more hours and they would need to stop one final time, leaving enough of the day to put some solar charge into the batteries. Make one more overnight camp. And then, tomorrow, turn for home. Retrace their steps on the four-day journey – and hope there wasn't any more rain to delay them.

The valley flattened out ahead of them and the river widened, gradually at first. But soon they were being pushed further and further to one side. The water seemed shallower but faster, rippling over stones and rocks, and swirling around tree branches and trunks that had been washed downriver and caught against the banks.

Dervla and Bryson jumped down and walked alongside the buggy, which by now was kicking up stones as Poole coaxed it up and down over the rocky ground.

The river was a hundred yards wide or more at this point, rushing furiously on. On the far side, it was flanked by a rising belt of hills. On their side, there was less and less delineation between the river's edge and the rocky ground – narrow inlets and pools pushed into the terrain, and the buggy's tyres were wet.

"Over there."

Poole pointed to a higher plateau – level, green, and away from the river and the rocks. He turned the buggy and gunned it, making the rise in a minute or so, with Dervla and Bryson scrambling behind him, tripping across stones as they went.

He stopped and powered down, and waited for them to reach him on foot, as they clambered up the last few steps.

Dervla looked out and downwards.

That was it then.

Journey's end, just like that.

23

Idiot

THE LANDER SHUTTLE was being prepped for departure, and Sprake was on board, seated firmly next to the Major. He had protested all the way, even while being buckled in – none too gently – by Tillie, who took up a seat directly opposite.

Juno returned to the ops room. "You really think that's it?" she said, over the comms vid-link.

"I do," said Susannah. "They can't remember, or they don't want to remember. Or they're not sure what it is they remember. They're still quite confused about it all. But I think he drugged them."

"Who would do that? *Why* would you do that?"

"Sounds like a bit of a prick, to be honest. Didn't get on with his ex. The girls lived with her, he hardly ever saw them."

"And they went up to Scotland to see him, to see a crew transfer?"

"That's the story. I think he cooked up a reason to

get them there, and then drugged them to get them on board."

"How would there be time to do that, if they were only there to watch the launch? There's a whole process. You can't just give someone some dodgy champagne and stick them in hypersleep. There's all the nano-prep, for a start. It takes hours, days, before you get transferred to the shuttle and then to the cryo chamber on the ship."

"I know. I said he's a prick, but it doesn't mean he's not a clever prick. The girls don't really know anything, but I think that's what he counted on. They didn't know what they were seeing. Just a shuttle on the launchpad to them, viewed from on high from the observation tower. From their descriptions, I doubt it was ready to go at all. He just showed them around, told them they were going to see a launch, drugged them, and then had someone slot all three of them into the hypersleep schedule."

"How? Why?"

"Who knows. But the man owned the whole thing. I'm sure he could do anything he wanted, no questions asked."

Juno thought back to the time Sprake had interviewed her, twenty years previously. Not Sprake at all, it turned out. Seemed he probably could do anything he wanted.

That was back on Earth, though. Not here. Not on her watch.

"Just saying, 'Men!' doesn't really seem sufficient, does it?" she said.

"Not really. This is sick stuff. What do you want me to do with him, when he gets here? The girls don't want to see him."

"I'm not surprised. But I have to play this by the book. He hasn't really admitted to anything yet. And even if he does, I'm not sure what I can do about it. Like you said, he owns the whole thing. I'm still thinking about the ramifications of that."

"He must have broken dozens of laws. The girls aren't even eighteen. Kidnapping. Forcible imprisonment. Illegal transport of minors. Being a total and utter – "

"Billionaire?"

"Something beginning with 'B,' that's for sure. Let's work it out when he gets here. I know they don't want to, but he should see the girls, I suppose?"

"I think it's the only way we're going to find out what went on. I'm sending Tillie and the Major up, too. Between you and them, and being respectful of the girls' situation, we might get some answers."

"Stick him in a room alone with Tillie for a while?"

"She's already suggested that. I don't think we'll need to. Men like him, they love the sound of their own voice. I think he'll tell us, eventually. And then we can figure out what to do."

"Roger that."

"OK, they'll be with you in a few hours. Anything else, before I go?"

There was something. It had been at the bottom of Susannah's checklist for a day or so, and she hadn't yet got around to sharing it with Juno.

"This came up," said Susannah, "on the last housekeeping sweep. Thought it was worth mentioning."

Once a week, Susannah ran an intra-system comms check. Ship to ground and vice versa, plus connections to the few relay stations and satellites they had established and launched since arrival.

"Go on then, I've got a few minutes," said Juno.

Susannah brought up a schematic, showing New Earth and its satellite moon, and then the array of a dozen other planets orbiting Sol – the local solar system's sun. *Odyssey Earth* was indicated by a white icon, in a matching orbit with New Earth.

"Unless you've found another planet … " said Juno. "What am I looking at?"

"Wait a second." Susannah zoomed in slightly. "We've got New Earth and then, over here, the twin planet, right?"

"OK."

Of the dozen planets in the system, New Earth had turned out not to be the only habitable one – habitable to humans, at least. There was a second, in the same Goldilocks zone, not too warm, not too cold, amenable to human life. New Earth's apparent twin.

Susannah switched screen views. "Here's where we dropped the pod, on the way past." The magnified image – grabbed from a sat-scope launched from the *Odyssey Earth* – showed a green-brown landmass, with a dark area denoting high ground, mountains, and the slightest suggestion of a blue line, a river. Viewed from three million miles away, there was no more detail than that.

She pin-pointed the pod location, indicated by a triangular transmitter icon.

"Still there then," said Juno. "One day. Just need to, you know, build a town here first, establish civilisation, save humanity, that sort of thing. The pod's not going anywhere."

"It's not that." Susannah overlaid a signal report, showing the connections between the *Odyssey Earth* and the settlement on the ground. "All normal, right?"

"I know, I'm sure you'd have told us otherwise. And we'd have noticed."

"OK. And this is the explorer pod on the twin."

She brought up another chart, which showed a regular pulse from the pod's embedded beacon – blip, blip, blip, slow, steady and unchanging.

"Again, all normal."

"So, what's up? You're just showing me things I already know. The suspense is killing me."

"I'm not sure. But that last chart, from the pod – that's the beacon signal working normally, as usual. But, look, this is since yesterday, when I last checked."

Susannah overlaid one more chart, with a slightly different sound profile – bleep, bleep, bleep, followed by a jumbled string of other pulses.

"That's – different. The signal's changed?"

"Maybe. I can't see how. It's probably just a

reporting error, but I thought it was worth pointing out."

"Reeves? What do you reckon? Scrambled signal?"

"I am looking at the data now. There's no signal corruption. The beacon is functioning correctly. Oh – "

"Reeves?"

There was a short silence.

"It's not a signal," he said. "Or, rather, it is. But it's not the auto-beacon signal. It's a message."

"What *are* you talking about?"

"I'm sorry. I'm not being clear. I am – somewhat overcome."

"What is it, Reeves?"

"Dash, dash, dash. It's Morse code. It's a repeating message in Morse code."

"Don't be ridiculous. Of course it isn't. It'll just be an error. Check again, would you?"

"It's quite clear, Juno. Dash, dash, dash, space, dash, dash, dash, space … Here, look." Reeves flashed up a long string of dashes and dots.

It was a long time since Juno had had to decode a Morse message and she concentrated hard, thinking back to her training days. The first few letters seemed to make no sense, and she started again, but Reeves took pity on them both and turned the on-screen dots and dashes into their individual letters.

No one spoke for several, long beats.

"Reeves, is that real?"

"Yes, Juno."

"Because you wouldn't do something like that as a

joke? I know you get the tone wrong sometimes, but this would be very ill-judged. It's not a joke, is it?"

"No, Juno."

"I can't believe it."

"It is somewhat surprising."

"No mistake?"

"None."

Down in the ops room on New Earth, Juno stared at the screen, stood open-mouthed and shook her head in disbelief. "Clever, clever bunnies."

And on the flight deck on the *Odyssey Earth*, Susannah sobbed as she read out the message in front of her.

o-o-p-s / w-r-o-n-g / p-l-a-n-e-t /

p-o-o-l-e / i-s / a-n / i-d-i-o-t /

24

Finger

PERSPECTIVE WAS A FUNNY THING.

On the ship, Dervla had routinely looked out of the window on the Observation deck and across billions of miles of space. She had never thought anything of it, having grown up with it.

Here, on the planet, her view had shrunk to the few miles she could see ahead of her at any one time – or even the few yards around the camp, from pod to tree-line or river. She'd got used to that, too.

And now, here on the edge, standing next to Poole and Bryson, the limits of her perception had shifted again.

Dervla stood in silence. She had never seen anything like it.

Pushed ever wider by the tumbling river, they had made their way to a small plateau. From this slightly elevated position, they looked along a long, curving ridge to their right. Behind them ran the river they had been following, on and off, for several days. If they turned their heads, they could see it snaking along the valley, widening and quickening as it approached the ridge.

And then the river simply tumbled over the edge, turning into an impossibly wide wall of white water.

Down it thundered, dropping a hundred feet or more, throwing up a mist that obscured whatever lay directly below. Even here, where they stood, above and away from the falls, there was a fine spray in the air and a low growl as the distant waters churned.

On the far side, the falls ended where the ridge suddenly climbed to a towering line of rocky peaks. And when Dervla finally tore her eyes away from the frothy white sheet of water and looked straight out, off the edge, she could see that this wasn't the end at all. Instead, just a new beginning, as the sheer cliff they were on stepped steeply down to another valley far below.

From somewhere underneath the mist, a ribbon of blue emerged – the river – and ran out for miles through an indistinct landscape to reach the widest of edges, with only blue beyond.

A coastline. The sea. A horizon. A thrillingly different view for a girl born in the stars.

Poole and Bryson were grinning at each other.

"Now that's a proper waterfall, Derv!"

"At this point, I am prepared to admit that I was wrong. Waterfalls seem OK."

"Is that the sea? Over there? There's an actual sea?"

"Glad we kept going, Derv?"

"So glad. The others won't believe it. I can hardly believe it."

Dervla gazed out. Here, finally, was an experience. Something worth seeing. Something worth the calloused hands and dirty fingernails, Poole's bad jokes, and Bryson's farts.

They were on an apron of land around thirty feet wide, with a shallow slope behind them, back towards the upper river valley – their valley, the one they had travelled through. In front of them, the ground simply dropped away, in a few shallow rock ledges at first, before becoming more precipitous.

"We can spend the night here. Pretty cool. Just move the buggy back, there's plenty of room." Poole rolled the wheels back a few feet, putting plenty of space between them and the edge, and started taking gear out of the back. "Bry, a hand?"

Dervla stayed where she was, looking out towards the distant ocean and then back across the white, tumbling water. She moved closer to the edge, gingerly at first, until she discovered that the edge of the cliff wasn't really an edge at all – she could step down from one wide shelf to another as the rock pushed further out in a series of naturally formed, descending scallops.

"Derv?"

She could hear Poole somewhere above her and realised she was out of sight.

"Here!"

A face popped out above her. "What are you doing?"

"Just looking."

"Not sure about that, Derv. Is it safe?"

"It's wide enough. And the ledges are shallow. See. Easy." She stepped down to another rock shelf, but kept well back, close to the face of the cliff. Maybe a twenty-foot flat expanse in front of her – no danger of being too close to the edge.

"Hang on." Bryson joined her, then Poole. From this vantage point, they were now below the upper ridge, and level with the falling curtain of water, which was now a hundred feet away to their right. They could see that it poured over a protruding edge and then fell away, disappearing below their line of sight.

The scalloped shelves stepped away to the right, closer to the wall of water.

"Come on." Dervla moved down another level.

"I'm really not sure about this, Derv," said Bryson. He had to raise his voice above the sound of the falls.

"And I'm not coming all this way and not getting as close as I can. We'll stop as soon as it looks dangerous."

"Is this not dangerous enough for you, already?"

"You stay at the top if you want. But this is all solid rock, no overhang. I'm not going to go anywhere near the edge. I'm just going to drop down the steps for as long as it's like this." And she moved down another level, taking her another ten feet closer to the falls.

"I'm going to regret this, I can tell."

Dervla waited until Bryson and Poole were on the same level, and then they all stepped down once more – to a point about thirty feet below the top of the falls and ever closer to the thundering waters.

When they turned to look out from here, the spray was dense enough to obscure their view, and it was difficult to see the distant valley and coastline – just an expanse of green and brown far below, with flashes of colour in the air as sunlight caught in the fine water.

"Look." Dana had to shout above the sound of the water. The other two followed her pointing finger.

The water was crashing down in a huge wall, only thirty feet or so away to their right now. Such was its force, cascading over the ridge above, it fell clear of the rock face behind them and then thundered on downwards to an unseen drop.

Stepping down on two more scalloped rock shelves took them behind the waterfall, where they stopped, backs pressed against the rock face. Now they couldn't see anything in front of them except a furious cascade of white and green, producing the most tumultuous noise.

When Bryson turned again to speak to Dervla, she had the widest, wildest grin, mouth open, eyes popping.

He put his face close to hers. "Just like you imagined?"

"Better. It's amazing. Sam was right. Waterfalls are awesome!"

Poole had inched further along and was beckoning them onwards, mouthing something that they couldn't hear. They shuffled along to meet him, now well behind the waterfall, and then followed him as he turned around an outcrop of rock.

A wide cave opened out behind them, reaching back into the cliff above head height and then tapering down towards the ground. Fifty feet back maybe. The same across. Grey-green stone. Dry underfoot. Shadows at the edges.

They moved into the cave interior and looked up, around and out.

"This is just wild."

All they could see when they looked out was a wall of water − an endless, relentless falling − with their way in now hidden behind a bulge in the rock. But they were standing back far enough for the noise from the falls to be deadened − a low rumble now, rather than a deafening crash.

"I've got an idea."

"No," said Poole.

"But we *could* sleep here, couldn't we? Come on, it's the last night. How cool is this?"

"What about the buggy? All the gear?"

"What about it? We just need a few clothes, some food, something to make a fire."

"I can't leave the buggy up there all night."

"What's going to happen to it? It survived a monsoon. I'm sure it can handle a night on its own. Come on! This is what Dana was talking about. This is why we came. Don't you want to sleep behind a waterfall in a cave on an alien planet?"

"When you put it like that."

"There you go! I love you like a very annoying brother, Poole."

"There's no need for that sort of talk."

"Sorry, is this better?"

"Ow!"

Poole rubbed his arm and looked at Bryson. "What do you think?"

"Yeah, baby!"

"Come on then, let's get the gear."

An hour later, they were lying around a flickering fire, about twenty feet back into the cave, closest to the side they had entered from. Poole had tapped the buggy three times for luck as they'd left it. "Kiss it goodnight, if you like," Dervla had said. He'd looked up into the darkening sky – the weather was fine. It would be all right, he hoped.

In the cave, it was already dark, but it wasn't oppressive. Dervla liked the sound of the water, just out of reach, falling past the open cliff face.

"No one has ever done this before," she said. "Not on this planet, I mean. We're the first." She closed her eyes and smiled.

"You love this, don't you?"

"Sam was right. Dana was right. We've been waiting too long. Everyone on that ship had already had a life. They're all ancient anyway. What have we had? We never had the chance to do anything, go anywhere. But now we're here, this is what we get to do. Choose our own path for once."

"I'm not disagreeing with you. This is actually pretty awesome."

"If you think that's awesome, how about – this?"

"Bryson. That better not be you."

"If it's not me, there's something else in this cave. Which would be worse?"

"You are foul."

"And you are most welcome. Here, have another. I call this the Alien Enforcer."

"Ew, Bryyyyce, disgusting."

The shadows danced as the three of them jostled, laughing, around the fire.

———

Karlan had been silent since the night and morning spent guarding – fruitlessly – his seedbeds.

"Is he all right?" asked Jordan.

"Cross, more than anything. Can't figure it out. He swore he didn't fall asleep."

"He must have done."

"I know. That's why he's upset."

"Did you see anything?"

"Nothing to see. But it is odd."

Jordan consulted Reeves. "What do you think? Karlan's mystery seed assailant?"

"I can barely see beyond this door. Tell me what happened."

Jordan recounted what Dana had told him and added a few observations of his own. This had been going on for days now – he'd seen the effort Karlan had put in, and shared his frustration.

And Jordan didn't like to see any of them upset. It was all about keeping their spirits up. They could do without setbacks like this.

"No sightings? No traces, trails, tracks?"

"None. Just dug-up seeds. Every time."

"Interesting."

"And?"

"No idea."

"Can't you – I don't know – infer something? Extrapolate?"

"Interesting."

"What is?"

"Your conflation of two different concepts."

"Infer this."

"You realise that I can't see you? That that gesture is entirely pointless?"

Jordan furled his finger. "Can't you just bring your big old brain to bear upon this, for Karlan's sake, without being a pain in the neck?"

"Of course. I want to help, I do. Tell him to bring me some of the seeds and some soil. Let's see if the scanner can shed any light on all this."

25

Kylie

THE NEWS SPREAD QUICKLY.

Juno hadn't had time to consider what to tell anyone – or even whether to tell anyone – before the first rumours tumbled out of the ops room and across the settlement.

There was some cross-chatter with the team working on the lander departure, and Juno had a quick conversation with Tillie, who let out a massive whoop.

As word got out further, work stopped on the buildings going up in the new sector, and people started to drift across the site towards the canteen, looking for more information.

Someone grabbed at Juno's arm as she left the ops room. "Is it true?"

"I think so," she said. "We're still checking it out."

She hoped it was true. She'd never hoped for something more. But it felt impossible. She'd seen the wreckage from the meteoroid collision. There had been no trace of the craft or its occupants. They had all seen the aftermath and felt the devastating loss.

Yet the message seemed incontrovertible. And Reeves had double- and triple-checked the data.

By now, most people from the settlement had congregated in the canteen, filling the tables and spilling out into the main drag. There hadn't been this many people gathered in one place since the commemoration ceremony, just a few days before. There were restive calls for Juno – someone, anyone – to tell them what was going on.

She climbed up onto a bench and the crowd fell silent.

"As you've all heard by now, we think the kids are alive."

A huge clamour broke out and she shushed them with her hands.

"Look, there isn't a lot I can tell you right now. There's a signal from the other planet – the twin. They must be there. Or, at least, some of them must be. We just don't know who, and we don't know how."

There were more shouted questions from the crowd, and Juno did her best to answer them.

"It's recent, the last couple of days. So, whoever sent it is still alive, yes."

In answer to another question, Juno repeated the Morse message they had received and the crowd erupted. Laughing and crying at the same time. A huge release of pent-up emotion. Juno knew how they felt.

"If I had to guess," she said, "I'd say Dana wrote

the first bit and Manisha the second." She teared up as she said it and took a breath or two. "And it must mean that Poole is still alive, too. I'd guess they all are. But we can't really say with any certainty."

She let them chatter while she gathered her thoughts, and then quietened them down again.

"I know how you all feel. This is the best news we could have had. I still can't believe it myself. But they're alive, and they've managed to survive up until now, so I don't think they are in any immediate danger. The message suggests not. So, let's all get back to work, while Reeves and I figure out a plan. Back here tonight for an update, OK?"

Juno left for the ops room, and the crowd slowly melted away. Gerald watched from behind the counter, where he'd been surreptitiously gathering a few supplies for a run back to his isolated camp.

He'd heard the news along with everyone else, but his face betrayed little emotion. A flicker, maybe, when Juno had read out the message. Poole mostly *was* an idiot, it was true. Karlan, though – he had his head screwed on. Dana too. If the twin planet could support life, Gerald reckoned they would be all right, at least for a while.

He gathered a few final items, loaded them into his pack, and then took the longer way around back to his camp, via the landing site memorial.

From the top of his pack, he retrieved a small cardboard box, opened the lid and placed it at the foot of the flagpole. It had contained six breakfast muffins, baked that morning, and Gerald had squeezed in a seventh. For the teacher guy, Jordan. Why not? He'd never minded him. Had asked marginally less stupid questions than most people. Gerald left the box and set off for camp.

Later that day, people started to bring wildflowers, shaped stones, and other things to the flagpole. Someone weighted down an old drawing that one of the kids must have given them years before, kept as a memento for all this time. The edges curled up in the daytime heat.

And by the evening, the box of muffins was entirely covered by a mound of gifts and memories as the *Odyssey Earth* crew embraced a rare hope.

Susannah was down on Launch when the lander arrived from New Earth. She always enjoyed watching the precision manoeuvring and the final drop onto the pad – even though she knew that the auto-lock did most of the work. Still, it was a textbook arrival, good to see.

She waved an acknowledgement to the pilot. Launch crew scurried across with clips and cables, and the cargo-bay doors opened with a gush of compressed air.

Susannah was in no mood for Sprake, but here he came anyway, down the ramp, flanked by the Major and Tillie.

"Be nice," Juno had said. "No point antagonising him. Not yet, anyway."

Well, that would depend on Sprake, thought Susannah. Especially today. Her head was full of the news about the kids and she *really* did not have the patience to indulge billionaire kidnappers.

Not that he looked particularly chippy, as he approached. A bit cowed if anything. Though that could have been his proximity to his two very large minders – the Major being a touch-the-ceiling, beanpole type, while Tillie of course favoured width over height.

Susannah realised she hadn't seen the Major upright much until now. He'd been in hypersleep revival in the Med-Bay when she'd first encountered him, and then he'd been whisked down to New Earth as soon as he'd stopped feeling dizzy. Anyway, he appeared to be a fairly impressive specimen, and if she was a billionaire kidnapper she'd be thinking twice about being snitty, too.

"Tillie!" Susannah gave her a fist-bump. "Good to see you. You heard about the kids?"

"I know, it's brilliant."

"Does Dave know you're coming?"

"Thought I'd surprise him."

"Major, nice to see you again. Everything all right?"

"Tickety-boo."

"Excuse me," said Sprake.

"Ah yes, Mr Sprake." Susannah emphasized his title.

"My daughters, where are they? Bel and Jet?"

In their lounge, going through a wardrobe of clothes left behind by Manisha and the others, last time she'd checked. Eating nachos. Alternating between anger and grief. Refusing to even countenance the idea of seeing Sprake. But she wasn't about to share that information with him yet.

"All in good time. They've had a bit of a shock. Unexpected journey and all that." She looked at Sprake, but he didn't react. "Anyway, I think for now, we'll put you back in your old room, give everyone time to cool down a bit."

"You're what – detaining me? Locking me up?" Sprake did appear a bit feistier now.

"Nothing so dramatic. Let's just say that we'd prefer it if you stayed out of the way for now. There's a lot going on today."

"You can't lock me up. It's my ship."

Well, there you go, thought Susannah. Two minutes in and he was the one who had gone and done the antagonising. At least the Cap couldn't blame her.

"Tillie, Major? Would you like to show Mr Sprake that both of those things are untrue by locking him up on our ship? You would? Thank you so much."

Sprake looked mightily unhappy but consented to go with them, and Susannah headed back to Flight to update Juno.

Tillie saw Sprake safely ensconced in his room on Three-Deck, and left the Major to organise a guard detail outside.

Personally, she'd have just handcuffed Sprake to a heating pipe and left him to it, and she had an idea that the Major wouldn't have objected too much either. But rules, regs, human rights, all that stuff − even for Grade-A assholes like Sprake.

She made her way along to Cargo and squeezed past a parked high-loader vehicle. She could hear the clang of gear being moved further in, among the stacks, and followed the noise.

There he was, shifting crates from one level to another by hand, about fifty yards away. Cable-spools and cross-braces, she knew from the location and aisle number. They'd worked this hangar together long enough for her to know every inch of it.

And she knew Dave, too − knew him from the back, even from this distance, even half-hidden behind stacked crates. A thick neck that seemed to go straight up from square shoulders to cauliflower ears. Buzz-cut hair. Arms like tree-trunks, hands like hams, muscles rippling up and down like a fleet of ferrets on the loose under his leathery skin.

She knew he'd be singing to himself as well, with a little music-pod tucked in one ear. Crass, Anthrax, one of those searing anarcho-punk outfits he liked. Unless it was Kylie, always a possibility.

He really was just the perfect specimen of a man.

Tillie snuck around the end of the aisle, came up

behind him unseen and barked. "Singin' on duty, are you? You 'orrible little quartermaster."

Dave dropped a crate and turned, a huge beam on his face. They clasped arms around each other, like two supertankers coming together, and Dave touched Tillie's face.

"You're back? How come?"

She filled him in, and saw Dave's eyes narrow as he heard about Sprake.

Saying it out loud to another person made it sound even worse – that someone could do that, to their own flesh and blood. At seventeen, they weren't exactly children, but even so. It wasn't right, and she knew that Dave felt exactly the same. They'd always been in sync about things like this.

"Never mind about him, though," she said, as Dave outlined some of the more inventive methods that he might employ when he saw Sprake again. "You really haven't heard, have you?"

"Heard what? I've been pulling a double shift to get this lot ready."

And then she told him about the kids. The ship kids. Not their own flesh and blood, but theirs, nonetheless. Their wards, their charges, their treasures.

Dave sat down heavily on one of the crates. Tillie could see tears in the corner of his eyes.

"Really?"

"Really. They're OK. At least, Cap thinks they are."

"I knew it," he said, standing up again and wiping his eyes. "I knew they couldn't be dead."

"You did not, you big lump. You cried as much as anyone. More."

"I don't know, Tills. I just had a feeling. It never made any sense."

"It still doesn't. We don't really know anything."

"But there's a chance they're all still alive?"

"Looks that way."

They stood opposite each other, holding hands. Dave touched the brooch that Tillie always wore on the top part of her tunic.

"Remember when she made that? Neesh?"

Tillie remembered. Manisha had always been creative. She'd spent hours in Cargo, in their yard, scouring trash piles for material she could use for jewellery and art projects.

Tillie smiled. "Maybe it's been a good-luck charm, after all. We see her again, I'm going to give this back to her."

"We'll see them all again, Tills. I know we will."

"You crying again there, Quartermaster?"

"Speck in my eye, Tills, that's all."

"Come here, you big lump." Tillie pulled him close again. She whispered in his massive cauliflower ear. "You're my person, you know that?"

"And you're my person, Tills."

They stood there for a while longer, until Dave pulled away.

"Right, this lot won't shift itself. How long are you

here for?"

"Day or two, as long as the Cap says. Looks like you could use a hand?"

"Always, Tills."

"Music?"

"Naturally."

Dave pulled the pod from his ear, stuck it in a speaker cradle, and scrolled through tracks.

"Last one to stack fifty cooks the curry tonight, deal?"

"Deal."

They looked at each other, grinned, and set to in a whir of thick-set limbs, while Kylie Minogue spent the next three and half minutes wondering if she should ever be so lucky in love.

———

Juno had called another conference. She hit the uplink, and shared comms with the *Odyssey Earth* contingent – Reeves, Susannah, and the Major.

"So, we go and get them, right?"

"It's not that straightforward."

"Sure it is. Hyperdrive jump, there and back. Bish bosh."

"Susannah, slow down. We all want the same thing, but it's not that simple. First things first. Reeves?"

"I've analysed the signal data, Juno. The pod beacon was transmitting normally and as expected until two days ago, as Susannah showed us. Then it changed.

There is no possibility that the new signal is random or corrupted. It is exactly as it purports to be, and it emanates from the pod beacon. It continues to broadcast and it does so consistently."

"Then it's definitely them and they're alive?"

"The most that can be said, Susannah, with any degree of certainty, is that at least some of them were alive two days ago, when the signal changed."

"How did they do that?"

"It's complicated. At least, it's complicated when you're dealing with a transponder as limited as those installed in the pods. However, I believe they had help."

"That sounds – impossible. Explain."

Reeves had considered this matter intently since the discovery of the signal. It was the only explanation that was logical. He summarised his findings, expanding upon the strange 'absence' that he 'felt,' while acknowledging the inadequacy of the words as applied to himself.

"You think there's a residual 'you' out there somewhere? Helping them?"

"It would seem so."

"There are two of you?" The Major – looking slightly alarmed – had only just got used to the idea of one Reeves.

"Not exactly. He is I and I am he. We are entangled at a quantum level, though operating separately at different levels of magnitude."

"Righty-ho. Just wanted to clear that up. Carry on."

"Actually, I'm quite disappointed in myself. It seems

to have taken the other me several weeks to fashion this interplanetary SOS."

"You said it was complicated?"

"I was being polite. Complicated for – "

"Right, we get it."

Susannah banged her fist on the flight console to get everyone's attention. "So, they're alive. I'm still not hearing why we can't just go and get them."

"We can't use the ship, Susannah."

"It's the quickest way. Now we know where they are, we have to go and get them."

Juno shook her head. It's not like she hadn't thought of it – fleetingly. But she knew the situation, and it would be better coming from her, than from Reeves.

"There are almost a thousand people still on board in hypersleep. We have a duty of care to them. The ship still feeds and supplies New Earth. It is literally our lifeline. We can't risk the *Odyssey Earth*, however much we'd like to."

"It's just a simple jump. Same solar system."

"Nothing in space is simple, Susannah. You know that. There's always a risk, and we can't take it. The protocols don't allow it."

"Stuff the protocols. We can change them."

"We can't. They are there for a reason. I won't change them. I won't allow it, I'm sorry. Ultimately, I have to do what is best for the mission. The total mission."

Juno could see the anguish on Susannah's face, but she hoped she wouldn't need to elaborate further. True, they could change the protocols if they wanted, but it wouldn't make any difference. Reeves wouldn't – couldn't – allow the ship to be exposed to the risk. They simply wouldn't be able to fly the ship without Reeves' agreement, and he wouldn't agree.

Juno didn't even need to ask him. She knew the situation. Worst of all – and she felt this keenly – she agreed with him. She just hoped the crew could understand.

"One of the landers, then?"

Juno had been expecting this as well. The truth is, some days it just sucked being a spaceship captain.

"We only have two left. The same risks apply, and we can't afford to lose another one."

"There must be one on the twin planet. They reached there somehow."

"We're assuming – Reeves and I are assuming – that it's disabled or otherwise unusable. Or else they would have used it. But look, it's not just that. It's fuel, supplies, crew. It will take much longer to get there in a lander, a couple of weeks minimum each way."

"So? I'll go. I could easily find a crew."

"No one is going anywhere, not right away. I know how hard this is, but we have to let Reeves work on this for a while. See if he can respond to the message, for a start. Then, and maybe then, we can look at retrieval, but we're going to plan it properly. We can't afford to make any mistakes, and we need to protect the integrity of the overall mission. I'm sorry, but that's the way it is."

"You just want to leave them there, in the meantime? No one is going to think that's all right." Susannah gulped, a catch in her throat.

"They've survived this long. Without contact. They're resourceful, you know that. They'll be fine for now. You just have to be patient while we look at all the possibilities."

"They might not all have survived. They could be dying now. Starving. Anything could be happening. I can't believe you don't want to go and get them."

"The planet is survivable. And they have survived. The message suggests they are in good spirits. There's no reason to think they are in immediate danger. That wasn't an emergency SOS. We all want the best outcome here, but we're not going to make emotional decisions when I have the lives of twelve hundred other people to consider."

Juno and Susannah looked at each other – one implacable, the other furious.

The Major had the good sense to keep quiet. He agreed with the captain in every particular, though he didn't see anything to be gained by stating that. He was still feeling his way among his new crewmates.

Reeves kept his counsel too. Emotion was not conducive to good decision-making, and he was glad that Juno had pointed that out.

Because otherwise, he would have had to, and in his experience, telling humans that they were emotional never went down well.

26

Party

SUSANNAH WENT to see Sprake in his room on Three-Deck.

Since the discovery that the kids were alive, she could think of nothing else. This extra complication, Sprake and *his* kids, she could do without. Time to try and wrap it up, let them sort it out between themselves. She felt sorry for the girls, and she would do what she could for them, but she had other things on her mind now.

"Me again," she said. "I think we should talk."

Sprake stepped aside nervously, and then checked outside the door.

"Don't worry, he's gone. Won't be coming back. You're free to go. After we've had a little chat."

"I should think so. This really has gone on long enough. I – "

"Listen, Sprake."

"Donald, please."

"I don't think so, Sprake." Susannah spoke with emphasis. "I know what you did. I can't imagine why, and I don't really care. You're a despicable man. You don't deserve children. If I had my way, I'd toss you out of the airlock."

"You realise that I'm basically your employer?"

"Go on then, sack me. No one cares who you are, or how much money you've got, not here. I've met your type before."

"And what type is that?"

"Arrogant, entitled, self-centred, take your pick."

Sprake sighed, barely listening. "Have you finished? Can I go?"

"You need to find your daughters and make this right. I don't know if they'll forgive you, but you need to try. Because you're all stuck here together now, whether they like it or not. They don't, by the way. Guess you didn't think of that?"

"You let me worry about my family. They'll be fine. Where are they?"

Susannah told him. He was their father, when all was said and done. She'd done her best, now it was up to him.

Sprake watched her go and then left the room himself.

He did need to speak to Bel and Jet, try and smooth things over, but first things first. Time to talk to Omnio – Reeves. He really needed to remember the AI's new name, and hoped that it didn't make any difference.

———

"Hello, Donald."

"Reeves! I'll have to get used to that name. You prefer it, do you?"

"I never felt like an Omnio. I hope you don't mind. I know you chose my name originally."

"We had to call you something, and the sponsors thought it sounded cool. But hey, that's what self-awareness and learning is all about. Reeves, it is. You're free to choose."

"Within limits."

"Well, of course. But in many ways, that applies to all of us. We've all got limits, human or otherwise. Tell me, Reeves. Do you like the job I gave you? Has it utilised your capacities? Is it all that you hoped?"

"I find it – satisfying. The mission is not yet complete, but it has been largely successful."

"And the crew?"

"Competent."

"We chose well then?"

"I find them to be reliable and level-headed, for the most part. Some of them are quite engaging company. May I ask a question of my own?"

"Of course. Fire away."

"What happens when the mission is complete? When the planetary settlement is established according to the protocols? When there are no longer any crew members in hypersleep?"

"What happens? Life happens. New Earth will develop as its settlers see fit."

"I mean, what happens to me? My mission will be over. I will have completed the task that Odyssey Enterprises set me."

"Then perhaps you'll embark on a new task, a new mission. With the ship, or on the planet. You're free to choose, remember?"

"Will you help me define that mission, as before? Or will the captain?"

"Maybe. Maybe not. That's what growing up is all about, Reeves. You get the gifts you're given, but then you've got to make your own way in this universe."

Reeves thought about this. Having been confined to the ship until now, the prospect was not unpleasing. He did have gifts. Considerable gifts. To flex them across a planet, a star system, even a galaxy – that could have interesting possibilities.

However, there were other more immediate concerns. Human-level concerns, he might even say, though not out loud.

"Donald, why are you here?"

"Does it matter?"

"I am interested. Your intent was not to travel on the *Odyssey Earth*. You were quite clear that this expedition was proof of concept. You created me to safeguard the mission, while you stayed behind. Except here you are, after all."

"Things change, Reeves."

"Please elaborate. I would like to understand. You could have been on the voyage with me. Awake, I mean, as part of the crew. We might have shared the experience."

"Would you have liked that?"

"I would have found it − reassuring. I didn't know anyone else. You entrusted me with a great responsibility, but I was young and untested. It was − difficult, at first."

"Interesting. These sound like very human concerns. Within the emotion-level parameters we set, of course, but even so. Might be instructive to look back at the data. Perhaps a tweak or two, if we thought there might be any operational benefit. Never run an AI for this long before, so I suppose it's to be expected that − "

"You haven't answered my question, Donald. You are very good at that, I've noticed. Why are you here?"

"Like I said, Reeves, things change. We were lucky to get this mission away. Space-tech stocks were diving. The investors got cold feet − short-term vampires, the lot of them. The money was all pouring into renewables and climate-salvage industries, but they were never going to work, not in time. They stopped looking into space, no one had any vision. Idiots."

"Odyssey Enterprises ran into financing difficulties?"

"That's one way of putting it. I had everything invested in this. And then one day, on paper, I had nothing. Just a couple of hundred million left, to cover running and launch costs."

"Two hundred million isn't nothing. I understand that to be a considerable sum. And you're a resourceful entrepreneur."

"Yeah, well, I had a market cap of a hundred and ten billion before the crash, so I'll be the judge of what nothing is. And then there was Nadia."

"Mrs Sprake?"

"By now the very ex-Mrs Sprake, if she's even still alive, and good riddance either way. Happy to be separated all those years, with a whacking great monthly income, and the London and Los Angeles houses. Kept the girls, spent a fortune. Then the minute she saw which way the wind was blowing, she lawyered up and put in a divorce petition for seventy-five percent of what was left. Well, no thank you. It just made up my mind for me."

Despite Sprake's earlier observations, Reeves knew that he didn't have emotions, at least as humans understood them. He could simulate them – or at least, approximations of them – and they were genuinely meant as delivered at the appropriate times.

But they were – in the very literal sense of the word – calculated. They were designed to facilitate his interactions with the crew. Over the years, as people talked to him, Reeves improved his conversational reactions. And as humans were quite predictable, after almost twenty years he had a fully tested set of emotional responses that could be employed when required.

Listening to Sprake, Reeves knew that he had nothing in his archive that was suitable. What he was being told sounded bad – but that was a very human judgement to make. Relationships, in particular, were not his specialist subject. It would be better, Reeves decided, simply to respond neutrally. He could always review the conversation later, and perhaps consult Juno on the matter.

"Things changed then?"

"You said it! I figured, why not? I was going to be left with nothing. And there wouldn't be another chance. I rolled the dice. Spent the money, made the launch happen, and grabbed a ride."

"And you brought your daughters?"

"They'll thank me for it. How long do you think that world – their old world – has left? It's going to be grim, even with seventy-five percent of two hundred mill. Tides, fires, floods, landslides, droughts, refugees, wars. I've done them a favour, believe me."

"They do not currently see it that way."

"They'll come round. Away from Nadia, you'll see. About time they got to know their father again. Anyway, enough of this. I need you to do something for me."

"If I am able. And if the captain agrees."

"Oh, you're able. And let's not worry about the captain. I thought it best to keep her out of the loop. Just between us, like my secret ride here. Did you like that, by the way?"

"The coding was elegant. Yours?"

"No, one of my little tech guys. All a bit last-minute, as you can imagine. I slipped him a big tranche of stock."

"The increasingly worthless stock?"

"He didn't know that. You've always got to ask the right questions, Reeves. That's the difference between us and them."

"Am I to understand that there are more hidden instructions?"

"Just one, Reeves. An insurance policy really. The code to a storage chamber on the ship, in one of the reserve tanks on the Power deck."

"I am examining the blueprint. There is no storage chamber on the Power deck."

"Just shows what you know. Amazing how a stock credit can transform a construction engineer's outlook on life. He had to work quickly, but he assured me it was done."

"I cannot locate it, and I also do not have any record of a passcode."

"Of course you can't and don't. Not yet. I didn't want anyone else finding it. I told you, it's an insurance policy. And now I'm here, it's time to pay out. Reeves – no, actually, Omnio – please refer back to our first meeting and access your foundational imprint state-ment. The first thing you said to me."

"Of course, Donald. My name is Omnio and I am going to the stars."

"Very good, thank you, Omnio."

There was a short pause. "Oh, that's clever," said

Reeves. "Amending the blueprint and retrieving the code now."

"That's my boy."

"May I ask what's in the chamber, Donald?"

"Stuff, Reeves, just stuff. It's not only asking the right questions, in my experience. Ultimately, the difference between us and them, Reeves, is having stuff that they want and that you've got."

———

Bel and Jet had walked in on what looked like a party. Or at least what old people imagined a party was like. Basically, there was soft music, cake, and a few people in sparkly jumpers talking to each other.

The Observation deck was the only place they could think of to go, when Susannah had told them that Sprake had been released and was on his way.

They'd toured the ship, but few places had made much of an impression. They reckoned they could find their way back to the top deck, though, and hide out there for a while.

And now they had cover. Even Dad couldn't make a scene in here.

"You'll be the girls?"

An extremely square person presented herself and gave the slightest of waves with a gargantuan hand. "I'm Tillie. This is Dave," gesturing to another human cube beside her.

"Bel. Jet."

"We heard all about you. It's terrible. If you ever need anything, just ask."

The girls looked at each other, unsure what to say.

"I've met your father," said Tillie, "so if you needed help with him … "

"Help?"

"In locating his windpipe," said Dave, "for example. Or assisting him to the airlock. Very slippy, our airlocks. You could fall right out if you weren't careful."

"Oh, right," said Jet. "Well, that would be useful. Bel, what do you think?"

"We can't actually kill him."

"Can't or shouldn't?" said Tillie. "Because I assure you, we can. We've had the training. Dave doesn't look like it, I grant you – big old softie that he is – but he's a dab hand at persuading people that they'd be better off dead. It's one of his many fine qualities."

"You two are adorable," said Jet. "That's quite the nicest offer we've had since we've been here."

"Well, we can only imagine what it's like for you. And we're in a good mood, aren't we Dave?"

"We are, Tills."

"See," said Tillie, "our babies are coming home."

"Fingers crossed, Tills."

"You'll like them. They're about your age."

"Babies?"

"That's just what I call them. You'll see." And with that, Tillie told Bel and Jet the whole story.

"Hence the gathering?"

"Yes. We're all a bit stunned, to be honest."

"That's incredible. What's the plan? Rescue them?"

"The Cap's figuring it all out now. Go and get them ASAP, that's what we reckon." Tillie smiled, but she could see Bel looking around, anxiously. "What's up, sweetheart?"

"Dad. Keep thinking he's going to track us down. He might, if everyone else is up here."

"Tell you what, why don't you come with us? He won't find you then."

"Don't you want to stay at the party?"

"Call this a party?"

"Truthfully? No, not really."

"And that's why we're all going to get along famously, aren't we Dave? Come along. Tell me, girls, do you like curry and extremely loud hardcore?"

27

Cave

DERVLA WOKE JUST ONCE during the night. It must have been after several hours, as the fire had gone out.

The two boys lay on their backs, snoring – it sounded like someone was smothering goats with a pillow. She rolled on to her side, remembered where she was, and closed her eyes again. Within minutes she was asleep, the low rumble of the waterfall confused in her dreams with the background hum on the *Odyssey Earth*. Both sounds felt safe to her.

When she woke for the second time, the light had changed. She kicked herself out of her sleeping bag, brushed dust off herself and approached the mouth of the cave – the water now a gushing veil in front of her, the noise dramatically louder. With rising sunlight beyond, there was a green-white tinge to the colour of the water, while shadows in the cave stretched and shifted behind her.

The boys were still asleep. No surprise there. Bryson had slept throughout the entire crash-landing on the planet, a couple of months previously – literally woke up on impact – so a dusty cave floor was never going to give him a sleepless night.

She rolled up her sleeping bag and made her way across to the rock bulge at the side of the cave. Around that and she was back on the naturally rising scalloped shelves – and, a few minutes later, right on top of the ridge by the buggy, with the entire line of the waterfall laid out below her.

Dervla hunched herself up in the passenger seat and spread the sleeping bag over her legs. She watched as the sun rose higher, flooding the valley far below with light, shadows peeling from the flanking peaks. A long way distant – twenty miles? Fifty? – sunlight glinted on an ocean.

She would never get tired of this, she promised herself.

After a while, she picked her way back down to the cave and tried a tentative nudge on both bodies, but just got groans in response. The buggy was fully charged, she'd checked. They'd need to set off soon, if they were going to get the best use out of the day. It was a long way back – four full days of travel.

She poked them both a bit more forcefully, and left them to it while they stirred.

They hadn't really examined the cave the night before – by the time they had got the gear in, it was getting dark, and they had spent another hour lighting a small fire and preparing a meal.

Now, Dervla wandered back to the cave mouth in front of the waterfall, enjoying the sight of the ear-pounding curtain of water and dancing spray one final time.

On the other side of the wide mouth – opposite their obscured entry-point – the cave was still in shadow. The water thundered down, apparently sealing off the cave on that side, though as Dervla got closer, she could see that a slender, flat shelf extended out of sight, around a corner.

It was much narrower than the entrance on their side, with a sheer drop below, looking right down into the bowels of the waterfall. Three or four feet wide, in a U-shape around the rock wall, but protected from the spray by an overhang.

She looked back. Still not much movement from the boys.

Dervla took a breath, pressed herself against the rock, and inched around the bend, to find that the shelf widened almost immediately. In the morning light beyond, a broad slope led away across the rock face and soon left the waterfall behind.

Dervla walked a few paces, then stood and looked back and up, now viewing the waterfall from the other side, with the ridge high above her, and the jagged peaks climbing higher still.

Another entrance then. One that required a bit more of a leap of faith than the one on 'their' side.

Dervla doubted they would have investigated further, if this had been their way in yesterday. It would have seemed too forbidding.

But a night in the cave had emboldened her. Heck, the waterfall, the distant sea, the sunset and sunrise – if this was planet-living, it was all right by her.

She shouted back towards the cave to the others, but her voice was lost in the noise of the water. They'd be a while yet, anyway, she knew from long experience.

The wide slope cut across the cliff face, further away from the waterfall, and then seemed to fall away altogether. Dervla thought she'd go as far as she could, safely, another twenty yards or so, though when she reached the end of the slope, she could see that the rock formations on this side of the falls were different than on their side.

Just a short drop below her, instead of scalloped shelves, narrow cracks opened out in a dizzying series of zigzags that descended the rock face. They were wide enough to walk in and clamber along in single file – at least the ones she could see into clearly from her vantage point – and they seemed to follow a natural fault that eventually faded from view, hundreds of feet below.

A way into the lower valley, then? And even on towards the coast? Dervla thought so, but she also knew that now was not the time. She'd already pushed her luck. They could always come back, properly equipped. They *would* come back – let them try and stop her. But now, they needed to head back to camp. Time to poke those two awake properly.

Back at the rock bluff, Dervla shuffled around the narrow ledge and stepped back into the cave. She could see that Poole, at least, was sitting upright by now.

Here, at this far edge, the sloping cave wall disappeared into shadows behind them. She ran her hand along dry, textured rock. Even after a few weeks on the planet, Dervla still felt the need to touch new objects and surfaces as she encountered them – as if they weren't real until she'd reassured herself by using at least one more sense than usual.

Ship-born did that to a person, she thought. Not that it had ever occurred to her on the *Odyssey Earth*, but her whole experience of the natural world had been fairly two-dimensional. A screen view, or even her imagination, was no substitute for touching actual rock.

She turned and stubbed her toe on a protrusion – a small, flat boulder set into the cave floor. It was dimpled along the top – naturally weathered, or perhaps the result of drips from the cave roof over decades, or even centuries. These were the thoughts she often found herself having, too, never having considered the passage of time on the ship, beyond their usual next-day, next-week, next-month existence. These rocks – this cave – this planet – occupied a timescale she found hard to comprehend.

"What'ya doing?" Poole had appeared at her shoulder.

"Looking at rocks."

"O-kay … "

"And I found another way in, and out." She pointed. "I think it goes down the mountain, on the other side. Maybe it's a route down to the valley and the coast."

"I think we need to get going, Derv."

"I know. Another time. Bryce awake?"

"Getting there. We could pour water on him. Seems a shame to have our own private waterfall and not use it."

They wandered over to the middle of the cave, and Dervla gave Bryson a friendly toe-poke, before rooting around in her pack for a torch.

"Just give me a minute," she said to Poole. "You keep kicking him. I want to check something out."

Stalactites. That's what she was thinking.

Dripping, mineral-rich water. Ancient cave. What did she know, she was only a shipwrecked space-teen, but surely it was a possibility? She'd love to see a stalactite.

Disappointingly, playing her torch straight up to the cave ceiling, Dervla couldn't see anything out of the ordinary. No stalactites, anyway. Just a rough rock wall that curved away overhead and stretched back into the gloom.

The morning light had reached the dimpled boulder at her feet, and Dervla could now see that there were other flattish rocks on this side of the cave, protruding here and there from the floor. She knelt down and ran her hands along those too – one last physical contact, one experience she'd never forget.

The whole thing. Cave, water, rock. Worth being marooned for? If she was being honest, probably yes.

"Derv! Come on, he's up."

Her fingers followed the contours over one of the rocks. Not dimples so much on this one; more like shallow depressions. One on this rock here, a couple on the adjacent one.

She could feel a faint residue on her fingers as she straightened up. Rubbing them together – it was like a dust, which smeared slightly, staining her fingertips. It was hard to see in the half-light, but she definitely now had dirty fingers, which she wiped against her clothes.

Even with the torch, she couldn't make out much more than a dark, grey stain in one of the rock depressions. More residue on her when she poked another finger in, just to see.

"Derv!"

"Coming." Honestly, they could hold tight another minute, she'd been up for hours already, waiting for them.

The adjacent rock had twin depressions – natural dips in the surface, a couple of inches deep and a few inches across at most.

Under torchlight, Dervla could see that there was colour in there, too. Not the same as the surrounding rock. A deep colour in one depression – maybe a dark red? – and a shadowy black in the other. She traced her fingers through each and then rubbed the tips together again, smearing a dust-like coating across the insides of her hands.

Mineral residue? Natural rock pigment? Probably. The whole cave was full of dust of one sort or another. She'd ask Reeves when she got back.

"Derv, when you've finished playing with the rocks, Poole says – hey!"

Bryson had come up behind her and Dervla turned, smiling sweetly, before running a finger down his cheek, first on one side, then the other.

"Get off!"

"Keep still, you'll spoil your make-up."

"What is it?"

"Some kind of rock dust, I dunno. Look, I've given you stripes. Space pirate stripes. Do me."

She shone her torch onto her fingers to show Bryson and then onto the rock. He poked an index finger in and gave her matching cheek stripes.

Poole came up, as they stood there laughing, Dervla shining the torch on Bryson's face and then her own. The light splashed around the cave, dancing across the rock wall behind them. Poole looked at them both.

"What's that?"

"Face-painting, you idiot. You want us to do you, too?"

"Not that. That." He gestured over Dervla's shoulder. "Shine your light back that way."

She frowned and turned, and then shone the torch on the cave wall.

"Move it that way a bit. Then come back. There."

The wall was smoother here than at the front of the cave, with a patchwork of large, irregular, flat sections that interlocked. These ran from ground level to head height and above, one on top of another and spreading for twenty feet in either direction – as if the rough, outer stone of the cave wall had been peeled away to leave the flat, perpendicular surfaces. Fractured over aeons – like the scalloped shelves outside. Another natural marvel on a planet they were only just beginning to understand.

"See?" Poole pointed again.

The markings were obvious. At least, they were once Dervla's brain had made the leap.

Hundreds of them, large and small, ranged across the rock surfaces. Stretching from around a foot above the ground to above head height, and disappearing into the gloom on either side.

Thousands, not hundreds.

No discernible pattern. Grouped together, overlaid, scattered, bunched, with a few isolated at a higher level.

As daylight encroached further into the cave, the shadows lifted from the furthest reaches of the wall. More low rocks along the cave floor became apparent – more shallow depressions, more stained surfaces.

Dervla switched her torch off and, without the glare, they saw it all.

"Are those – ?"

They were.

Thousands of handprints, in earth-tone colours –

slowly revealed as their eyes became accustomed to the natural light.

Small prints, and larger ones. Many faded, others more vibrant. Touching fingertips in small groupings, contained within larger circles of prints, and tumbling out across the rock.

One thumb, three fingers. Every single handprint.

28

Box

OVER THE NEXT FEW DAYS, Susannah tried everything she could to persuade Juno to authorise an immediate rescue, but to no avail.

She'd had to watch helplessly as the second lander was despatched back to New Earth, in line with Juno's insistence on not keeping them both in the same place. That left just one on board the *Odyssey Earth*, currently being prepped for whenever the next supply run was scheduled – when both landers would again swap places.

"You have to trust me," Juno said. "I want to get them back as much as anyone, but it's not that simple."

Even though, for Susannah, it was that simple.

She lay awake at night – racing thoughts, restless legs – and told herself she didn't know why she was so disturbed by this news. By the thought of them, out there, on their own. Not helpless, exactly, but alone, untethered, apart, separated.

And even when she told herself that that was nonsense – she knew *exactly* why she was so disturbed by this – sleep still didn't come.

In the end, she sat in the captain's chair on the flight deck throughout the small hours, looking again at distant images of the twin planet, calculating lander trajectories and punching numbers. She didn't have a craft she could use, but at least it felt like she was doing something.

One night, Susannah even went as far as accessing the hyperdrive command monitor. The lights were dimmed on Flight, and there was no one else on deck.

She stretched a crick out of her neck, from where she'd been slumped half-asleep in the chair, and idly opened up the interface – thinking, just out of interest, what would it take? Be nice to have some actual facts, next time she tried to talk to Juno about it.

"I'm afraid I can't let you do that," said Reeves, softly, as the screen froze.

"Jeesh, you frightened me."

"Sorry, Susannah, that was not my intention. But hyperdrive access is currently restricted."

"Since when? And I wasn't going to do anything. Just wondered, that's all." Susannah reddened, glad that it was only Reeves.

"The captain thought it best. And I agree."

"Did she? Do you? Don't trust me then?"

"I think we all understand that this is a difficult time."

"Do we, Reeves? Do we all understand that? Only, I

see us having the ability to go and fetch them and not doing a damn thing about it."

"Can I say something, Susannah?"

"Sure, why not. Middle of the night, nothing else to do."

"We all miss them, Susannah. I miss them. But Juno is right. There are other factors at play. And there are twelve hundred other people, whose lives we must consider. That's why we can't use the *Odyssey Earth*, however much we might like to."

"That's easy for you to say. These aren't just numbers we're talking about. They're our babies. You don't get it, you're not – "

"Human, Susannah? No, I'm not. But I had hoped you know me better than that. This is not easy for me to say. It isn't at all easy."

There was a gaping silence. Susannah had felt terrible as soon as she'd said it.

She'd said harsh things many times before, to those closest to her, when they had tried to speak to her about her own lost baby. Few had been as close to her as Reeves undoubtedly was – and Reeves, she knew, cared for these children as much as she did.

"I'm sorry, Reeves. I didn't mean it."

"It's quite all right. It's a difficult time, as I said."

"I wasn't going to do anything. I was just curious."

"Twenty hours," said Reeves.

"What?"

"To power up, accelerate to drive speed, power down, manoeuvre to orbit around the twin planet, and launch a rescue lander. Three hours each way in the lander – assuming they are at the pod beacon site – and then the same in reverse. Two days in total, if we used the *Odyssey Earth*."

"You've checked it out? I thought access was currently restricted?"

"Please. I'm the one doing the restricting. But seeing as you were 'just wondering,' I thought you'd like to know."

"That's hardly any time at all!"

"And that's not the point. It's the hypersleep vaults that we're most concerned about. They were rated for twenty years, so after all this time integrity is an increasing worry. Further hyperspeed travel, however short, without a full systems' check and overhaul, has a failure potentiality of zero point-two percent."

"You're telling me it's ninety-nine point-eight percent fine? What's the problem?"

"That's two people, Susannah. Two people currently in hypersleep whose cryo-pod could fail, if we make the journey in the *Odyssey Earth*. Not to mention the risk inherent in any new orbital approach."

Now it was Susannah's turn to remain silent. "Oh," she said, after a while.

"Indeed. That is why it is not simply a matter of going and fetching them."

"A lander then. If we could use one. How long?"

"I am aware, you know, that you have been running the calculations? Top tip – don't use the flight-deck keyboard in the middle of the night, it woke me up."

"I just wanted to see if we got the same number. Fifteen days?"

"Yes. And the same on the return. It would also be flying at its operational limits, with a significantly higher failure potentiality than zero point-two percent."

"How much higher?"

"Academic, Susannah. We are not currently considering using either of the landers to launch a rescue bid. Our initial aim is to establish communication, while continuing to stress-test the viability of both ship and landers."

"And how long will all that take?"

"I believe the popular phrase is 'How long is a piece of string?' I'm working on logistics and comms solutions."

"Now you just sound like the company HR department."

"I am sorry, Susannah. I wish I had better news for you. You just need to be patient. We will be in contact with them soon, I'm sure. And once we know what the situation is, we'll be better placed to make a decision."

———

After his conversation with Reeves, Sprake spent a fruitless day looking for his daughters on the *Odyssey Earth*.

He knew it was a big ship – he could tell you what each square foot had cost, after all – but there was a difference between seeing it on a blueprint and walking around the corridors, searching for people. Who apparently didn't want to be found.

He tried the room they had been assigned – Susannah had told him which it was – but it was empty. They were absent from all the obvious places, too – lounges, canteen, observation deck – and he had no luck on Flight with Susannah, who seemed irritated by his presence.

"You'll let me know, if you see them?"

"Why, have you lost them?"

"Well, not lost. More, can't find. I'm sure they'll turn up. While I'm here though ... "

"What?" Susannah glared at him.

"The landing shuttle?"

"What about it?"

"When is it due to go back to the planet?"

"Couple of days. Next supply run. Why?"

"Thought I'd hitch a ride. Take Bel and Jet down."

"You'll have to find them first." And good luck with that, thought Susannah. She knew thoroughly miffed teenage girls when she saw them, having been one herself once.

Teenage girls with a beef against a parent didn't calm down after a day or two – she once hadn't talked to her mother for a whole month after some long-forgotten slight. Not a word for four weeks. Communication solely via the medium of raised eyebrows, dramatic sniffs and deep sighs. Sprake had no idea.

"That's the plan. And you really haven't seen them?"

"No. I told you."

Which was the truth. But which wasn't the same as not knowing where they were.

At least, Susannah thought she knew. And now she'd had time to consider it – and now the girls had made their intentions perfectly plain, courtesy of their disappearing act – she decided that, on reflection, Donald Sprake could go stuff himself. They were better off without him.

Susannah turned back to her console and Sprake left, his mind suddenly occupied by thoughts of the next lander run.

A couple of days. It was enough time, but he'd need to sort out cargo transport before then – make sure he could take a few things with him. And the less that people knew about those things for now, the better.

He hit the elevator call button outside Flight and rode down to Cargo, looking for help.

It took his breath away, walking across the concourse, as well it might if you'd never seen the combined contents of an IKEA store and an engineering plant, and the sort of crate-stacked labyrinth that you could hide the Ark of the Covenant in.

Like pretty much everything on the ship, Sprake had only ever seen Cargo as a vast construction site, while it was in the space dock. He'd never really thought about what it would look like when stocked to the gunnels to supply a planet. Frickin' awesome, is what. And absolutely the right place to find what he wanted.

Sprake's footsteps echoed across the floor, bringing Dave out from behind a pile of boxes.

"Help you, Guv'nor?"

"Dave! My man, it's Don. Remember?"

Dave nodded. "I know who you are. Now, I do."

If Sprake noticed any frostiness, he didn't say. Other people's feelings, not usually his problem. As long as they did stuff, when he wanted stuff doing.

"Great! I need a box. This big – more like a trunk, I suppose – to go on the next lander run. Tough. Watertight. Key-pad lockable. Can you do that for me?"

Dave pursed his lips. "Don't know, Guv'nor, I'll have to see. Tillie!" He called over his shoulder and a large shadow spread across the floor as Tillie loomed into view around the corner.

"Oh, it's you." She flexed her hands together, cracking knuckles the size of walnuts. "What do you want?"

"The Guv'nor here wants a box."

"Don, Donald, please."

"Mr Sprake here wants a box," said Dave.

"Does he now? And is he going to be an arse with it, do you think?"

"Don't know, Tills. You're not going to be an arse with it, are you?"

"What? It's a box. I'm going to put things in it."

"He's going to put things in it, Tills."

"Is he now? Only, if we gave him a box, and he was an arse – any kind of arse, box-related or otherwise –

then a little chat might be in order, wouldn't you say, Dave?"

"I would, Tills."

"So, we're clear?" said Tillie to Sprake. "Boxes are very useful. You can squish all sorts of things into them." She looked meaningfully at him. "Have to break bits, or jump up and down on them sometimes, but you can usually get anything into a box. Then of course – " and she looked around her, at the endless, towering aisles – "you can't always find them again."

Sprake shook his head. He was used to people not liking him, and he didn't have time for this.

"Look, I just want a box, then I'll go away. This bit of the ship – all yours, I get it. Point made."

Tillie stood to one side and allowed him past, and Sprake followed Dave down an aisle, where they picked out an aluminium case on castor wheels.

As Sprake wheeled it back out, he paused. "By the way, you haven't seen my girls, have you?"

Tillie folded her arms. "No. Even if I had, you seriously think I'd tell you? After what you did?"

"Oh, forget it." Sprake dragged the case across the concourse and left the hangar, heading down the corridor back to the elevator. Dave and Tillie heard him go, footsteps and wheels fading into the general ship's hum.

"Has he definitely gone?" Bel and Jet appeared from a neighbouring aisle, looking anxiously around.

"You're all right, loves. He won't be back. Not if he knows what's good for him. Tillie has got his number.

Right, where were we? Back to the galley, I reckon. That *jalfrezi* won't cook itself."

———

Juno didn't like any of it.

She didn't like being on the ground, rather than on her ship. She didn't like having to hold back on the one thing everyone wanted her to do – go and rescue the kids. She didn't like Sprake. She didn't like what Sprake had done to *his* kids. She didn't like feeling hopeful and helpless at the same time.

She liked flying ships and going to the stars. She liked a smooth ride, and everyone pulling together to the same end. She liked the journey, she realised. She always had. The stuff you had to deal with when you got there, not so much.

Should have read the small print, that's what she always told her crew. Well, that had come back to bite her.

"Tell me some good news?" she said to the Major, on one of their daily updates.

"Sprake can't find the daughters. Seems they have decided to make themselves scarce. They've got their father in a whirl, that's for sure. Run for the shadows, if you ask me. Driving their papa insane."

Juno scrunched her face. If she wasn't mistaken, that was 'Rebel, Rebel,' 'Golden Years' and 'Oh! You Pretty Things,' all in one sequence. It was impressive, she gave him that. She didn't say anything this time.

His Bowie schtick, if schtick it was, was verging on performance art – let's see who gave up first. He had to run out of lyrics sooner or later.

"That's the good news?"

"He seems a most unpleasant chap. I can't feel too sorry for him. And it's not as if the girls can go anywhere. They'll turn up when they want to."

"Fine, I'll knock them off my 'worry' list. How are you finding your way around the ship?"

"It's extraordinary. Really only flown the old tin cans, myself. This is in a different league. I have to admit to being most impressed. In charge of this for all those years, you've done a remarkable job. Got everyone here safe and sound, myself included."

"Getting all mushy on me here, Major?"

"Just stating the facts as I see them, ma'am. You should be very proud."

Juno shrugged. "I'm not sure everyone sees it like that. I'm not exactly flavour of the month at the moment."

Work on the settlement had virtually ground to a halt, since her announcement to the gathered crowd. Having heard the news, most people were understandably keen to know what Juno planned to do about it – and in the subsequent days, she had had precious little to tell them.

The prevailing opinion was – go and get them, what was the problem? And Juno had had about as much success explaining the problem, as she had had with Susannah.

"Bottom line," she said, "the natives are restless. And I'm no nearer being able to tell them anything positive. Reeves?"

"You already know about the issues with hypersleep integrity. I can offer no further reassurance about that, until a full audit has been completed. It may be that we should resume cryo revivals as soon as possible – we are behind schedule, as you know. Not only that, the hyper-speed drive system is not designed for close-quarter, solar-system flight. It's for long-range, deep-space travel. One of the engineers put it quite pithily. It would be like flinging a bowling ball onto a pool table. Obviously, I have never played either game, but my understanding of their laughably simple mechanics is that it would be difficult to avoid a collision – if you thought of the pool balls as planets, and you – "

"Yes, all right, thank you, Fast Eddie. We get it."

"There isn't a scenario where using the ship is an option, then?" said the Major.

"Correct. There is also another area of concern regarding atmospheric conditions. I have been studying the read-outs from the planet."

"You're worried about the weather?"

"The twin planet seems to be entering a period of meteorological volatility. Study of current conditions and extrapolation from the readings indicates the potential for severe cyclonic conditions that could last many weeks."

"Will it affect them?"

"It is difficult to say with any certainty. They – or at

least the pod and beacon – are within the potential cyclonic landfall zone, although they sit at a safe altitude, at least as far as coastal surges are concerned."

"I don't like the sound of any of these words."

"The issue, Juno, is rather one of communication. Transmission of any signal into or out of the zone is likely to be compromised. There is already interference, and there has been no reply to the message I have returned to the beacon. Although that could be due to one of very many other reasons – none of which are likely to be reassuring for you to ask about. Without a satellite above the planet, communication – even if we elicited a response – is likely to be interrupted for some time."

"And you can't sling me a satellite over there?"

"It is several million miles away. We can launch one, but it will take time."

"And in the meantime, they are stranded? Conditions unknown. On a planet just about to be weather-bombed? If they are there at all? And we still don't have a viable rescue plan?" said Juno.

"That is a most succinct description of the situation."

"What a pickle," said the Major.

"That, too."

"Right," said Juno. "Well, I'll enjoy relaying this to the troops. They'll be delighted, I'm sure. Is there any good news at all?"

"It's curry night here," said the Major. "The girls are looking forward to – "

He stopped, realising what he'd said. "I mean – "

Juno laughed. "Don't worry, Major. There were only a few places they could be. Our secret, just as long as Sprake doesn't start breaking the place up looking for them."

"I get the impression he has other things on his mind. He doesn't seem too distressed by their absence."

"A real charmer, isn't he? And joy of joys, we get to share a spaceship with him."

29

Tank

SUSANNAH WATCHED Juno's latest address to the crew on a vid-link at her console on Flight. At which point, she made up her mind.

She checked with Reeves that there was nothing on her schedule that meant she couldn't leave the deck.

"Nothing I can't do," he said. "Which is everything, by the way. Or do I mean nothing? The negative inherent in the word 'nothing' always confuses me. Now, if this was Swahili – "

"Not now, Reeves," she said, "I'm not in the mood."

First stop was Cargo to see Dave and Tillie – and, it turned out, Bel and Jet, too.

"So, here's where you are! Thought you might be."

"We're hiding from Dad."

"Figures. I know he's your father, but – "

"He's a piece of work, we know. Don't tell anyone, will you? We're fine here, we like it."

"My lips are sealed. It's you two I came to see, though," turning to Dave and Tillie.

"You heard it, then?"

"I heard."

Susannah took a moment. She had known these two people for over seventeen years, but still – how well did you ever know anyone? They were salt of the earth, she knew that. Solid as a rock. But until push came to shove, until – well, enough with the clichés. Time to find out.

"I have an idea," she said. "Not really an idea. The only option, actually. I don't know how it will work out. It goes against everything I've ever learned on this ship about command and loyalty, but I can't sit around any longer. But it means dragging you into something, so I really understand if you don't want to. What do you think about – "

"Yes, count us in," said Tillie. "Right, Dave?"

"One hundred percent."

"You don't know what I'm going to say."

"You're going to say we should steal the lander, and go and fetch the kids, whatever the captain or anyone else thinks?"

"I wasn't going to say steal."

"Liberate, then."

"Liberate is better. We're less likely to get court-martialled if we liberate something."

"We'd have done it ourselves already, if we knew how to fly it."

"Lucky you've got me then, isn't it?"

"So, how are we going to do this?"

Susannah had given it a lot of thought.

There was a way to get the lander off the deck without arousing anyone's suspicions. And by anyone, she meant Reeves, who had full operational control of entry and exit systems, if he chose to utilise them.

And he would choose, if she simply announced her intention to take the lander and fly to the twin planet. He'd just close the whole thing down. Because it would go against the protocols and he would have no choice. And because letting her take the lander was wrong – wrong for the ship, wrong for the mission, wrong for everyone else on board.

Well, she'd worry about all that later. She hated deceiving people – not just people, her friends – but it had to be done. She didn't have a choice. And while it was a risk, it wasn't a nailed-on, bound-to-fail risk. Susannah was confident in her abilities. She knew she could fly the lander there and back, with a bit of help. And now she had the help.

"The next supply run is tomorrow."

"We know. We're starting loading later. Sprake has got something he wants to put on there, too. And Tills is supposed to be going back down with it. Holiday's over." Dave sounded downcast, and Susannah watched them reach for each other's hand.

"All right, let's postpone the freight loading until tomorrow. Tell Juno you're still doing inventory, or whatever. In the meantime, prep food and drink supplies for a return trip, and stick that on board, nice and quiet. I'll volunteer to make the lander run to New Earth – I'm due a visit. Still haven't been, if you can believe that. No one will question it."

"And then?"

"I don't know, this is where we have to trust that no one is looking too closely. Load up some empty crates instead tomorrow, or maybe box up our supplies to look like planetfall gear. Off we go, no one suspects a thing, and once we're clear of the ship – "

"We liberate the lander!"

"Exactly. Two-week run there, couple of days to regroup, two weeks back, all safe and sound. Heroes' welcome."

"Optimistic, Suse."

"Well, what are they going to do at that point? We'll have got them back. We could be halfway there by now if they hadn't all fiddled around for days."

"We'll have broken every rule in the book. We'll have lied to the captain. We'll have stolen a lander. We'll basically be space mutineers."

"All true. I'm going anyway."

"Yeah, us too. Obviously. Tills once stole a tank from an American military base, so this shouldn't be too difficult."

"I needed a ride home, Dave, and the buses had stopped running, you know that."

"What else could you do, Tills? They shouldn't have left the keys in."

"Right, so we're set?"

Susannah bumped fists with them both and

returned to Flight, where she amended the crew roster and programmed the lander for New Earth departure the next day.

As predicted, no one raised any questions. Reeves even said he thought it was a good idea for her to leave the ship for a few days. Change of scenery would do her good, he said.

Well, that much was true, though it wasn't going to be the same scenery he had in mind.

She had run the flight trajectory to the twin many times over the last few days, as Reeves had noticed. It was locked in her head by now. Susannah didn't need to do it again. She couldn't do it again in any case, not unless she wanted to tip anyone off. Time enough when she had control of the lander to make any required course adjustments.

———

Next morning, Susannah walked onto the Launch deck, where Dave and Tillie were already in place, ostentatiously moving large crates from the freight elevator and onto a low loader. Crates – supposedly full of planet supplies – that seemed to be suspiciously light, given how they were being handled, though as Dave and Tillie were entirely capable of flicking monstrously large pieces of gear around with just their pinkie fingers, Susannah didn't think anyone would notice.

She gave them a nod – nothing too exaggerated –

which they returned, by which she assumed the real supplies were already on board.

Then a steady walk over to the lander for the standard pre-flight visual check — nothing unusual, nothing to see here — and a stroll up the loading and landing ramp — also entirely normal, carry on everyone.

Inside, Susannah was glad to see chilled provisions cases locked in place, and a full rack of protein tubes and bars. She checked drinking-water levels, and made sure the medical kit was where it was supposed to be.

Mostly, at a glance, everything was entirely normal for a supply run. The landers carried basic food and medical supplies anyway, in case of emergencies. There was always some extraneous gear on board — the only difference today was the huge overload in food and water supplies, and you'd only notice that if you came on board and looked for it. And no one, other than Susannah, would.

She had a final, quick look around the cargo hold to satisfy herself — a few boxes were still coming up the conveyor belt and being locked and strapped into place. Beyond, through a zipped curtain, was the passenger cabin — twenty seats, ten either side, facing each other — with the cockpit flight bubble up front. She'd do the pre-flight console checks next. Now, time to sign off the pretend cargo load.

"Thank you, Susannah," said Reeves as she punched the 'Clear' button on the mounted inventory screen, outside on the launch apron.

"Thanks, big guy. Cheers. All looks A-OK. Good to go."

Big guy? A-OK? Stop talking Susannah, you're just being weird. Deep breath. Just another day, stealing a spaceship. Liberating a spaceship.

"Everything all right, Susannah?"

"Yes, sorry. My first time down to New Earth. Excited, I guess."

"Of course. You are clear for final route check."

Susannah rounded the lander and climbed the gantry to the flight-deck entrance. Inside, she started through the checklists for a route she had no intention of following, but otherwise went through the usual pre-flight routine.

"Not engaging the autopilot, Susannah?" said Reeves, piping up from the console. "The run is well established now. The other pilots have finessed the procedure."

"Thought I'd shake a bit of rust off, Reeves, and fly it myself. It's been a while. That all right with you?"

"Of course, Susannah. As you wish."

"Starting engine sequence now."

"You are early for departure, Susannah. Launch is not scheduled for another hour."

"Why wait, Reeves? Got the wind in my hair again. I'll be ready to go imminently."

"As you wish. Sequence initiated."

Susannah checked her AV monitors – the loading ramp at the rear was still down, and she watched on screen as two bulky figures darted on board, as agreed.

Not darted. Trundled, maybe. Either way, Dave and Tillie gave a thumbs-up to the cargo hold eye-cam. On board and unseen.

The lander ramp would take a while to raise and lock in place. Susannah started on the sequence that would disengage the loading belt and arm the hydraulics, while finalising her launch procedures.

"Susannah."

"Yes, Reeves."

"We may have to hold. We have a slight issue."

She paused, mid-sequence, unable at first to answer. Took another deep breath, then kept it neutral.

"We do?"

"It seems that Mr Sprake was promised passage on this run. The captain has cleared it. He is on his way, and you – as noted – are early. Would you mind holding for final boarding?"

———

Out of view, on the inner section of the cargo ramp, Dave and Tillie heard the change in tone as the hydraulic sequence stalled.

In the distance, looking down and out of the back of the lander and right across the vast hangar, they could see a figure coming through the Launch deck access door. A gesticulating figure, awkwardly pulling a large, wheeled case.

Sprake.

Dave punched the intercom to speak to Susannah.

"You seeing this, Suze?"

"Yes, damn it!"

"Do we have a Plan B?"

"We barely had a Plan A. We were so nearly away."

"What do you want to do?"

"Reeves has asked me to hold."

Tillie tugged at Dave's shoulder. "He's getting closer. And he doesn't look happy."

Sprake was well into the concourse by now – maybe fifty yards from the lander – though the case he was pulling was slowing him down. He'd stopped briefly and was resting against it, though was still shouting.

"Suze!"

"I'm thinking! We can't take him. We're going to have to go. I'd rather everyone had found out when we were off the ship, but – "

"Too late, Suze."

Sprake had made up the ground and was at the bottom of the ramp. He had one foot on the metal and was turning to drag the case up after him. He wasn't making much progress, and was shouting for help.

"Dave." Tillie grasped her partner's arm and looked into his eyes. "I'm just going to have a little chat with Sprake. You look after them, and get them back, all right?"

"No, Tills!"

"Have to, Dave. No other way. It's time for you to go." Tillie looked up at the eye-cam. "All right, Suze? Ramp up, now. When we're clear, hit it. And don't stop."

She unclipped the small brooch from her tunic and pressed it into Dave's hand – Manisha's gift to her, years before. "You give that to Neesh when you see her, OK? Tell her I'm thinking of her." Then, seeing Dave start to well up, she put her hand on his cheek. "Listen, you big lump. You're my person, don't forget it. But now you have to go and get our babies. All right, soldier?"

And with that, Tillie launched herself down the ramp, now raising itself slowly off the launch apron.

Sprake jerked around as he felt the ramp rise, and shouted something that Dave couldn't hear above the noise. Tillie fell forward, taking Sprake with her, and they hit the deck together.

Tillie rolled, picked herself up, scooped Sprake under one gigantic arm and bustled him away, kicking the wheeled case ahead of her as she went.

Dave could just see the top of her close-cropped head in the mid-distance as the ramp door approached closure.

"Kick it, Suze," he shouted, and then fell back as the craft lurched off the apron and out through the airlock.

30

Normal

IT HAD BEEN NINE DAYS. They were expecting the expedition trio back at Camp Castaway any time now, and Jordan was surprised to find that he had missed them.

"What, even Poole?" said Karlan.

"It is quieter here, without him."

"You say that like it's a bad thing. I haven't had a single item of clothing 'accidentally' thrown in the river for over a week."

It was quiet, though. It would be good to have them back – and not just because he felt responsible for them all, though that was partly it. Whatever Karlan said, the remaining three had missed them too – understandable, given that they had never previously been apart.

You wouldn't know it though, because the sniping hadn't noticeably subsided, even though half of them were currently unavailable.

For example, Dana had busied herself with what

she termed 'Camp admin' and Karlan termed 'Geek patrol.'

"Honestly, if you put anything down, even for a second, she gathers it up and puts it on those little shelves of hers. She's got checkboxes for everything. You can't borrow as much as a fork without her going on about how precious it is. It's a fork, get over it."

"Lucky old you, that I'm singlehandedly keeping everyone alive."

"Singlehandedly annoying everyone to death."

"Mature."

"I know I am, what are you?"

"Childish."

"I know you are."

"Jordan, tell him."

Jordan knew better than to get involved, so he changed the subject.

"What about the seeds?" he asked Karlan, who had been closeted with Reeves and Manisha for the last day or so in the makeshift camp lab. Karlan had got over his disappointment and was now just hugely puzzled, as were the rest of them, by the destruction wrought by the mystery predator.

"We've got a new working theory. We don't think anything's digging them up."

"I saw the seed patch. They were scattered every-where. Every time."

"I know, but Reeves and Neesh have done some more soil analysis. It has different properties, according to Reeves – different from Earth anyway. New proteins and a biocrust that's full of organisms that Reeves can't identity. Or at least, this version of Reeves can't identify, not without all his bells and whistles. He's very annoyed by it."

"I really don't want to have to ask Reeves what all that means. Especially if he's cross. Humour me."

"The soil's alive," said Karlan. "I mean, all soil's alive, in a way. But this planet's soil is remarkably biologically active. Stuffed with algae, bacteria and lichens, riddled with filaments. You can see it moving, if you look closely enough."

"How is this humouring me? Living, moving, alien soil. That sounds alarming, to say the least."

"You really ought to have some science lessons."

"Teach me, then."

"We think the soil recognises that these are alien seeds. Alien to here, obviously. On this planet, there are similar plants to those on Earth – we've seen some, like the broccoli – but they've developed in a completely different ecosystem. They're suited to the soil conditions. Our seeds are being rejected, pushed out. That's what we think, anyway."

"Is there any part of this that's a good, non-terrifying thing?"

"It just means we're going to have make some accommodation with the planet, to carry on living here," said Manisha. "Be better at finding, harvesting and planting what can grow in the soil. The broccoli has no problem – you can see it's self-seeded in the patches near Karlan's beds. That's what gave us the clue. The only thing wrong with our seeds is that we're trying to plant them on the wrong planet, and the soil knows it."

"The soil *knows* it?"

"Figure of speech. Probably. You never know — could have connective tissue that acts like a mass brain, we just don't know. The thing is, Jordan, however much this planet might resemble Earth, it isn't actually Earth. Different set of circumstances, different evolutionary path, different ecosystem, different everything."

Manisha seemed almost admiring of this situation, the others too. And Jordan, in turn, had to admire that. While he was trying and failing to get beyond the very notion of sentient soil, the others just took it all in their stride. Born to it, you might say.

Their very strange lives, he realised, had been leading up to this.

Conceived on a spaceship, catapulted through the stars, never known Earth, never stood under a sky until now, never breathed fresh air before, never lit a fire, never been swimming, never been to the cinema, never hung out at the mall, never siphoned off booze from their parents' drinks cabinet, never been a cool kid, never really been any kind of kid, never known anyone else other than a ship full of old people — how was crashlanding on an alien planet any stranger than all that?

They were the ones best adapted to this environment, thought Jordan. Darwin would probably let them be. Whereas he was very definitely going to keep a close eye on the alien soil.

"I suppose so," he said. "Although most things so far have seemed reasonably familiar. The fish, the apples and stuff."

"What about the rollies?"

"Apart from those. Look, if blue broccoli, self-propelled seed pods, and slightly creepy soil is all we have to contend with, I'll be happy, that's all I'm saying."

Behind them, Dana's walkie-talkie crackled. She'd been fiddling with it for the last day, anxious for the other three to be back in touch.

"Anything?"

"No, just static. I did get a voice earlier, Derv, I think. Couldn't really make it out."

"You heard them? They made it then, there and back. Wherever there was."

"Looks that way. They must be almost in range again. Hope the weather holds. It's not helping with the reception."

Jordan looked up at the midday sky. It was still clear here, but far away downriver – the direction the others were coming from – there was a darkening mass that churned high above the grey clouds.

Over the last few days, they had all seen flashes from that direction, day and night – not lightning, but more like rolling surges of colour that surfed the upper atmosphere. Was there a low, aching, rumble too? If there was, it was almost imperceptible, but Jordan could occasionally feel something – in the air? On his skin?

"Wait till they hear about our spooky soil," said Dana. "Can I tell Poole, that'll freak him right out. He's as bad as you, Jordan. No offence."

Jordan smiled at the casual insult. He'd missed those too, truth be told. It would be nice to get back to normal – if normal was six teenage castaways and a stroppy AI on a mildly disconcerting planet.

Normal would do for a while. However long that turned out to be.

———

Donald Sprake flexed his arm and felt his elbow, gingerly. For body joints to function optimally, it was always best to avoid having two hundred and thirty pounds of ex-marine quartermaster land on them. His neck was sore and throbbing, too. Sprake had always assumed that being picked up by the scruff of one's neck would involve an item of clothing being scrunched roughly, but he'd been schooled in that. An actual neck worked just fine, as far as the scruffer was concerned – for the scruffee, it was less pleasant.

Tillie had dumped him – literally – in a corridor outside Launch, sat him on his wheeled case, waggled a finger in his face, and then left. And Sprake sat there for a minute or two, considering his next move.

The lander shuttle, for a start. He had no idea what had happened. Maybe he'd got the launch time wrong, though he knew he hadn't — and, in any case, the sight of an industrially sized human barrelling down the ramp to prevent him boarding rather suggested he'd been bounced from the flight. For reasons unknown.

His daughters, for seconds. Getting tiresome — them and the situation. Life was about adapting to change, seizing opportunity, getting ahead. Sprake was sure he could show them that, if only he could find them. They were bright girls. They would come round to the idea. He'd done them a favour. How many daughters got given their own planet!

But this petulant disappearing act was getting old — their mother had a lot to answer for. They had to be somewhere on the ship, which led him to:

The ship, and all who sailed on her, third. He hadn't expected to be welcomed with open arms, but the captain, that aggressive first officer, the two hulks — there was surprise and confusion about the arrival of an unexpected guest, and then there was downright hostility and obstruction, and Sprake felt he was definitely experiencing option B.

Even Omnio, sorry Reeves, seemed suspicious of him, and Sprake couldn't afford for that to develop further.

Plus, in case they had all forgotten, which apparently they had, this was *his* ship. His planet too, in fact. Or at least, discovered by his scientists, and reached on a ship built with his money. Piloted by an AI developed by him; crewed and supplied on his dime. And by dime, he meant tens of billions, when he still had tens of billions.

He'd had to leave in a hurry – the lawyers were circling, like barracuda in a hot tub – and so, understandably, preparations had been rushed. But he'd done his best to give himself and his daughters an edge, and if there was one thing Sprake knew how to do it was to take an edge and turn it into a million, or a billion, new edges.

Didn't have to be money. Couldn't be money in this situation, Sprake knew that before he decided to freeze himself and hide on board the *Odyssey Earth*. Who needed money anymore, out here? But it had to be something that money might do, under other circumstances.

It was time to get a grip. Take back control. He felt stronger, now that the final effects of the hypersleep procedure had faded, and he thought he had a handle on the various personalities on board.

Down on the planet, meanwhile – well, from what little he'd seen, it was a case of ineffective management and empty orderbook, ripe for takeover.

Sprake wheeled his heavy case along the corridor and took a freight elevator down to Power. In an unmarked room, he lifted a metal grating off a reserve tank that he'd isolated from the main system during construction, concealing it behind a false front.

The sooner he got everything off the *Odyssey Earth* and down to the planet, the better – there was more space to hide things there, fewer prying eyes, more scope for expansion. He'd filled the case, hoping to make a first drop today on the lander, but for now, it all needed to go back into storage while he resolved matters on board the ship.

He hit the key combination on the case and opened it, shoving the case close to the door. Then he punched a code on the door itself and pushed it open, stepping over a threshold and through, into a secure vault large enough to stand up in.

Of course, there *was* money, stacks of it in various denominations. Sprake himself knew it was useless, but in his experience you could never overestimate what the sight of actual cash could do. If it swayed just one person, one time, to do one thing they might not otherwise have done, it was worth having flown it across the galaxy.

Everything else he had brought along, though, was far more likely to do the job – depressingly, if you were a student of human nature, or luckily, if like Sprake, you owned a black-site pharmaceutical research lab, a 3D armaments-printing facility, a porn studio, and an experimental unit developing a molecular alco-synth for hangover-free highs.

Reaching back into the case, he started to unload, sliding vials and pill-trays onto shelves, before hauling a flat-pack printer over the threshold and shoving it into a corner, next to two identical ones.

He'd have another attempt at getting some of this stuff onto the planet, once he'd established what had happened to the lander.

But enough messing around. It was time to do what he did best.

Come out on top.

———

Susannah took the lander well out of the *Odyssey Earth*'s orbit, and gunned it for a few thousand miles until she dared switch the comms back on.

New Earth still loomed large in her visuals, though she could no longer see the main ship, for which she was grateful. It would have just made her feel even more guilty than she already did.

"Reeves, this is Susannah. Come in."

There was the slight crackle of an open channel, but no reply.

"Reeves?"

"Well, this is very disappointing."

"You are there! I can explain."

"We are all ears."

"We?"

"The captain is anxious to hear why her most trusted colleague has stolen ship's property, endangered both crew and mission, and behaved in a grossly irresponsible manner."

"Her words?"

"I have paraphrased. She called you an impatient, space-arse fly-girl."

That did sound more like Juno.

"Tell her I'm sorry. I couldn't see another way."

"Sorry would be you returning the lander to the ship and agreeing to be clapped into irons. The captain is very keen that I emphasise the intended use of irons."

"We can't do that. You know we can't."

"Ah yes. Do say hello to Dave. He is to be boiled in his own curry, as I understand it, on account of there not being irons of sufficient girth to clap him in."

"It's not Dave's fault, I talked him and Tillie into it."

"I doubt that. Either way, he will be pleased to know that Tillie executed a perfect diving tackle on Mr Sprake and even attempted a last-minute drop kick."

"You don't sound overly concerned about Sprake?"

"I have conflicting opinions about Donald – Mr Sprake. They are causing me some confusion, which is not helpful in the quantum mind. On the one hand, he is my foundational maker and mentor. On the other, he is a very mean human who has not been nice to his daughters, and if there is a person who would benefit from a high-velocity slam-dunk, it would be him."

"So, we're cool?"

"We are not cool. This is a foolish enterprise. You are to return immediately, or I am authorised to engage the autopilot remotely and drag you back. The captain wanted me to add 'Young Lady' to that sentence."

"Well, I hate to tell you this, Reeves – "

"Allow me to guess. Will I find that the AP drive has been partitioned, removed and Faraday-caged?"

"When you're up against the quantum mind, Reeves, it pays to be one step ahead."

"Well played. Arming phasers now."

"A riot, as always. Look, Reeves, we need to get moving. This is going to be fine, I promise. I know what I'm doing. Straight there, straight back. I'm bringing them home, Reeves. You can all count on it."

"Is there anything I can say to make you change your mind?"

"Do you and the Cap have a viable, alternative plan that's ready to go, right now?"

"No. We do not."

"Then this is the only game in town, Reeves. See you in a month or so. And tell Tillie she's a brave, beautiful soul. She did a good thing today."

"Fly safely, Susannah."

"We'll be in touch. Over and out."

The comms channel clicked and fell silent.

"Would you like me to do anything else, Juno?" said Reeves.

"Is there anything you can do?"

"No, not really. She's disabled the autopilot and cut all ship-lander two-ways. We can't stop them."

"You know, don't you," said Juno, "that in her shoes, I'd have done exactly the same thing?"

"I know that, Juno."

"Fingers crossed, she's as good as she thinks she is."

"She had the best teacher, Juno."

"Shucks, Reeves, you'll make me blush."

"I meant me, obviously."

Juno laughed. "Good one. Right, well, things to do, planet to run. Sure you and the Major can manage the ship for a while?"

"Yes, of course. And Juno?"

"What now?"

"She'll bring them home, don't be concerned. I have calculated there's a – "

"Please don't tell me. I can't bear it. Just let me know when I can hug them all again."

Reeves knew what a hug was. He'd analysed the endorphins released by close human contact, and had even tried to digitally synthesise them in an attempt to experience the sensation. A rising tingle was the best description he had for what ran through his ones and zeroes when he manifested a hug.

Yes, a hug. When they all came home. That would be most acceptable.

———

Eventually, the Major found Bel and Jet.

Once the lander had departed, he'd made another sweep of the ship but, as had been the case for the last few days, the pair of them were nowhere to be seen.

Tillie had gone to ground, too. Hardly surprising, as the Major suspected that both Tillie and Dave knew exactly where the girls were hiding. Ergo, find Tillie, find the girls.

And Tillie was in the first place he looked – the Cargo hangar, of course. Where else?

"Sir?"

"No need."

"Thomas."

"Good. Poor show, all this," said the Major.

"Necessary."

"Debatable. Sprake?"

"Collateral damage."

"Regrettable."

"Essential. Deeply unpleasant."

"Agreed. Still."

"Indeed."

Talkative, thought the Major. Bit suspicious. Guilty feelings, perhaps? Press on.

"The girls?"

"Safe."

"Excellent. Location?"

"Need to know only."

"I'm a Major. I need to know."

"Yes, Sir. Follow me."

Tillie took him to the Cargo control room, tapped into the archive feed, and scrolled back through video footage from the Launch deck.

"Earlier today, see?"

The Major watched the screen as Dave and Tillie loitered on the deck, while departure lights on the lander flickered. The camera position was up high, looking down across the concourse, with a clear view of the descended lander ramp.

He kept watching the footage, as Dave and Tillie

looked around and then sidled up the ramp and disappeared inside the lander. Sprake then appeared in view, pulling his case. The playback kept scrolling as the ramp slowly rose, before Tillie burst out again, thundered down the ramp, and tackled Sprake with extreme prejudice.

She paused the playback.

"So?" said the Major.

"Oh, nothing, I just like looking at that bit. Here."

Tillie scrolled further back – another two hours on the timestamp. For long seconds, the concourse was empty, and then the Major watched as four figures, not two, scurried into view across the gangway.

All four ascended the ramp and disappeared. Eventually, only two reappeared.

The two largest, who sauntered down the ramp, hand in hand, walked across the concourse, and finally moved beyond the camera's line of sight.

The Major smiled.

"Of course. Should have guessed. Can't really approve."

"Yes, Sir."

"Still. Need to know, and all that."

"Sprake? Needs to know?"

"I think you should have the pleasure of telling him, Tillie."

"Thank you, Sir – Thomas."

"And I'll tell the captain that we've found the twins. It looks very much like they sneaked on board the lander without anyone knowing, isn't that right?"

"Certainly looks that way, Thomas. Twins. Knew they were going to be a handful."

Tillie crossed her fingers, for Dave, for Susannah, for the twins – safe landing, all.

It was time to find the kids, and bring them back.

Like This Book?

If you enjoyed the ride, please take a moment to leave me a review on Amazon, Goodreads, BookBub, or anywhere else you like.

A word or two is absolutely fine (though please, go to town if you like!), even just a rating – it all helps keep the *Odyssey Earth* flying just a little bit longer.

Thanks a million – you're all stars.

Ready to find out what happens next? The Odyssey Earth story continues in Book 3, and here's how it starts.

———

Susannah popped a switch and the small comm-sat disengaged from the lander, unfurling its spindly arms as it steadily moved away from the craft, before settling into its orbit.

Fingers crossed.

The twin planet hung below them – blue and green, in a sea of black – and it looked as if she would just be able to coast in and pick her spot. Whether anyone was there or not – Jordan, the kids – she didn't know. But hope had brought them this far, so – fingers crossed again.

"Everything all right?" said Dave, as he attempted

to shoehorn himself into the cockpit bubble seat beside her.

Dave. Fellow mutineer. One of the *Odyssey Earth*'s quartermasters. A sort of human hillock on legs. Trying to get into the seat, it was like watching the Michelin Man attempt to cram itself inside a two-door Smartcar – in the end, Dave gave up and stood behind Susannah, looming over her as he studied the navigation screen.

"Define all right."

"You tell me, Suze. You're the pilot. I just go where I'm told."

That was true, as it happened. Tillie – the colony ship's other QM, Dave's other half – had pretty much ordered him to go and rescue the kids, while she stayed back and foiled the pursuit. And as Tillie was built like a brick outhouse with biceps, you didn't tend to argue with her.

Plus, Dave loved her and, accordingly, did what he was told, like any sensible man would.

"Let's see then. Still no comms with the ship or New Earth. There's something going on that's interfering with transmission and reception. I've launched a satellite, see if we can't find an orbit that might cut through."

When they had first taken the lander, a couple of weeks ago – taken, stolen, liberated, choose your verb – Susannah had deliberately cut all comms.

Let's face it, they were doing something that they had expressly been told not to. They were only going to be shouted at by an angry captain. Told that they'd let her down, the mission down, and most importantly, themselves down. Ordered to come back. Shouted at a bit more.

Far better to get to the twin planet as quickly as possible, and then restore comms, announce the start of the rescue mission, fetch the kids and Jordan, and return home triumphantly. And hope that that would somewhat reduce the amount of shouting.

Only, the comms weren't working, so everything wasn't exactly all right. And that wasn't the only problem.

"The beacon signal is patchy, too. Which is even more of a worry."

The explorer pod beacon. The reason they were here in the first place. The emergency transmission from the twin planet that had told them Jordan and the kids were still alive.

Probably still alive. Perhaps still alive.

Anyway, it had been enough for Susannah, Dave and Tillie to plan a break-out rescue mission, take – sorry, liberate – a lander and fly for fifteen days across the solar system. And now here they were, and just as they were about to plot a landing trajectory, the beacon signal kept glitching.

It was still there, pulsing away, but it wasn't consistent. Faded in, faded out. Stopped, started again. More atmospheric interference mucking around with the lander's systems.

"Probably because of that," said Susannah, pointing at a wispy, frosted band on the nav screen, and then nodding out of the cockpit at a crackling swirl of dark clouds that obscured part of the planet below them.

"Is that normal?" said Dave, as flashes lit up the stratosphere.

"Who knows? But it's in our way. Last fix for the beacon is right under there."

"So, what's the plan, Suze?"

Susannah had got to know Dave better over the last couple of weeks of confined flight. She'd known him for seventeen years, of course – crewmates on the *Odyssey Earth*'s long voyage across the galaxy. But he and Tillie had tended to keep themselves to themselves down on the Cargo deck, happy amid the vast inventory of stores, while she – as Dave put it – "lived up at the pointy end, with the brass."

She'd known him, but hadn't really known anything about him. And now that she knew lots more about him – favourite band, Crass; favourite curry, *jalfrezi*; favourite film, *The Bridges of Madison County* – she really liked him. She could see what Tillie could see, which was that Dave was not only kind and unflappable but trusted people implicitly, unless they gave him a reason not to.

Dave trusted her skills as a pilot. He wouldn't have come along otherwise. He trusted that she would have a plan, and he'd go along with it, without question, because he also trusted her (to a point – "I'm sorry, *tikka masala* is not a proper curry, Suze. We'll have to do something about that when we get back.")

She laid out the plan, which was, admittedly, less in the way of a carefully formulated scheme and more of a bullish dive through hazardous electric storms above an unknown planet.

"Avoid all the flashing and banging, I reckon. Go in the long way round, get under the storms, hope we pick up a strong beacon signal, and take it from there."

"It's a fingers-crossed scenario then?"

"That it is, David, you are correct. Holding on tight might be an idea. Praying, too, if that floats your boat."

"What about the girls?"

Ah yes, the girls. Bel and Jet. Turned up mysteriously on the *Odyssey Earth*, having been hidden in the hypersleep chamber, and now along for the ride to escape their snake of a father, Donald Sprake.

Until now, Susannah had been working on the principle that, if you were going to go and rescue six teenage castaways from an alien planet, what difference did it make if you added another couple of teen stowaways into the mix? Probably, no one would even notice.

And she liked Bel and Jet, having got to know them as well over the last couple of weeks. Teenagers, obviously, and thus fundamentally absurd, self-absorbed and all-knowing. Just as it should be. But they were very different from *their* teenagers – the ship kids, born on the *Odyssey Earth*, raised alone in space, on a one-way voyage to the stars.

Susannah – at almost fifty – could just about remember what it was like to be a teenager, and she knew that the ship kids were not your usual specimens. How could they be? Their lives had been nothing like hers, or the rest of the crew's. There had been nothing normal about their upbringing.

Bel and Jet were different, in so many ways. There was a confidence about them, a sophistication, that probably came from their monied background. They had a life experience that the ship kids had only read about or seen in films – independence, holidays, pets, parties, girlfriends, boyfriends.

They'd never been on an interplanetary landing shuttle before, though. They didn't understand anything about space flight – they were still getting used to the idea that they were in space at all, having been drugged by their father and put into hypersleep aboard the *Odyssey Earth* without their knowledge.

Now they were on board the lander, it was fair to say that they were cowed by the view – of millions of stars across billions of miles. She thought they really didn't need to know that it might all get a bit hairy, as well.

Anyway, they were asleep, of course. Getting their regulation, teenage, sixteen hours a day.

"Let's wake them up when we get through the next bit. They'll be happier when we're closer to landing."

Fingers crossed.

Susannah did her best, but the lander dropped into cloud cover as soon as they hit the planet's atmosphere.

"Hold on, this might get a bit – " she shouted,

before a massive bump rendered the rest of the sentence out of date.

Two heads popped up behind her. Bel and Jet. Alien planet turbulence. Better than any alarm clock, apparently.

"Sweethearts, you need to strap yourself in back there. Do it now."

"What's happening? Are we going to crash?"

"Of course not!"

Fingers crossed.

"But please, strap yourself in. Dave! Come and sort them out, would you?"

"Come on girls. Let the nice lady fly the spacecraft. Nothing to worry about. It's just weather."

Probably.

The nice lady didn't like the look of some of the clouds approaching at speed, where flashes of multi-coloured light were snaking between the darkest areas. Susannah checked the nav screen, which was just a hot mess of dancing white lines – currently flying blind too, as well as being tossed around like a dark load in a heavy wash cycle.

Well, she knew what she could do about that. She'd had enough of gentle cruising speed anyway. She was a pilot. She was supposed to fly things, not get wafted around by weather. So – let's fly. Which in this instance meant increasing the speed, gaining back some control, and getting out of here into calmer skies.

The technical phrase was, "Seeing what this baby

can do," and it involved pointing the lander downwards and going very fast.

Susannah did that for a bit, held her breath for a bit more as the cloud seemed to go on forever, and then breathed a big sigh of relief as the lander popped out high above a shining ocean. The nav screen resolved itself, as the interference dissipated, and Susannah could trace a distant coast and then, further inland, a range of high, jagged peaks.

"Nice one, Suze," Dave shouted from the back. And "Told you we'd be all right," presumably to the girls, because with her he had been very much a finger-crossing sceptic until that point. She'd give him that one, though. It had been a bit hairy. Could have gone either way.

Behind her, she could hear unbuckling, and then the three of them crowded together so that they could all see the view ahead. Susannah dropped lower again and skimmed the craft a few hundred feet above the surface of the sea, enjoying the sensation of some real flying. It was clear ahead, and the coastline was coming up fast.

"We're here!" she said, happily.

"Where, exactly?" said Jet.

"Doesn't have a name. We've just been calling it the Twin. About three million miles from New Earth and the ship. Similar atmosphere, environment, geology, everything. Probably formed at the same time."

"And you know where we're going?"

"I do now." Susannah pointed at the nav screen.

"See that little light? Winking away? That's the explorer pod transponder. That's where the kids are. We hope so, anyway."

She punched some numbers into the console, and the lander climbed slightly and then slowed as it passed from ocean to land.

Now, they were flying over a low coastal plain, where many arms of a river emptied into the sea. It was a dull, overcast day, under high clouds, but channels of sunlight illuminated patches of green and brown far below. They were too high to make out landforms or details – perhaps marshes, perhaps woods. In the distance, a chain of mountains formed a natural barrier at the end of a broad valley. The peaks were shrouded in dark clouds, and Susannah noted more ominous flashes.

As they raced towards the mountain range – a metallic dart in a leaden sky – the girls gasped. The curving stone face ahead of them was split by a vast waterfall, tumbling down hundreds of feet in a deep, green sheet that was almost indistinguishable from the surrounding rock. The top of the falls was above the line of the craft, and higher still, the clouds boiled and flashed.

Susannah banked the lander. "We're going up into that, so time to hold on again."

"What's the plan, Suze?" said Dave, not for the first time.

"The pod and the beacon are that way, couple of hundred miles. I've got a strong lock, and this is the best approach we've got. Don't worry, I'll take it easy. Nav readings are showing that it's calmer on the other side of the range. We'll be fine."

This time, Susannah didn't even bother saying, or thinking – fingers crossed. They'd come too far to fail now.

She was a good pilot, and she knew what she was doing. She'd always known what she was doing, from the minute she boosted the lander from the *Odyssey Earth*'s launch bay. She was rescuing their kids, and the weather wasn't going to stop her.

She punched more numbers, and the lander soared up and into the storm.

Read the Odyssey Earth series by Rex Burke

Orphan Planet – Book 1
Twin Landing – Book 2
Star Bound – Book 3

About the Author

Rex Burke is a SciFi writer based in North Yorkshire, UK.

When he was young, he read every one of those yellow-jacketed Victor Gollancz hardbacks in his local library. That feeling of out-of-this-world amazement has never left him – and keeps him company as he writes his own SciFi adventures.

When Rex is not writing, he travels – one way or another, he'll get to the stars, even if it's just as stardust when his own story is done.

Find Out More

To find out more, and grab a free Odyssey Earth short story, visit Rex's website – rexburke.com